THE CONFESSIONAL

Also by Anthony Masters

THE
CONFESSIONAL

Anthony Masters

St. Martin's Press
New York

THE CONFESSIONAL. Copyright © 1993 by Anthony Masters. All
rights reserved. Printed in the United States of America. No part
of this book may be used or reproduced in any manner
whatsoever without written permission except in the case of brief
quotations embodied in critical articles or reviews. For
information, address St. Martin's Press, 175 Fifth Avenue,
New York, N.Y. 10010.

Library of Congress Cataloging-in-Publication Data

Masters, Anthony.
The confessional / Anthony Masters.
p.   cm.
ISBN 0-312-10956-3
1. Terrorism—Spain—Fiction.   I. Title.
PR6063.A83C6   1994
823'.914—dc20   94-710   CIP

First published in Great Britain by Constable & Company Ltd.

First U.S. Edition: July 1994
10 9 8 7 6 5 4 3 2 1

To Diane Fisk with very many thanks

There's not a nook within this solemn pass
But were an apt confessional for one
Taught by his summer spent, his autumn gone,
That life is but a tale of morning grass
Withered at eve.

William Wordsworth
Yarrow Revisited. 6. 'The Trossachs'.

Here, beside the naked water
I'm searching for my freedom, my human love;
not for the flight I may have, light or searing lime,
but my present moment lying in wait on the sphere of the
    crazed breeze.

Federico Garcia Lorca,
Double Poem of Lake Eden.

No man is an island, entire of itself; every man is a piece of the
continent, a part of the main.

John Donne
Devotions upon Emergent Occasions. XVII.

Prologue

The water in the pool was lukewarm and far from refreshing, and he noticed that the mosaic tiling at the bottom was cracked and occasionally discoloured. Yet the old walled garden, with its sun-bleached statuary, ancient palm trees and fragrant herbs, gave him the all-embracing contentment, even entrancement, of at last being at home; and for a man who rarely was, the feeling was wonderfully sustaining.

Eduardo Tomas swam luxuriously. Months in Madrid, then travelling in both Europe and America, had exhausted him, and the threat to his life, now almost a year old, had been sharp and unrelenting. However good the security that surrounded him, however vigilant his bodyguards, the shadow of his potential assassin was always there. If only he could imagine a face, an identity, then somehow the threat would be more containable, but the facelessness – that was the appalling thing. It could be anyone: anyone in a crowd, anyone close to him – even one of his bodyguards like Mrs Gandhi's assassin. Eduardo would spend hours tormented by conjecture, never free of the fear which gnawed at him, dominating his every waking moment.

Here on the island, the slow erosion of his nerves and confidence sometimes temporarily eased, but Eduardo knew that this was self-delusion. The threats continued wherever he was; letters typed on a machine that couldn't be identified, phone calls that were seemingly impossible to trace. There were a number of reasons why he could have been singled out for this long campaign of lethal promises, but it was impossible to be sure who was responsible. The sheer number of permutations both shocked and terrified him. To keep calm

7

was Eduardo's main preoccupation, but it was far from easy. His mind seemed to be permanently in overdrive. In a long political career there were so many things in retrospect he wished he had handled differently. He was conscious that even on Molino – on the island – he had made wrong decisions. However, at least he knew that Anita would go on loving him whatever happened. Eduardo never ceased to wonder at the way his wife blinded herself to everything – except her love for him. She had ring-fenced him, compartmentalized everything. Of course it was claustrophobic, but it was also pleasurable in a way. The words of a Lorca poem drifted into his mind. *But like love the archers are blind.* The trouble was that as far as he was concerned they weren't. He was being sought out.

Eduardo increased his pace, his arms cleaving the water with neat precision. As he swam he thought of the English writer, Salman Rushdie, his isolated life protected from Muslim extremists. Could he ever be trapped in that same situation? No, the thought was absurd. Surely his tormentor would be caught soon, or give up. Please let him give up.

For months his only comfort had been frequent telephone conversations with his old friend Marius Larche, whose logic and reasoned arguments gave him strength. A high-ranking officer in the French branch of Interpol, Larche told him he was sure he had nothing to fear, that his persecutor was bound to be a crank – someone obsessed with a public figure. It was a fairly common neurosis, he said, and the whole affair wouldn't have lasted so long if whoever it was really meant business. Larche made him feel better – a little cosier – both as a staunch friend whose views he had always respected, and also as a professional whose experience he knew he could count on. But Larche didn't know about Sebastia, nor did he know about the tensions in the family, and Eduardo knew that he would never be able to tell him.

Father Miguel, his father's friend and an old family confidant, had also made light of the threats. 'Just a symptom of the age we live in,' he had pronounced. Eduardo nursed the cliché to his bosom like a hot water bottle. Miguel was an acknowledged pessimist, often an alarmist, so it was good to hear his vague optimism.

Eduardo turned over on his back in the tepid water and stared up at the deep meridian sky; he listened to the sea and the crying of gulls and closed his eyes. In the darkness he saw a shadow detach itself from an insubstantial landscape and flutter towards him. He opened his eyes and stared up towards the sun.

Security on the island of Molino – the beloved home of the Tomas family – had been doubled, and even now guards were sitting in the shade, drinking coffee, watching the fence, no doubt noting his every move, every stroke, as he glided up and down the pool. They would know if he picked his nose, hear him break wind, probably make jokes about him.

Eduardo dived deep below the surface, touching the intricate design of the cracked mosaic tiling at the bottom of the pool, opening his eyes and dimly seeing the translucent centaur, half horse half man, that it represented. He stayed down as long as he could and then, with lungs bursting, broke the surface. One of his guards lifted an acknowledging hand, as if welcoming back an adventurous child, reassuring him that he was still enmeshed in the web that contained his every move.

Detective Superintendent Alison Rowe left the squash court in the New Scotland Yard Club as irritated as she had anticipated. Her immediate superior, Chief Superintendent Blake Mackintosh, was not a good loser, particularly to a woman, and the whole process of playing a game with him was utterly predictable. Once Mackintosh realized that he was unable to win fairly he had used every tactical ploy he possibly could, and his childish insecurity had been pathetic to witness. Yet the game at least brought his dislike of her out into the open, and the snide comments, the lascivious looks, the unbearable patronage were not so pronounced.

As she showered Alison reflected that, as a university entrant to the Met, she should have known that she would have to face extreme prejudice. She had joined at twenty-three and her promotion to Detective Inspector had been fast – another reason for her unpopularity with men like Mackintosh.

She stayed in the shower as long as she could, delaying the moment when she would have to face /him in the bright morning bar. She had always been fit, but it was her mental resilience that had saved her, helping her to endure her friends' derision when she had elected to join the police, and then cope with the male chauvinism of her colleagues. Her determination, her quality as a police officer, her professional achievements, her foresight, had put her where she was, but it had been a continuous battle.

As Alison dressed, an image of her father drifted into her mind. Long retired, he had been Chief Constable of Dorset and the family home near Lulworth had once been one of the great bastions of a form of country house life that was now almost dead. To Alison, Seawrack represented a world of almost mystical perfection – a place she loved more than anywhere else. When she was sixteen, George Wise, a disgruntled gardener sacked by her father, had set light to the house and one wing had been completely destroyed. Wise had been caught and the wing restored, but the fire had seemed like an assault on her very soul. The later discovery that Seawrack had been underinsured and that most of the family money would have to be ploughed into the rebuilding had been an appalling shock. It was as if George Wise had won after all, and the injustice of it still rankled with her. The final blow came when she was at university. Her mother died and her father, unable to manage without her, decided to sell Seawrack to the National Trust, and ironically he now lived in the wing where the arson attack had taken place. Deep down, Alison felt that none of these changes would have come about without the intrusion of George Wise. It fuelled her passionate belief in law and order, and when she came down from university the police force had been her next logical step.

The image of her father stayed with her as she pulled on her track suit and dried her long dark hair. Her emotional life had come a poor second as she ploughed her career furrow. Single-minded was what she called herself; Lady Alison was the name chosen for her by her colleagues. Unable to find anything else to occupy herself with in the changing room, Alison resolutely picked up her squash bag. She would have to face Mackintosh.

A fountain played at one end of the pool, monster silver fish heads spewing water ,from gaping mouths. Eduardo swam lethargically towards them, climbing out and standing up behind the shimmering screen. He could no longer see his guards clearly from here, and could only catch shifting glimpses of the large white colonnaded villa with its Palladian pillars and bell tower, its straight lines softened by bougainvillaea. In this house he had been born, played as a child, awkwardly entered into his privileged youth. From here he had launched his political career.

As he stared at the building through the distorting mesh of water, Eduardo heard the running of feet through the house, echoing over the tiled floors. At first, he was simply curious. No one ran here; everyone walked, sedately, discreetly, almost tentatively. The servants moved like shadows, the family, when they were here, were low-key, sheltering from public life, wanting peace.

The first painful stirrings of unease quickly became raw fear; the sweat broke out on Eduardo's brow and panic seared his stomach. He wanted to hide, to run, but as in the traditional nightmare he couldn't move and anyway there seemed nowhere to go. He stood completely still, knowing he was a target; but amidst everything he felt another, conflicting, emotion: a slight sense of relief. Had it come at last? Was he going to be able to put a face to the threat? Could he negotiate – finish it once and for all? Like a child he clung to the unlikely hope, but gradually the terror swamped him. He was going to die – he knew that. He was going to die. And only then would it all be over.

Numbly Eduardo saw his two security men rise silently to their feet, drawing guns, holding them in both hands, balancing themselves, feet apart, knees bent, hands solid on the butts of their weapons. Unreality suffused him; he had never seen this

11

happen before. In his mind's eye, a shadow detached itself from a dark forest and began to run towards him.

An intruder was scrambling over the security fence. Eduardo turned silently, unable to shout out, to warn. There seemed to be a solid block in his throat that could not be dislodged. Then he saw the dark head of a man, hauling himself up the fence, gesticulating, waving a gun in his hand. He was shouting something but Eduardo didn't wait to hear. With an undignified little squeal of fear, instinct made him dive, thrashing his way down to the mosaic centaur in the deepest part of the pool, clawing at the water, screaming inside and shitting himself at the same time.

The bar was all plastic and formica, with imitation leather chairs, glass tables and musak. Mackintosh was sitting before a pint of bitter looking broody, but when he saw her he assumed an expression of careless *bonhomie*. Alison smiled wearily.

'What can I get you?' He was tall, rangy, with a bushy moustache and slightly affected side-burns.

'I'll have an orange juice.'

'Right away.'

When he returned, she could see that he would have to justify himself before they could get down to business. She looked around her; the club was crowded, mainly with men, all talking police shop. Alison sighed.

'Bit off form today.' He put the glass down gently on the table, as if a loud noise would affront her. 'Got a bit of wrist strain.'

She nodded politely, trying to achieve a sympathetic smile.

'Awful bore – might get a bit of physio.'

'Why not?'

'Thrash you next time.'

'I expect so.' She looked at her watch and Mackintosh shifted uneasily. He had a nice wife, she reminded herself. She had met her at some function or other – a young-old little doll of a woman with china blue eyes and an anxious smile. 'Pleased to meet you,' she had said and had rattled on about their new house – a little box amongst other little boxes. But the kids had sounded less orthodox: Tony, a student at RADA, Emma playing the clarinet in the National Youth Orchestra. She had been surprised, and had immediately condemned herself for being a snob.

'Better get down to it,' he said, lighting up a cheroot. 'I wanted to talk to you about something that might be a little delicate.'

'Who for?' she asked curiously, pleased to discover the conversation was going to be more meaty than she had imagined.

'You,' he replied gently, with just a hint of patronage. 'Ever heard of Eduardo Tomas?'

'Isn't he a minister in the Spanish government?'

'Home Affairs. There have been threats against his life over the last year which the Spanish police are taking seriously.'

'Basque Separatists?' she asked vaguely, wondering what was delicate about this for her. The suggestion had made her slightly tense and she realized she sounded over-casual, as if she knew he had an edge on her. Was this his way of getting one up on her after losing the game, or was she becoming totally paranoid about him?

'I don't know anything about Spanish politics,' he said, making them sound like the inner workings of a Third World dictatorship.

Alison didn't reply and there was an awkward silence.

'Hooper's flown to Barcelona,' he said at last, looking at her speculatively. 'He's using Irish papers but MI5 are sure it was him. They need corroboration though.'

There was another long pause and Alison felt as if she had been touched inside, somewhere private, by a cold, reptilian hand.

'How many years ago was it?' Mackintosh prompted tentatively.

'Five.' She could feel the blood rushing to her face. The shock was tremendous and it vibrated inside her with a painful resonance.

'Heycroft wants you to go out there. You're the only one with a chance of identifying him – you know that.'

'He'll change his appearance,' she replied, her words tumbling over each other. 'Surely that's obvious.'

'We know this is a very long shot,' snapped Mackintosh. 'But your description of him was so detailed, despite what happened,' he added hastily, 'that we think you could still recognize him, even with a disguise. His voice maybe – an inflection – the way he walks.'

'Perhaps . . .' She was hesitant, still shocked, unable to bring herself to an acceptance of what he wanted her to do. She'd recognize Hooper, Alison was sure of that. She would recognize the bastard all right.

Mackintosh went on hurriedly, slightly brusquely. 'I know a member of the Spanish government is an unlikely target, but Hooper does seem to specialize in politicians. Heycroft's certain he killed Sir Montague Peters – and James Reeney; the description of the assassin in both cases does seem to tally. Heycroft's got this theory he's one of those arrogant bastards who doesn't bother with a disguise for the actual killing but goes to earth very effectively between assignments. If MI5 are correct he's not been so careful this time and we could be one jump ahead.'

While Mackintosh was talking, Alison's mind registered a series of shock waves that were so intense that she felt an almost physical pain. She had put Hooper in a sealed compartment some years ago. It had taken a long time to get him in there – a very long time – and now Mackintosh had deliberately forced him out. Jagged images filled her mind and she was back in the patrol car, sitting with Mike Stanley in Balham High Street. There was a noise, a bang, and the images sharpened, yet became more fragmented. The side street, the man lying outside the front door with another lying in the road. Minutes after, they had stopped a car – a small white Nissan – and questioned its driver. His square, slightly pock-marked face had a small purple birth-mark on the chin. Then there were the eyes, slate grey, rather large. Memorably large. They had been about to search the Nissan when he had shot Mike, then herself, and had driven off at high speed. He had never been caught.

14

The memories became hazier. Mike reeling about with the blood and brains coming from the side of his head. The impact in her chest. Later a nurse told her that Mike Stanley had died from his injuries. The bullet had gone through her breast and out through her back. The scar was still there, livid and puckered. Weeks passed. Pneumonia came and went. Then the visit from the man with MI5 and the knowledge that she had surprised a hit man who had been code-named Hooper. They hadn't got anything on him, and no knowledge of who he was. She was able to give him a brief description.

Over the years Hooper and Wise, the gardener who had set fire to Seawrack, had merged, had formed a solid mass of pain and fear that she had to keep in that sealed compartment. They were a demonic double-act: one had attacked her home; the other had tried to destroy her body. She had survived both, but only just. Now she was being asked to reach back into the past, to pursue one of the dark pair.

'There's a lot to talk about,' said Mackintosh. 'And Heycroft wants to see you tomorrow morning.'

'Are they sure?' she asked, her face expressionless.

'Yes.'

'Why didn't they arrest him?' But she knew the answer.

He sighed impatiently. 'They wanted to know why he was going to Barcelona. There's a complication though.' He paused. 'The Spaniards lost him of course,' he said with satisfaction and Alison could have hit him for his insular superiority.

'Are you saying he's been sent to Spain to kill Tomas? That they've let him go and now I'm to join Tomas's bodyguard in the hope that if Hooper arrives I can identify him before he strikes?' she asked incredulously.

'I'm not saying anything. But you'll be seconded to Interpol. There's one of those smooth Frogs who's friendly with the Tomas family. Heycroft's planning to ask him to help you.' Alison caught a knowing look in Mackintosh's eyes and rose abruptly to her feet.

'I'll think it over.'

* * *

15

Eduardo surfaced, dived again, but was soon forced back to the blinding light. The sun reared above him threateningly, burning white, merciless in its Mediterranean intensity. He gasped, stared round, panic making him nauseous. A man was lying on the patio, moving a little and then lying still. He was surrounded by servants and security men. Caterina, the maid, was standing to one side, shouting and being shouted at, but the sound seemed a long way off, as if everything was still under water. Eduardo swam to the side, looking round him like a trapped animal. Was he in shock? Why couldn't he hear properly? Then he realized he *was* hearing, and that a number of people were yelling at each other without making any sense. Eduardo could stand it no longer. 'What the hell's going on?' he roared, pulling himself out of the water. He turned back for a moment and grabbed at the towel that was lying on the side of the pool. Gathering what little dignity he felt he had left, Eduardo walked towards the milling confusion, all too conscious that he had soiled both his trunks and the pool. But in the light of what was happening embarrassment was irrelevant.

'I'm very sorry, señor. It was your maid's boy-friend.'

'Who?' Eduardo stared at the security man as if he was an imbecile.

'They had a row and he ran out of the house. But he ran the wrong way and started coming towards the pool. His name is David Arias.'

'What have you done? Shot him?' Eduardo was beginning to shiver.

'No – Luis – he pistol-whipped him.'

'Who was that who came over the fence? I thought he was going –'

'It was Enrico. He's just been drafted in. We radioed for assistance –'

'And Enrico came over the fence,' said Eduardo acidly. He felt an acute sense of anti-climax. Depression swept over him; there was no resolution.

David Arias was a callow-looking youth with an incipient moustache. He lay there with his eyes closed, a great bruise coming up on his forehead which the maid Caterina was tending nervously. The three security men hovered over them like a flock of anxious hens.

'Get up,' shouted Eduardo and the boy struggled to his feet.

'I'm sorry, señor. Very sorry.' Caterina was beside herself with anxiety. 'He ran the wrong way –'

'How many times has he been here?'

'Many times. You said I could have my friend visit me. You said –'

'Shut up.' Eduardo turned to the guards with sudden angry realization – that not only had he just received a terrible shock, but now it looked as if he was going to have to apologize for it. He felt desperately tired; if only they would all go away and he could just fall asleep somewhere. 'This looks like my fault – I should have told my secretary to inform you . . .' He paused, impatient at the convoluted chain of command. 'I should have told you that I said she could have this visitor.' He turned back threateningly to Caterina. 'You see what trouble you've caused.'

'I'm very sorry –'

'You're lucky you're going to keep your job.'

'Thank you, señor.' She looked as if she was going to embrace him and Eduardo took a couple of steps backwards.

'Does he need medical attention?'

'No – no, señor. He will be fine.'

Arias was on his feet now, his hand to his face, his eyes on the ground.

'He's not to come to this house again,' snapped Eduardo. 'Do you understand, Caterina?'

'Yes, señor.'

'And do *you* understand, young man?'

Arias nodded dumbly, though Eduardo could not tell whether the boy was merely inarticulate, or as deeply shocked as he was, or simply overawed by being harangued by the Minister.

'Get out then – and Caterina . . .'

'Yes, señor?'

'Bring me a large vodka – I'm going to change.' He looked

17

back into the pool and saw a small turd floating into the shallows. He would get Paco to inform one of the gardeners.

Two security men had settled back into the shade while the third returned, via the house rather than the fence, to patrol outside. His vodka finished, Eduardo lay, eyes closed, near the fountain and as far away from his guards as he could get. Anita, his wife, was in Girona, doing a little gentle shopping with their chauffeur/bodyguard in attendance, and his son Salvador was wind-surfing, watched by more security men in a motor launch. It just couldn't go on. Now this absurd mistake, the unbelievable trauma of it all, a ludicrous climax to a year of misery – and no resolution or relief. Larche would have to come out here – he was the only policeman he trusted. Larche was discreet, calm and civilized; the kind of urbane Frenchman he would like to have around him at a moment like this. They had known each other at the Sorbonne and had seen each other from time to time ever since. They weren't close friends, more good acquaintances, which was just what he wanted. He'd ring him now, talk it all through with him again. He needed the calm, still voice of reason immediately, even if it was only on the end of a telephone. But maybe his request would be a painful one for Larche, who had suffered his own family tragedy last year.[*] Eduardo shrugged. He could but ask him. He levered himself up on one elbow and felt for his towel, but before he could go inside and make the call in the privacy of his office, the telephone was brought to the poolside by his secretary, Julia Descartes.

'Who is it?' snapped Eduardo. 'I've had an appalling shock and I want to relax – not prattle on the phone.'

'I know, sir.' She was all professional sympathy. 'But it's Father Miguel. I thought you might like to have a brief word as he said it was very urgent.'

Impatiently, Eduardo took the phone. 'Miguel?'

The old man's voice was faint and halting. 'Eduardo?'

* Murder is a long time coming

'I'm here.'

'We've got to put an end to all this speculation.'

'I wish we could.'

'I have certain information that may interest you.'

'What sort of information?' asked Eduardo guardedly.

'I can't discuss it on the telephone,' said Father Miguel more sharply. 'I want you to make the journey to the valley urgently. Tomorrow at four. I'll see you in the confessional box, the one with my name on the outside.'

'Isn't that a rather strange place to meet?'

'It's the most private,' Father Miguel replied firmly.

'But there are rooms, offices . . .'

'All buzzing with other priests. Think what a flutter it would cause if the Minister for Home Affairs talked to me in such places. But in the privacy of the confessional – what could be more natural?'

'Very well,' Eduardo agreed reluctantly.

'So you'll be there?'

'I'll be there,' replied Eduardo slowly. Maybe there was some hope, he thought, but, afraid of being disappointed, he was determined not to be too expectant.

Eduardo telephoned Larche from his study which overlooked the Medas islands with their bird sanctuary and reef, now regularly despoiled by rapacious divers. His own island was thankfully a considerable distance from the tourist beaches and hotels on the mainland and was screened by the observatory on the highest rocky crag of the Medas. Seabirds perched overlooking Molino like so many thousands of spectators, but the human variety, even if they came in the largest of their yachts, were not allowed to penetrate the line of buoys festooned with warning notices.

'Marius, it's Eduardo.'

'Very good to hear from you.' Larche's voice was warm, welcoming, and Eduardo could picture him, sitting in the airy office at the top of the building with a coffee – a good coffee. In fact he was trying to cope with a hangover acquired at an Interpol conference followed by a dinner the night before, and was drinking a clandestine cognac.

Eduardo began to tell him what had happened, realizing his voice was uneven, his shock all too apparent. He had forgotten, however, what a good listener Marius Larche could be – quite unaware, in reality, how comatose he was that particular morning.

At the end of Eduardo's flurried explanation Marius said, 'You can't go on taking the strain like this. You're in a miserably isolated position.' He swallowed the last of his cognac and wondered about having some more. It was obviously going to be a day when people demanded things of him and he wasn't up to it.

'I almost feel like resigning.'

'Will that make it go away?'

'Good question. I even shat in my own pool – I expect they're draining the water away now and removing the turd I left in there. No doubt they'll find some face-saving cover story for it all.' He could hear Larche chuckling at the other end and then smiled himself, but the smile didn't last long.

'Is there anywhere you can go for a while?'

'It won't blow over, Marius. If I can't get away from it on Molino, where can I? What's more – I don't have any faith in the way I'm being protected, or the action that's being taken over the bombardment of threatening letters and calls I'm getting. They've been going on a long time – too long. I want you to join the investigation. I know Interpol is involved; it can be arranged for you to come. You're a good policeman – a good organizer. And you're my friend.'

Larche sighed. 'I can't just come in and take over a high-powered case like this. Have you forgotten who you are?'

'No,' said Eduardo bitterly. 'I just think other people have. What happened today was such a bad breach in security.' He began to tell him about the swimming pool incident all over again and Larche listened patiently and sympathetically.

'I'm on another case, that's the problem.' His heart sank at the thought of it. He was trying to cope with the case of a child abducted to Venice by his Italian father – a man

20

who was a known pederast. He was on the run with the boy in the city and so far there was no trace of either of them.

'I want you to come, Marius. I've got to have someone I can trust here – and in an official capacity. I can't *take* any more of this.'

There was a short silence, during which Eduardo could sense Larche thinking how unwelcome he would be to the Spanish police.

'If you could speak to Sabier I could be with you in a couple of days,' he said at last. 'I could delegate what I'm doing. Can you wait – hang on for a day or so?'

Eduardo felt a surge of relief. The local police, the Cesid, the army, all shrank into insignificance beside Larche. And why? The answer went back a long way to a night in a Parisian back street when they were staggering home together after a drunken party. The gang of muggers had pounced suddenly – three of them – and Eduardo, terrified, would have handed over everything he possessed. But Marius had been angry and with remarkable fury had despatched all three youths with his fists and his head and his feet. Eduardo had never seen anything like it, would never have expected such blind temper from anyone as ostensibly civilized as Marius Larche. But his single-mindedness had reassured him – the sheer force and thoroughness of his attack. Afterwards Marius had said, 'I hated them – they were violating me. That's what used to happen at school – I'd go crazy.' It was this passion, this protection that Eduardo so desperately needed now; someone close to him who would keep him in the picture, not just guard him but interpret what the hell was going on. Maybe he just needed Larche as some kind of symbol – a talisman – but he needed him very badly and he was determined to get him, whatever anyone said, however much bureaucracy railed against the decision.

'I've just had a call from Father Miguel,' continued Eduardo uneasily. 'And that's another mystery. You remember him? He says he has some information for me – and I have to go to the Valley of the Fallen tomorrow to see him. Of course he's an old

21

man so whether or not he's talking nonsense I couldn't say. But he's a good friend, even if he is going senile, and I reckon I should go.'

'I don't know if that's such a good idea,' said Larche. 'You're still in shock. Where's Anita?'

'In Girona.'

'Will she be back soon?'

'Yes. The house is full of security men and servants. But you'll reassure me more than any of them,' he added persuasively.

'What good can that old rogue priest do you?' Larche sounded admonishing.

'He has his ear to the ground . . .'

'Maybe he isn't functioning . . .'

'I've decided to go, Marius.' Eduardo was adamant. 'However enfeebled he is nowadays he still knows what's going on. And that's what I don't.'

'The Valley of the Fallen?' Larche mused. 'That place gives me the creeps. Are you sure the security will be tight enough?'

'I thought you believed the risk was minimal – that my persecutor was a crank, a psychopath?' But he was only goading Larche now, trying to make him uneasy, paying him out for being busy and too preoccupied with his own affairs.

'I'm sure that's the way it's going to turn out,' said Larche as reassuringly as a brisk nanny. 'I think the threats will probably tail off – that there'll be no resolution.'

'I suppose that's what I'm most afraid of,' admitted Eduardo, his flash of temper giving way to honesty. 'Then I'll never know who it was, and whether they've really gone away – or not.'

'I'll come as soon as I can,' said Larche, 'but I warn you, they'll resent me.'

Eduardo Tomas rang off, leaving Marius Larche feeling puzzled. For a man who was so much in fear of his life, it was odd that he was proposing a long trip to Madrid to see the old priest. He might be a family friend, but he had a dubious reputation. What could he have to tell him? And if it was so important, why didn't Miguel disclose it immediately? Did Eduardo have some other reason for asking him to drop everything and run to his side? But despite his curiosity and compassion Larche knew he couldn't drop his current case indefinitely. He would, however, go to Molino and be supportive for a week or so.

For a while he ruminated on his friendship with Eduardo Tomas, if being chums at the Sorbonne so many years ago could really be called friendship. That's when they'd been close. Over the last few decades they had met infrequently – been friends at a distance – acquaintances really – and the closeness had largely evaporated.

Late that afternoon, whilst still dealing with paperwork at his desk, Larche received another call, this time from London and a senior Scotland Yard officer with whom he had been in contact for some years.

'It's Alan Heycroft, Marius.'

'Very good to hear from you.' Larche was always at his most benign when uneasy and he went on to pursue enquiries about Heycroft's nearest and dearest.

When these exchanges were concluded Heycroft said, 'This Tomas affair?'

'Yes.'

'Are you connected?'

'I've been asked out there.'

'By the police?'

'By Eduardo Tomas. I'll be resented, of course, but –' He broke off as Heycroft interrupted him.

'As ever your reputation precedes you.'

'Thank you.' Larche waited for the favour Heycroft was about to ask.

'This is a very long shot but I'm sure that a hit man, code-named Hooper, flew to Barcelona last night. Our people thought they saw him at Gatwick, but the Spaniards lost him the other end. It may turn out to be a red herring but I've got this – this hunch that he could be after Tomas.'

'I see.' Larche suddenly felt extremely uneasy. Hadn't he just dismissed Eduardo's anxiety – practically told him that he was being hysterical?

'We have a very bright young female.' Heycroft somehow made the compliment patronizing. 'Her name's Detective Superintendent Rowe – Alison Rowe.' He paused. 'Some years ago she was injured in a shooting incident when her colleague was killed.' He paused again but Larche made no comment. 'The gunman was Hooper and I'm sure she can identify him. I'm sending her to Barcelona right away, but I want her to go further than that.'

'Where?' asked Larche, but of course he knew exactly what Heycroft was going to ask him.

'I know you can get her on to that island.'

Larche was about to minimize the problem again, to emphasize that many politicians received death threats every day of the week, then he stopped himself.

Heycroft continued as persuasively as he could. 'Obviously we're not asking Rowe to lead a hunt for Hooper – that's up to the Spanish police – but we've been after this bastard for five years now and I would like her to have access to the island. In the mean time, the Spaniards are finding her a hidey hole . . .' Heycroft's voice died away and there was an awkward silence. 'Would you be prepared to help?' he said eventually and Larche felt a stab of compunction at making it so difficult for him.

'I'll do my best,' said Larche shortly, wishing that Eduardo's call had not come when he was hung over and that he had agreed to help him with alacrity. 'I'll be going over there myself in a few days so I'll try and steer your Detective Superintendent in the right direction.'

'Thanks,' said Heycroft quickly. 'That's very good of you.'

'Do you know where she will be staying?' asked Larche wearily.

'No – but Jervier will.'

'I'll ring him and arrange to see her on my way through.'

When Larche put down the phone, he sat back, trying to assess the implications of all that Heycroft had been telling him. Then the telephone rang yet again. Larche picked it up, only to hear his Chief's voice, asking him urgently for news of the missing boy. He gave him the latest details, and most of his concern for Tomas vanished as he began to organize the stepping up of the hunt.

Part One

1

They had lunch next day at El Escorial in the gloomy coolness of the Hotel Santiago. For once, Eduardo ate with his staff. He told himself it would be an ideal opportunity to get to know them a little better; after all his secretary and research assistant had been with him for several years now. In his heart, however, he knew that it was really because he could no longer cope with being alone.

Carlos Mendes, his personal bodyguard, was swarthy and short, with powerful arms and shoulders and eyes that constantly travelled every rooftop and corner, every alleyway, each passing vehicle. Julia Descartes took down in shorthand his every thought, and Damien Alba, his research assistant, could produce full biographical notes on any Spanish or foreign minister or official – and could just as easily tell him a journey time, an airline schedule or where to buy a good wine even if they were in the remotest part of Spain or in a foreign capital. They were not stimulating company, but Eduardo felt a twinge of shame that he had never bothered to see them as people before, and was only doing so now to suit his own convenience. They had flown from Barcelona to Madrid, and Eduardo was pleased that not only had airport security been very tight but they had been tailed first to Barcelona and later to the Hotel Santiago.

Over lunch, Eduardo played the good listener, occasionally passing his hand distractedly through his soft wavy hair. He discovered that Mendes was a soap opera addict, Descartes didn't know what to do with her teenage daughter and Alba was worried about his weight, although Eduardo noticed with irony that this didn't seem to affect his liberal consumption of red Rioja. But Eduardo was only superficially attentive. At forty-eight, tall, commanding, physically dominant, he had rarely known panic. A few glimpses, perhaps – he remembered an incident with a horse as a child, later another in a speedboat race – but nothing permanent. Not like this. None of them knew – not Anita – not Salvador – not Marius – none of them knew how afraid he was, how the cold fear of being stalked filled his entire consciousness. But the worst thing was the breadth of possibility, the anonymity of it all.

Later, washing his hands and combing his hair in the wash-room, Eduardo pondered on his failure to cope. His thoughts slid as usual to the disastrous mistakes he had made in Sebastia. As if the death threats weren't enough, he had all that to worry about too.

Hurrying back to the rubber plants and polished tiles of the foyer, Eduardo found, as he had suspected, that his own staff were in a semicircle with their backs to the latticed picture windows, and the manager, under-manager, chef, head waiter and wine waiter of the Hotel Santiago were facing them, beaming ingratiatingly. He smiled blandly at them, wrung their hands and wondered if any of these bastards had ever been on the spot, as he was now. To hell with them, he thought. All they are is a bunch of grovelling arse-crawlers. Eduardo pressed the last palm and thought of Molino, his wife Anita and his son Salvador – Molino, the rocky wilderness with its lashing Mediterranean storms, the sunlit cave where he and Salvador dived – all contaminated now by what had happened on the island and, as a result, what might happen if it all came out. There could be no connection between Sebastia and the death threats, of that he was certain; he'd thought it through so many times. But Miguel, perhaps Miguel really did have some information for him. Eduardo hoped to God he had.

As Mendes drove the Mercedes out of Escorial and on towards the Valley of the Fallen, they listened to a tape of Anita playing the cello. It was a Schubert sonata and the haunting fullness of the sound soothed Eduardo. In no time they were easing into the valley and his first sighting was the gigantic stone cross that soared above the enormous cave church. Eduardo had attended official ceremonies there on half a dozen occasions during his political life, and the place depressed him just that little bit more each time. Not that Franco had not done the Tomas family proud; during his regime his father and uncle had both occupied high office. Now, ironically, although his father was dead, both he and his uncle had happily performed a volte-face to the left. Just under the cross, stark under the burning cobalt of the sky, was a series of large sculpted figures; lions, eagles, giants deep in thought or political lament cluttered the base of the steel-supported cross, which was reached from the valley by a cable railway.

This afternoon, despite the heat, the valley was swarming with frenzied-looking tourists who were being ferried by cable cars from the garish souvenir stand to the cross. Eduardo's official car drew curious stares as it purred on until it arrived at the paved area in front of the cave church. Just behind them, a large Peugeot also drew up.

'Julia and Damien, get yourselves a cold drink. I'll not be longer than half an hour. Carlos, you'll escort me as far as the confessional box, then I want to be alone with the Father.' Eduardo spoke authoritatively, brooking no argument.

Mendes opened Eduardo's door for him and a few onlookers watched the distinguished, beige-suited man leave the Mercedes and walk briskly towards the cave church with his short, swarthy companion just a few metres behind him, casually looking around. To some of the idlers, Eduardo's face was vaguely familiar, but such was the speed of his progress that they had no time to identify him.

They walked into the sudden welcoming coolness of the interior, down the highly polished floor towards the cross. The tunnel-like nave was suffused with the smell of incense and candle-grease as Eduardo and Mendes trekked past huge Fascist angels, each with an avenging sword, past dark chapels, wall paintings and statuary until they arrived at the plain, circular altar where Jose Antonio Primo de Rivera, founder

31

of the Falangists, was buried. Opposite his grave lay Franco's plain slab. This area too was full of tourists, some of whom were no doubt security men.

Eduardo had known Father Miguel almost all his life. He had been prominent amongst the churchmen who had supported and ministered to the Franco government, but he had also acted as an undercover agent to the Tomas family who had always wanted to know a little more than they were told. Eduardo remembered his father once saying, 'Father Miguel has gradually come to abuse the secrecy of the confessional. This has been very useful to me – to us as a family – but of course he is not a priest we confess to – will never be a priest we confess to.' The old man had childishly delighted in playing his double game, well paid by the Tomas family for his information which had so often allowed them to be one jump ahead in Franco's power games. Even today Father Miguel still had his ear to many keyholes.

Eduardo looked at his watch. Just on four. He wandered casually back from the altar and began to look for the box. It was not long before he found one with Father Miguel's name posted outside. As Eduardo entered, Mendes unobtrusively took up his position, checking with a security man further up the aisle.

Eduardo knelt down in front of the grille.

'It's Eduardo, Father Miguel.'

Father Miguel's familiar gravelly voice said, 'I'm happy to see you.'

'How are you?'

'Not good. But I'm glad you've come. I have some ... information for you which is not very pleasant.'

'What are you talking about?' asked Eduardo, unable to react immediately to what the old man was saying. He felt numb.

There was a short silence. 'Wait a minute,' Father Miguel said slowly. 'I think somebody else wants to see me.'

'What?'

He leant nearer the grille and caught a muttered enquiry. Then there was a dull thud and almost instantaneously Eduardo felt a crashing impact that knocked him forward. He looked up at the grille, saw that it was shattered and felt a strange mistiness of both vision and sound. There was an insubstantial luminosity to the confessional box around him, and a sense of unreality possessed him. Something warm was seeping down his shirt. Then everything stopped.

Mendes was dimly conscious of someone leaving the other side of the box, but his attention was distracted by a young woman who had just fallen to the floor, centimetres from the door that hid Eduardo. She appeared to be having some kind of fit, rolling and thrashing on the ground and emitting a high-pitched animal whine.

A small crowd gathered around her and for a moment, Mendes felt uneasy. Any one of these people could be waiting to kill Eduardo Tomas. Then he saw the trickle of dark blood seeping over the floor, between the feet of the onlookers. It could only be coming from one place. He knew that. For an instant Mendes froze – and then raced into frantic action.

Instinctively knowing what he would find, Mendes ripped open the door of the confessional box. Tomas was kneeling, facing the broken grille, his head resting in the aperture. There was a small hole on the side of his skull from which blood was slowly pumping, and a rather anxious smile on his face. His eyes were open, staring straight ahead, and one of his hands had grasped the broken scorched wood around the grille.

When Mendes numbly and automatically pulled open the adjoining door he gave a little grunt of disbelief. Father Miguel was also slumped forward, his shattered head against the partition. Unlike Eduardo Tomas, most of his face had been blown away.

2

The décor of the restaurant in Lyon promised more than good food; it provided an ambience that was both discreet and comforting. The light wood panelling of the walls, the occasional painting, the tiled floor, the heavy white tablecloths, the widely spaced tables, the total absence of background music – all produced an atmosphere of expectancy and sharpened the appetite.

Marius Larche was already at a table reading *Le Monde*, scanning an editorial. A subtle, inviting tang of garlic, herbs and strong coffee lightly pervaded the air. Several times he glanced at his watch, knowing Monique would be late, but wondering how late. Pushing a lock of his long grey hair out of his eyes, he sipped at his pastis. He was a good-looking man, slightly going to seed; there were bags under his eyes and his tanned face was lined around the mouth. But apart from these signs of ageing, Larche had a distinctive Roman head with strong features and unusually light blue eyes. They were memorable – steady, probing, discerning – but there was also a slight ambivalence to them.

'I'm sorry, darling.'

Monique had swept in, her tall figure in some disarray. She was wearing an elegant suit, but the small black box-like hat had come somewhat adrift, releasing strands of dark hair. She had expressive eyes that communicated her mood at once, and Larche could see immediately that she was slightly flustered – and behind the fluster there was worry. They had been married a year now and he had never ceased to marvel at how happy they had been. Yet he also knew how fragile that happiness was, and how much there was in his past that could easily destroy everything they had. She had no real idea of how powerful his relationship with Jean-Pierre had been and how, like a living force, it still intruded on the present, thrusting its way into their love and aching like a bad tooth. Larche knew that she didn't quite trust him, but he also knew how hard she tried to banish the fear from her mind. He loved Monique more than any woman he had ever loved in his life, but the power of the past dogged them, however much they both tried to put it in perspective. Larche's journey to Spain was to be their first real separation, and he felt uneasy about telling her that he was going. He also felt a sense of guilt, for not only had he put off telling her about it but he had suddenly found he was looking forward to this short breathing space. He loved Monique – he had no doubt about that – but he had been alone a long time and living with somebody had turned out to be a demanding experience.

'I went to Benoits,' Monique said, stumbling over her words.

She sat down and ordered a negroni from an attentive waiter. Larche didn't reply immediately and she gave him an appraising look, as if asking him to commend her initiative.

'I love their material. Whatever you choose I know it can only enhance those shabby old rooms.'

The waiter returned with her drink almost immediately and she put it to her lips, taking a sizeable gulp.

'We should have started on the house much earlier,' he said quietly.

'Well, Alain took a long time making up his mind.'

'Doing a life sentence may have lessened his sense of urgency,' said Larche drily.

'He offered.'

'Yes, but I never thought he'd honour the commitment.' Larche folded up his newspaper and put it on the floor. He began to toy with the menu.

'Don't let's order yet,' she said. 'I want to relax a little.'

He put down the long strip of card reluctantly; his stomach had been rumbling for some time.

'Just think,' she said. 'We can start the restoration immediately. Alain has been . . . generous.'

'For a man who killed my father. Yes.'

She gave a little shrug and he immediately wished he hadn't been so crude.

'I'm sorry.' He reached out and took her hand. 'I shouldn't have said that.'

'No. I'm being thoroughly insensitive.'

He increased the pressure on her hand. 'I want the house restored. God knows I want it. And with my mother in the nursing home there's nothing to stop us. We'll be living there one day.'

With our children, she wondered, and then buried the thought.

'What else did you spot?'

'Just some furnishings. Curtains.' She smiled. 'I'm really beginning to play the role of the little woman now.'

'You could never be that.' He lifted her fingers and kissed them. 'To see that place restored is everything to me. Everything. And our living there together would banish all those ghosts – all that . . .'

'We could go down there over the weekend,' she said, anxious to fill the awkward silence. 'Just to plan. If you don't want to stay in the house I could book the little pension in St Esprit.'

He frowned. 'There's a problem – one that I didn't tell you about last night. Procrastinating as usual.'

Monique looked out at the early evening street, with its crawling traffic and lengthening shadows, and Larche knew that she wished she hadn't been so quick off the mark.

'I may have to go to Spain.'

'Why?'

Larche searched for the right words. 'Do you remember meeting Eduardo Tomas at the Music Festival in Barcelona?'

'Yes, your old university friend. He's a minister in the Spanish government, isn't he?'

'Yes, and he's been receiving death threats. I have to go unofficially just for a few days.' He paused. 'There's an added complication in that British security think they've sighted a hit man on his way to Barcelona, and there's a young police officer who might be able to identify him . . .' Larche paused again, not really wanting to embark on a complicated explanation.

She gazed at him steadily. 'How terrible for him.' Then she said, 'You haven't seen him for a while, have you?'

'No. Shall we order?' he asked.

She gave him a bright smile. 'Yes, I'm starving. Tell me all about Eduardo.'

If only they could talk about Jean-Pierre as they used to, bring him into the open, thought Larche as he summoned the waiter again. But now it seemed impossible. It also seemed impossible to remember that her suspicions were natural enough. He had told her he was bisexual before they had married, and he had also assured her that he was always going to be faithful to her, but unless they talked about it a good deal, he felt vulnerable – and they hadn't talked for some time.

The waiter brought the phone over while they were eating mussels.

'Yes?' Larche sounded brusque. He was often interrupted at meals but still resented leaving addresses and telephone numbers with the office. He listened attentively and Monique watched the shock spread across his face. When the voice at the other end had finished speaking, he replied abruptly, 'Give me twenty minutes.' He looked down at his steaming plate and up into Monique's wary eyes.

'What's happened?' she whispered.

'Tomas. He's dead.'

They stared at each other in disbelief. Then Larche looked down at his plate again and focused on a piece of bread that was half buried in the sauce. He had dropped it there when the call had come and now it was slowly sinking. He watched it go down numbly.

'How?' she asked gently.

'He was shot.'

She gazed at him, unable to reach him. The bread had almost sunk now and he stared at its remnants in a puzzled way.

'I'll have to go immediately. I didn't – I didn't take the threats seriously. I told him some crank was responsible. God – why was I such a fool?' He looked up at Monique, his face working, the shock and pain and guilt stark in his eyes. 'I had an appalling hangover after that damned dinner. I suppose I just wanted to shut him up . . .' He couldn't go on.

'Did the hit man get him?'

'It would seem so. Well, someone got him anyway.' His voice died away and then regathered a little strength. 'There was apparently a good deal of confusion with a young woman having some kind of fit. He was in a confession box and no one heard the shots. The assassin escaped.' Larche stared at some distant point across the room and unintentionally caught the eye of an elderly woman. She darted an alarmed glance at him – and then returned to a detailed study of her cassoulet. As she did so, she made some remark to her older companion and he raised his eyebrows. Eventually Larche's distracted gaze returned to Monique and he began to speak rapidly to her again. 'I think he died at once. There was a priest killed too.' He paused. 'If only I'd damn well listened to him, insisted he didn't make that damned fool rendezvous, but he was just another interruption to a bloody awful day . . .'

Monique leant over and kissed him. 'I love you,' she whispered. 'I'm so deeply sorry – but you can't blame yourself like this. You have so much on – so many cases – that . . .'

'Eduardo was a friend.' He fought for control. 'They're sending a car.' Larche fiddled with his napkin and then threw it down. Around them, the restaurant was beginning to fill up and the near silence which had originally accompanied their conversation had been replaced by a discreet murmur.

'Have some more wine,' she said, pouring him a glass of claret before he could protest.

They were silent until the car arrived a few minutes later, pulling up at the kerb and sounding its horn. The soft evening light gave the Mercedes a kind of dusty sheen, and two children on skateboards paused to admire its subtle bodywork and gleaming trim.

'I've got to go.' He half rose and sat down again.

'I shall go down to Letoric,' she said with sudden decision. 'Phone me there.'

'Yes. I'll ring.' Larche rose again and the horn sounded a second time. He came round the table and clumsily kissed her. 'Waste of a good meal.'

'When will you call?'

'Late tonight.'

'I love you, Marius.'

'Kiss me again.'

She pressed her lips to his. 'Keep safe,' she whispered. 'You're so precious to me.'

As the DC10 circled Barcelona airport, Larche's guilt increased. He had advised the Spanish Minister for Home Affairs, an old and valued friend, that the threats on his life were no more than the work of a crank – threats that could be discounted with a derisory smile. He had done this because he had been hung-over, overworked and uninterested. Now the worst had happened, Larche's conscience was tormenting him as it had never done before.

As the plane came in to land, Larche closed his eyes. He never watched landings; it was all out of his hands so he preferred to physically dissociate himself from the entire operation. Normally he found closed eyes an effectively escapist antidote, but now all he could see was Eduardo's face.

Grimly, Marius Larche knew he was going to have a very bad night at his hotel – something he couldn't afford if he was going to have the difficult day he anticipated. Perhaps a few scotches would help him to sleep, but then he would wake with a hangover – just as he had done when Eduardo had called. All too often, he thought ruefully, as the DC10 touched down, life tended to be circular.

In the early morning, the dew was still heavy on the foliage that was now nearly engulfing the Château Letoric. Monique Larche gently applied the brakes of her little Fiat Tipo and pulled up at the battered oak front door. She had not been able to sleep, despite the fact that Larche had phoned just after midnight. He was staying in a hotel just outside Barcelona, he had told her, and was going to try to get some rest.

Rising at five, Monique had driven from Lyon without stopping, arriving at St Esprit just before eight. She had then taken the lower road past the lavender fields and bumped slowly over the rutted and weed-grown drive of the Château Letoric. Well, she thought, in a few months' time she could have restored some sort of order from the chaos, although she also knew it would probably take a couple of years to get the old château into the kind of shape that she and Marius wanted.

The heavy door opened before she could knock, and Estelle, the housekeeper, appeared wearing a stained dressing gown, with yesterday's rouge on her cheeks. Despite her sluttishness, Monique liked her knocked-about warmth, and wondered if her feelings were reciprocated. Somehow she doubted that they were.

'I saw you coming,' she said. 'I might have known you'd be early.'

'Is it inconvenient?'

'No, madame,' she said reluctantly. 'I know you can't wait to get started.' She looked past her. 'I thought Monsieur Larche was coming with you.'

'He's been called to Spain.'

'Police business?'

'Yes.'

'Anything to do with the murder of that minister?'

'I think so.'

'Ah – I wondered about that when I saw the television last night. He knew him, didn't he?'

'They met at university,' Monique replied rather shortly.

'I've made some coffee. But would you like breakfast?'

'Coffee will be fine,' said Monique as she stepped hurriedly inside.

* * *

40

Alison Rowe was slender, dressed like a student, Larche thought, in jeans and a T-shirt, but was probably somewhere in her thirties; and she had an air of authority. Her long untidy hair framed an oval face, and rimless glasses were pushed slightly forward on her nose. She looked as tired as he felt, but the reserve – the iron, too-stretched reserve – was her most obvious trait.

Glancing at his watch, Larche saw that it was just after two. They were standing in the rather unlikely setting of the ambulatory of the monastery of Sant Pere de Rodes, looking down on Puerto de la Selva where the mountains met the distant unwinking blue of the Mediterranean. The heat was intense here, and the stony flints on the rugged mountain path just below them seemed to reflect back even more. He put his hands on the broken masonry of the parapet and felt the rough baking stone.

'The whole area's alive with security people,' he said. 'I've never seen so much activity.'

'Part of the new airport building at Barcelona was sealed off yesterday afternoon,' she said. 'It took two hours to clear customs.' She paused. 'It's extraordinary to be in the middle of a huge public tragedy like this; there's a sort of muddling-through-the-blitz atmosphere here.'

'That's what you British did then – muddle through?' asked Larche.

'I don't know what we did,' she replied a little defensively. 'That's what we like to *think* we did.' There was a short silence and then she said, 'He was a very popular man – your friend Eduardo. I was met by a security man at the airport – someone high up in Cesid. He was crying.'

'Yes,' said Marius carefully. 'Eduardo commanded a lot of respect.'

'I gather you know the family well.' She was the inquisitor now.

'Yes, I knew Eduardo as a student and we've always been friends.' He tried to curb the flatness of his speech, but he had woken with the predictable hangover and spent the morning being briefed by the now extremely helpful Spanish police.

41

They seemed delighted to see someone from Interpol, as if his presence not only lent weight to the devastating importance of the tragedy but also gave them added support. They were all too clearly both mortified and frightened by their failure to protect such an eminent public figure. It was during this session that he was told the investigation at the Valley of the Fallen was well in hand but the Tomas family wanted him on Molino after he had met Alison Rowe and taken her to lunch with some high-ranking Spanish policeman.

'What were you told this morning?' she asked.

'That the family wanted me to come to Molino and that we would be given every facility.'

'We?'

'Naturally you'll be coming with me. It's essential you know the background.'

'But all I'm good for is identifying one particular assassin,' she protested drily.

'You can be taken off Molino at any time if necessary. Surely you don't want to kick around here on your own with nothing to do?'

'I'll come,' she said. 'But what's all this about some girl having a fit and covering up the assassin's escape? Was she some kind of plant?'

'They don't know and of course she's sticking to total denial, but I would say you were right.' Larche paused. 'She's a local whore who would do anything for a pay-off, but apparently there's no evidence of her having received any money. Yet.'

'But the fit,' said Alison Rowe impatiently. 'Surely some medic can decide whether it was genuine or not?'

'She's in hospital, under guard and having tests. But she *is* an epileptic.'

'I see.'

Larche looked at her curiously, wondering if she was trying to impress him. 'We can talk more later,' he said rather self-consciously. 'We're going to see a man called Casas over lunch. He's a Spanish policeman who's meant to be looking after us.'

They both gazed down uneasily at the old disused vine terraces that ran down the dry flinty mountain to the shimmering

Mediterranean below. 'Isn't this place rather dramatically out of the way?' he said suddenly.

'I think that's the idea; they bundled me out of the airport very fast. I got the impression they were worried that Hooper might be hanging around somewhere – might see me wandering the streets of Barcelona.'

'It's a large city,' observed Larche with irony.

'I don't think the police chief I met is very imaginative, and anyway he was in one hell of a panic. He wouldn't be able to handle another corpse.' She laughed for the first time and Larche liked the sound. 'Apparently they use this place as a hideaway for police informers.'

'A sanctuary,' replied Larche, looking at the hazy mountains.

'There's a small flat,' she explained as they walked slowly back down the shallow steps and out into the tiny courtyard. She paused. 'By the way, what rank has Casas?'

'He's in the Cesid. I think he feels he needs to keep an eye on us in case we show up the Spanish police and their security people.'

'Do you know the Tomas family well?'

'Yes, but not nearly as well as Eduardo. I've stayed on Molino before though.' He paused. 'His brother Blasco is a Benedictine monk. He belongs to a community on the island of Fuego – about twenty kilometres further down towards Blanes. The other brother is a marine archaeologist called Jacinto, whose wife Maria is a scuba diver. They run a rather chic diving school in Estartit.'

'I've heard about them. Aren't they macho adventure seekers popular with the rich and famous?' she asked rather abruptly.

'No comment.' Larche stared at her reflectively. 'The Tomas family have always been devoutly religious,' he said unexpectedly. 'They're a rock solid part of the old Catholic establishment in Spain. Do you remember Bishop Carlos?'

'Isn't he the priest who led the rebellion against the new Mass? He wanted to keep it in Latin, didn't he?'

'And clashed head-on with the Pope and lost,' replied Larche. 'But he's still a bishop and publicly licking his wounds courtesy of the family.'

43

'So they're powerful,' said Alison Rowe.

'Yes,' Larche replied, 'they're powerful in the old Spanish ways.'

'What's that supposed to mean?'

'It means they're insular and secretive.' He looked at his watch. 'It's time to meet Casas,' he said abruptly.

'Why were you asked to see me alone?'

'Heycroft,' he replied. 'I think he wants us to be a good team.'

'You asked me to start clearing out those chests in the study,' said Estelle, 'and I found some of Monsieur's old sketches. He must have only been a boy at the time, but they're rather good.'

Monique was surprised; there was a note of familiarity in Estelle's voice that she had not heard before. Previously Estelle had always referred to Marius in rather a remote way – not as a person she had known quite well over the last year when she had had to take over the running of Letoric and turned from housekeeper and nurse to Marius's mother, to caretaker of a crumbling old mansion.

'I must have a look.'

'Yes, I put them on the desk for you to see.'

Hurriedly, Monique changed the subject. 'How's the clearing up going?'

'Awful. I don't know what to throw away.'

'The clothes . . .'

'Oh, they've gone. And I've taken some of the old lady's stuff over to the nursing home. The rest I put in the cellar – just for the moment, in case she asks for it. You know what she's like.'

'Yes. How is she?'

'Rambling. She hardly knows anyone.' There was a tinge of bitter regret in Estelle's voice. Well, Monique thought, at least that's one person she cares about. She finished her coffee and stood up.

'I'll go and have a look at those sketches.'

'They might be worth framing,' said Estelle and Monique

44

looked at her sharply, certain she detected a hint of mockery, but Estelle's face was solemn.

The study was dim, but sharp, clear Provençal light thrust shafts through the ancient curtains, now worn so thin they were almost transparent. She and Marius had sifted through the contents of the desk and the bureau themselves, but they had left the trunks to Estelle. 'Father put all the debris in there,' Marius had said. 'There's nothing that's private or precious.'

He had been wrong. The sketches were laid out, face down, on the dusty surface of the desk, and as Monique idly turned them over she could see that Marius had had a talent for drawing. Many were of the château in better times, with the formal garden mellow and attractive. The fountain was clear of weeds and the lawns were smooth and verdant, dotted with statues and dominated by a summer house. There were other pictures of his parents, of a dog running across the lavender fields and of streets in St Esprit. Then she came to the bottom of the pile – to the pictures of the strapping young man on the tractor. This was Jean-Pierre, and as Monique turned over the sketches she became increasingly uneasy.

Casas was thin and elegant, a handsome sixty-year-old, clean-shaven and slightly defensive. He ordered a substantial seafood lunch which they ate in a small restaurant overlooking the sea at Puerto de la Selva.

'I gather you were a personal friend of the late Eduardo Tomas,' Casas began, 'and that he had already asked for your help. Perhaps unofficially?'

Larche briefly related the facts, although he was sure that Casas knew most of them already, and made no attempt to cover up his disastrous underrating of the situation. Casas then turned solicitously to Alison Rowe.

'I – I hear this assassin Hooper wounded you some years ago,' he said briskly.

'Yes,' she replied expressionlessly.

'And you would recognize him?'

'I believe I can.'

Casas turned to Larche. 'I understand the family have given you permission to be on the island?' His voice was neutral.

'Yes. I'm going to take Detective Superintendent Rowe with me.'

'You are?' Casas raised his eyebrows and smiled a ready-to-be-offended smile. 'Do you have the family's permission for that? Or the investigating officer's? Or the security services'?'

'No,' said Larche firmly. 'I shall take responsibility. Other members of the Tomas family could still be in danger from this assassin.'

Casas nodded, smiling faintly as if he was tolerating some degree of insanity in Larche. 'I think that's rather unlikely, don't you?'

'I wouldn't dismiss Hooper as irrelevant if I were you,' said Alison, irritated by his patronizing manner. 'We clearly don't know whether this is a political assassination or something more personal, something that might affect the Tomas family.' She paused. 'Or do you?' she challenged.

Casas shrugged impatiently. 'The investigation is at an early stage.'

Larche looked through the window at the flotilla of police boats surrounding the foreshore and the crowds of loitering spectators watching from the harbour.

Casas caught his glance. 'The island is swarming with police, secret service, intelligence – you name it, they're on Molino. There is more than adequate protection for the Tomas family. And please – I've not been asked to give you a briefing – just to assist with the logistics.'

And so that you could take a look at us and report back. Larche smiled slightly at Alison Rowe who smiled back.

Casas intercepted the exchange and frowned. 'I'm not in any way involved in this investigation,' he added.

'Just in us?' asked Larche jovially.

'You're our minder,' put in Alison rather over-casually and immediately looked as if she regretted the comment.

'I don't understand.' Casas and Larche both looked puzzled.

'It's just an English expression. It means you are here to look after us – to protect us.'

Casas relaxed and took a sip of the dry white Mâcon he had ordered.

'We're not going to be disruptive,' said Larche, 'and we're not conducting a separate investigation. We would like to liaise with the investigating officer, of course.'

'That would be Emilio Calvino. He's a pleasant fellow with a very fine mind.'

'And he's in charge of the whole investigation?' asked Larche.

'Put it like this – he is in charge of the police investigation. There are other enquiries going on but naturally everything is being co-ordinated. The government are looking for quick results.'

'So he could be replaced if he's slow in delivering the goods?' said Larche shrewdly.

'It's a complex business.' There was a slight hesitation in Casas's voice. 'Do you know Molino well?'

'I've known Eduardo well over the years, but I've only stayed on Molino for brief periods and that was usually as a member of a large house-party,' Larche explained. 'I always felt an outsider – rather like a poor relative – so I can't say I enjoyed the experience. I'm not a jet-setter.'

Casas nodded, clearly agreeing that Larche was no international playboy, but also pushing the remains of his sea bass around his plate as if he was ruminating about something else.

'So is there anything additional that I should know about Molino?' asked Larche amicably, aware that Casas was wondering whether he could confide in him.

There was a curious stillness in the air and Larche knew that Alison Rowe was also listening intently. She's very intuitive, he thought, and was suddenly glad that she was coming with him. Despite his need for space, he still needed the qualities of a woman that a man lacked. Larche forced his concentration back to Casas.

'The family is a very old one, as you know of course,' said Casas. 'Their roots are here – in Catalonia. I speak as a local man; my father was a Catalan fisherman. He's dead now, but there was a song he used to sing about Molino – the one his

47

father used to sing, as had *his* father before him. It's something very close to us here.'

'What is it?' prompted Alison quietly.

'I remember a few lines of that song – I can hear him singing it on the boat now after some rough, fresh wine.

> *'Listen to the pan pipes coming over the sea*
> *Pipes of love, pipes of lust*
> *Pipes of Molino – pipes of Sebastia*
> *Naked flames*
> *Leaping in Sebastia.'*

'Sounds like Bacchanalia,' said Alison. 'What's this place Sebastia?'

'It's a small fishing village on the very tip of the island.' Casas hesitated and absently rubbed a piece of bread round his plate. 'It has a rather dark history – a place where sex of various kinds could be had freely.'

'Sounds a real little paradise.' Larche was uneasy.

'I thought the Tomas family owned the island,' said Alison. 'Didn't they own Sebastia as well?'

'No,' replied Casas. 'It was always separate.'

'But how did a place like this exist in their back yard?' asked Larche. 'Isn't it a little – disreputable – particularly for such a distinguished Catholic family?'

Casas smiled. 'The two communities seemed to have co-existed quite happily – and separately over the years.'

But Larche was taken aback. 'I have to admit I'd heard the odd rumour, but I always dismissed it. Surely there isn't any truth in all this?'

Casas shook his head rather patronizingly. 'My dear Larche, I know it to be true for I used to go there as a boy. I lost my virginity in Sebastia – as many others had before me.'

'Right under the noses of the aristocracy?'

'*Right* under their noses,' said Casas with some pleasure.

The waiter brought coffee and Alison Rowe and Marius Larche refused cognac. Casas had a framboise.

When the waiter had gone Alison said, 'So – Sebastia was a sort of brothel – right in the lap of the Tomas clan?'

'It was more than that . . .'

'What else then?' said Larche impatiently, wishing Casas would come to the point.

'All things were allowed in Sebastia,' said Casas, looking at Larche very directly. 'The place is run by men – for men. But one day the women will step in and when they do I wouldn't like to be around.'

'What do you mean by that?' asked Alison curiously.

'Maybe nothing at all. It's just my own feeling – there's a special breed of woman in Sebastia.'

'Clandestine Amazons?' asked Larche brightly.

'Perhaps they have clandestine power,' replied Casas, 'like Islamic women. But they've been watching and waiting too long – seeing their own sex used, spat upon, exploited. One day . . .' His voice almost died away. 'One day, I've often thought, they might turn on the men.'

'I didn't realize you were such a feminist.' Now it was Alison's turn to be bright.

Casas shrugged. 'I'm not – I'm just a fatalist.'

'Why are you telling us all this about Sebastia? Is it *that* important?' Larche asked.

Casas drank some more of his framboise. 'Background,' he said quietly. 'Of course, on another level, the Tomas family have done a great deal for Sebastia. We know they've helped the community when there've been poor catches, bad times, storms –'

'Plague, pestilence,' cut in Larche impatiently. 'Come on, what is all this? More local rumour and speculation?'

'Are you suggesting that Eduardo Tomas's death could have some connection with the seamy side of Sebastia – and that brought about his murder?' Alison sounded sceptical. 'Surely a situation like this would have leaked out. I mean, it's not exactly *Hola* magazine stuff but what about your tabloids? And the rest of Europe's?'

Larche could see Casas was already regretting his frankness. 'As you say, it's most likely to be local rumour and speculation and dismissed by the media as the stuff of injunctions and libel suits, but I thought you'd like to know.'

'Eduardo Tomas was clearly murdered by a professional assassin,' pointed out Larche. 'I don't suppose he was hired by some woman from a fishing village.'

'True – but no one else is going to tell you about Sebastia. I'm a local – and you should understand a little of the local background.'

'Do your – other colleagues know about this? Those who are not locals?'

'Of course,' replied Casas. 'I considered it my duty to tell them.'

'I never went to Sebastia when I was staying on the island before,' said Larche. 'But then no one ever left the house and its grounds.' He paused. 'However – thank you for the information. It's certainly a mystery why the respectable Tomas family keep Sebastia on their doorstep if it's as disreputable as you say.'

'Go to Sebastia yourself. You'll find nothing – just an old Catalan fishing village. No more.'

'It all comes to life after dark?' suggested Alison.

'It only comes to life for those who know,' said Casas, draining his liqueur.

3

Half an hour later a short, rather dumpy little man with a straggling grey beard got out of a black Mercedes. He strolled across to the jetty where he was greeted with some deference by the security guards just as Casas emerged from the restaurant with his protégés and hurried across the road.

'Detective Superintendent Alison Rowe and Detective Chief Inspector Marius Larche of Interpol. This is Inspector Emilio Calvino who is in charge of the investigation for the Spanish police.'

There were formal handshakes while Larche tried to forestall the professional hostility he had anticipated in Calvino. 'I realize that you may see us as interlopers, but we shall both keep a very low profile.'

'The more help we have the better.' Calvino's voice was neutral; his eyes were expressionless and a bland smile hovered on his lips. 'Besides, I know the family are anxious to see you in their hour of need, Señor Larche. You are a friend, are you not?'

'I knew Eduardo Tomas,' said Larche guardedly.

'And I gather he was anxious for your involvement.'

Larche continued to make self-effacing noises, deeply conscious of Alison Rowe's appraising gaze. She's assessing how I handle this, he thought, and I'm not coming over that well. 'I just want to ensure our roles don't overlap,' he continued.

'But they will, señor. How can they not do so?' Calvino's professional smile widened. 'You are welcome to talk to whom you like, but at the same time you must, of course, keep me informed. You and Detective Superintendent Rowe will be our scavengers, toiling in the harvested fields. But who knows what you will find still growing, still festering. Naturally you will both receive our co-operation as I'm sure you will receive the family's. We shall disprove that English expression – too many cooks spoil the broth.' He laughed and then lit a small, rather noxious cheroot. 'The island's our fortress,' he said. 'Please ensure you don't try to leave it without my permission.'

The launch sped over a still, calm ocean which was sprinkled with yachts, many of them stationary whilst their occupants took the siesta. Calvino stood up in the prow, just behind the dapper-suited man at the wheel. He stared ahead, his broad back a clear indication that conversation was no longer required and that he had disposed of at least his initial duty.

Larche glanced at the receding coastline, at the cliffs, whose strange sinewy quality Salvador Dali, who had lived and worked at nearby Port Ligat, had captured so exactly. Leaning forward expectantly, he watched Molino grow bigger, the same rugged cliffs dropping sheer into the sea, the waves boiling at their base which was honey-combed with caves. Great pinnacles of rock, formed by the island's erosion over the centuries, rose from the surf, thickly populated by huddled gulls.

Police speedboats ringed the craggy shores, bobbing up and down on the rough water as it touched the outcrops of Molino – a magnificently barbaric sight, chillingly primeval in its grandeur. There was no sign of any buildings or even, so far, of a natural harbour, just the relentless lashing spume of the waves and the mournful cries of the seabirds.

Dampened by spray, sitting in the stern of the launch, Marius Larche and Alison Rowe watched the ancient shores with unease. It was as if a ragged monolith had been placed in the eye of paradise.

Slowly, lurching in a tide rip, the launch rounded the northern tip of the island. It was the first time Larche had ever approached Molino from the sea; his other visits had been made by the Tomas family's private helicopter.

Again he stared up at the towering water-drenched rock

formations and at the densely packed pine trees at the top. It *is* a fortress, he thought, but not of Calvino's making. It's always been sealed.

Alison Rowe was depressed; as they neared Molino she felt increasingly worried about her brief. If the Spanish police found Hooper in Madrid or Barcelona, then she would, no doubt, be swiftly called to identify him. Beyond that she felt she was uselessly hanging around, an encumbrance to Larche and to everyone else on the case.

She shivered involuntarily, cold in spite of the hard glare of the sun. The dredging up of the horror from her past was still causing her considerable pain. And there was something else; something that darted around in her mind – a little stab of worry that was growing larger and more irritating by the moment. Had Heycroft sent her to Spain to get her out of the way? Was there really anything valid for her to do here? Would she have a job when she got back? Was he already manipulating a variety of different situations against her? Alison pulled herself together and tried to shake off the paranoia.

Her thoughts turned to Tom. They had been friends for ten years now – almost to the day – and had been about to celebrate the decade with a trip to Pompeii. She suspected that Tom had planned the trip deliberately, for this was where they had met, on an archaeological holiday. Then he had been a barrister, divorced with two young children. Now he was still a barrister, divorced but with two older children. They had similar tastes, backgrounds, interests, and he had wanted her to live with him with a view to marriage, but she had put him off. Alison wanted to be single-minded, didn't want the conflict of interests that she knew marriage would bring. She was determined to battle to the top in the police, determined not to allow marriage to stand in her way, aware that her male chauvinist colleagues and competitors would undoubtedly interpret it as a sign of weakness.

But strangely, despite all her ambition, in the last few weeks she had not been so sure, and loving companionship – even babies – with Tom seemed less of a taboo. What would she do if Tom proposed to her in Pompeii? Would she amaze them both by accepting?

Larche turned to her and smiled as the launch nosed through the choppy waters, round another headland and on towards a harbour that suddenly appeared welcomingly through the silver sheen of the spray. It was a good smile, she thought. Strong and authoritative and almost mischievous, as if he wasn't prepared to be put down or patronized by anyone. In his well-cut jeans and open-necked shirt, Larche had a distinction that set him apart from all the other policemen she had met. It wasn't that he was French and therefore of a different culture to the hard-bitten, woman-shy, insecure and competitive men that she usually worked with; he just came over as more mature, a survivor. But a survivor of what, she wondered. The Roman head, the lines around his mouth, the bags under his eyes, the long grey hair, those light discerning blue eyes. What had he seen? What had he experienced to exude this strange aura of survival, of redemption?

'It rather strikes me that the situation in Molino has all the makings of a vintage Christie,' Larche remarked in his light brown voice with its slightly accented English. Suddenly Alison realized that he was trying to reach her more positively – that they were to be colleagues, sharing the light-hearted *badinage* as well as the evidence. Oh well, she supposed it would pass the time. 'Of course we need a storm,' he continued. 'The family, friends – and admittedly in this case half the security corps and a large number of policemen – trapped in an old house on a bare rock.'

'It's not very bare,' she observed. 'It looks as if there's a dense pine forest up there.'

'Mere detail,' he reprimanded. 'The victims are hurled to their deaths from the topmost pinnacle. Suspects multiply and are narrowed down by Hercule Poirot.'

'Is that you?' she asked.

He shrugged. 'In all modesty . . .'

'And I'm Captain Hastings?'

'In drag, perhaps. Later we confront everyone in the library, Poirot accuses and the murderer runs for the abyss.'

'Suppose there isn't a library?' she objected.

'There must be; it would ruin the whole plot if there wasn't.'

He watched her covertly as they laughed and saw her visibly relax for the first time, the intelligence radiating from her eyes, her dry humour already an ally. Yes – yes, he *had* grown used to the company of women and Larche was pleased that Alison Rowe had been persuaded to come to Molino.

'Well,' said Calvino, sounding slightly like a holiday courier. 'The harbour is the only way in – and out – to this part of the island – and there's no movement without security passes.'

The launch was nudging against the smooth, round, weed-hung rocks of the small natural harbour, and Larche looked up chipped concrete steps to the dark pines beyond.

'Señora Tomas is expecting you.'

'Obviously Detective Superintendent Rowe and I will work together at all times,' said Larche.

She smiled her gratitude and Calvino nodded quickly.

They walked up a narrow path between the pine trees with the late afternoon sun filtering down in latticed beams. The cicadas had begun to sing and there was a pungent scent of rosemary. Every now and then, flints and boulders pushed their way through the thick prickly undergrowth which continuously narrowed the track, and beyond was the darkness of the pines. Larche could hear the waves beating relentlessly against the rocks below them. A helicopter circled noisily and then began to roar over the trees and out to sea.

'You're keeping the island under wraps,' said Alison, attempting conversation.

'Yes.' Calvino seemed more at ease when he was talking to her. 'There's a big dispute about security boiling up. After all those threats, Tomas walked to his death almost alone, except for his bodyguard, Carlos Mendes.'

'Had he been with Tomas very long?'

'Only a few months.'

'You think he might be implicated?'

'We're checking him out, but he's an unlikely assassin.'

The path widened and Larche found himself out on a wide headland lit by a mellow sun, its warm, ancient stones an inviting respite from the dim claustrophobia of the trees.

The house was set on a slight rise, with a large wooden cross surmounting a small shrine just below it. Imitation Palladian, it was a substantial two-storeyed white villa with a bell tower enclosed by a high wall. There were two policemen with holsters lounging against the wrought-iron entrance gates. Both had an air of somnolence which changed to relaxed vigilance when Calvino came into view.

He nodded to them and rang the bell. The gate slid open electronically, and they walked up a flight of steps into a paved courtyard. To one side there was an oval-shaped pool with a cherubim and seraphim fountain, and looking round, Larche noticed that there were several pieces of sculpture, some of them abstract, including a ragged silver construction which reminded him of the cliffs on the coastline, and several metal spheres topped by small windmills.

Larche glanced at Alison, but before he could say anything he saw Anita Tomas coming towards them, walking slowly, and calmly. A woman of considerable physical presence, despite the fact that she was small and stocky, she wore a beautifully cut black dress and a pair of high-heeled, obviously extremely expensive shoes. A slow, slightly questioning smile spread across her impassive features.

'Marius. How good of you to come.'

Her smile had a luminosity to it that startled Alison. Why, she's beautiful, she thought. Really beautiful. And she has such power of personality. Was that part of her persona as a distinguished cellist, used to the international public platform? Or was it to do with being the Spanish Home Affairs Minister's wife? Or both? No wonder she could still insist that Marius Larche should be allowed to come to Molino. Yet Alison noticed something else about Anita Tomas. There was a shuttered look to her eyes and a reservation in her manner that gave her a rather detached air.

'Anita.' Larche stepped quickly towards her and they embraced. 'I should have come much earlier.'

'You're a busy man.' Her voice was clipped, authoritative, yet rather aridly polite.

Larche winced. 'I wish I'd taken Eduardo's telephone call much more seriously.'

'You weren't to know,' she replied without malice. 'Please don't blame yourself.' Anita sounded rather irritable, as if she didn't want to bother with anyone else's neuroses.

Calvino's fixed smile widened as he spoke. 'Señora, I have to speak to my security counterpart so I'll leave you with your new arrivals.'

'Thank you, Señor Calvino.' Her voice was brisk and dismissive.

Realizing he had failed to introduce Alison, Larche said quickly and slightly awkwardly, 'This is my colleague from England, Detective Superintendent Rowe. She is following up some information on a suspect we have and would like to talk to you about the threats Eduardo received.'

That was quick, thought Alison admiringly. She was wondering how he was going to explain her away.

'The letters? Señor Calvino has the originals but I have copies. There are tapes as well.'

'Thank you.' Alison shook hands with her. Despite the heat Anita's palm was cool and dry. That's how she seems as a person, Alison thought suddenly. Cool and dry and formidable. A hard person to know; probably equally hard to question. 'I'll liaise with Señor Calvino, but I would like to take a look at the copies.'

'Who is your suspect?' asked Anita crisply.

'An assassin who I've . . . had an encounter with before.'

'An English assassin?'

'Yes.'

'And you think this assassin could be implicated?'

'We don't know yet.'

The tears glistened for only seconds in Anita Tomas's eyes

and then began to roll down her dark cheeks. She made no attempt to brush them away and soon they were rivulets, seemingly unending. She made no sound at all.

I didn't expect this, thought Alison. For a moment she wondered what Marius Larche was going to do. Would he embrace Anita again? Calvino had already disappeared, striding back out of the gate, no doubt relieved to be rid, even temporarily, of his charges. But Larche did nothing, standing calmly, watching her silent tears. Then after what seemed like an eternity, he reached out for her hand and took it gently.

'I can't live without him.' The words were clipped, positive, almost authoritarian.

Larche said nothing, but went on holding her hand. Then the tears stopped as suddenly as they had started, and with all the dignity of Mediterranean grief, she released his hand and said, 'You must both come in.' Once again, Anita Tomas was her aloof, stylish self.

The room was cool and inviting, with a mixture of abstract and impressionist pictures on the walls. The furnishings were sparse – a few low-slung chairs and a sofa, a bar, a desk and a huge bookcase – on an enormous expanse of tiled floor.

'You've changed the old layout,' Larche observed.

'Eduardo had it done last year. He said he wanted less clutter in his life.'

'Do you like it?'

'I preferred the clutter. Please sit down. Will you have a drink?'

'A pastis,' said Larche.

'I'll just have something soft.' Alison's voice was tight with tension.

Anita poured the drinks herself and put them down on a glass-topped table. She brought nothing for herself.

'The servants usually do all this,' she said absently, 'but I can't stand them around me at the moment, so they're sitting in their quarters with nothing to do.' She laughed harshly. 'Eduardo wouldn't have liked that. He believed in using his labour force.'

There was a slight pause. Then Larche said, 'Anita – I'm obviously conscious of overlapping with Calvino.'

'Yes, I thought you would be.' She offered no reassurances.

'I expect he will have already asked you a lot of questions.'

'Yes.'

'I shall have to repeat them,' said Larche stolidly.

'Of course.' She shrugged. Clearly he was not ruffling a single layer of her reserve.

'Something puzzles me,' Larche spoke slowly, almost hesitantly.

'What?'

'Every politician gets death threats. Why did he take these so seriously?'

'That's easy to answer. The person who wrote the letters knew his movements exactly. Do you want me to show them to you?' She half rose to her feet.

'No – not yet. I just want to talk to you.'

'Very well.' She was sitting in one of the armchairs but her whole body was stiff and erect, as if she was posing for a bad photograph.

Anita Tomas was a very formidable lady, thought Alison. There was a dignity to her that would clearly brook no argument, but there was something else too – a perception that was quiet but astute. She knows what's going on all the time, Alison decided, and she's used to control.

'Detective Superintendent Rowe is investigating the presence – the possible presence – of a hit-man named Hooper in Barcelona. He may have no connection with the case at all.'

'Does Calvino know about this?'

'Yes,' said Alison.

'Detective Superintendent Rowe might be able to identify this suspect,' said Larche, 'so she has been asked to come out here and investigate a possible connection.'

'May I ask how you will recognise him?' asked Anita.

'Yes – he shot me.'

For the first time, Anita Tomas was taken aback. 'I'm very sorry.'

'I recovered – but my colleague didn't.'

'I see.'

'He's a very dangerous man.'

'And what makes you think he's mixed up in all this?'

'We had a report that he flew to Barcelona, travelling on Irish papers,' she said flatly.

'But you are not sure?'

'No.'

'Surely – he would have changed his appearance?'

'We suspect he's been involved in a number of recent assassinations of political figures.'

'May I ask who?'

'I'm afraid I can't tell you.'

'Did anyone come here?' asked Larche. 'A few days before Eduardo died? Has anyone come here since?'

'Only Bernard Morrison – the artist who was painting my husband's portrait. His credentials are impeccable.'

'When did he go?'

'He's here now,' she said calmly. 'He came today.'

'*Now?*' Larche looked shocked. 'Did Calvino allow him on the island?'

'Yes, Marius, he did. Because I asked him to. Like I asked him to allow you – and you allowed Miss Rowe.' She looked at him challengingly, her autocratic little frame stiff with indignation. 'This is my home – still my home. I realize the police and the security people have to do their job – and I appreciate the enormity of what has happened. I loved Eduardo, Marius, and he was very precious to me. His portrait – is more important to me than ever. I'm also used to getting my way – as you know – so I overruled everyone.' She smiled self-deprecatingly, as if defying him to argue with her. 'It's not difficult to do that in my position, I'm afraid. I'm used to having my own way. The finished portrait is being shipped over, but he brought photographs. You'll understand I needed them at this time – rather desperately. Oddly, I commissioned the portrait and my husband sat for it when he was in London last year.'

'So you never met Mr Morrison until now?'

'We've corresponded. He's written some wonderful letters

about Eduardo. They obviously struck up quite a strong relationship during those hours of sitting.'

'You mean you corresponded *before* Eduardo's death?'

'There hasn't been very much time afterwards, has there?' Her voice was icy but Larche carried on unabashed.

'How did you find Mr Morrison?'

'He was recommended by Sir Evan Taylor at the Royal Academy; one of England's most distinguished portrait painters.'

Larche turned to Alison. 'Have you heard of him?'

'The name's familiar.'

'Surely he could have sent you the photographs – rather than arriving here in person?'

'Yes, he could have done, but we'd made the arrangement for him to come and I saw no reason to break it.' She paused, looking slightly embarrassed. 'I'm giving him a new commission,' she added.

'To do what?' asked Larche.

'I want him to paint Eduardo here in the house – paint what he looked like here.' She turned away from them for the first time, fiddling with a bracelet. 'You must think me very foolish,' she said, but Alison thought that she sounded more angry than defensive.

'No,' she said quickly. 'I don't think that at all.'

'Well, I *am* foolish, trying to perpetuate his memory in any way I can. I mean . . .' She hesitated and then quickly recovered herself. 'I'm quite able to watch him on video, or to listen to him on audio tape. It's not painful – in fact, it's very necessary. I do it all the time.' She pressed a button on the table and part of the wall slid back to reveal a huge screen. Anita then turned a switch and Eduardo came into view, looking as confident and as charismatic as ever. He was being interviewed on a chat show but Anita quickly pressed another button and the screen went dead again.

They're the same, Alison thought; the one dead and the other alive. Both special people in powerful worlds, supremely confident of themselves – until a couple of bullets put paid to everything.

'Did Eduardo have any personal enemies?' asked Larche.

'Not in the course of his career; he was a very popular man. I know the police and the security believe this to be a political assassination – perhaps ETTA or the Separatists. No one's claimed responsibility yet.'

'Isn't that very odd?' asked Alison. 'Surely they'd be only too pleased to benefit from the publicity. I mean, that would be the point of the assassination, wouldn't it?'

Anita shrugged. 'It *is* strange.' She paused again. 'Have the police briefed you?'

'We know the basics,' said Larche.

'But your Interpol presence is official?'

'Yes.'

'Marius – I wanted you to come here and I'm happy that Detective Superintendent Rowe will be working with you. I'll do anything I can to help.'

'Did you have *any* idea what Father Miguel was going to tell Eduardo?' asked Larche.

'No. And I'm sure it was a mystery to Eduardo as well.'

'But he went very willingly?' asked Alison curiously. 'Wasn't that a bit odd? There he was, bombarded by death threats, and he went calmly off to Madrid with minimum security.'

'He didn't have minimum security,' said Anita quickly. 'His aircraft was covered and so was the drive to the Valley of the Fallen. There were security men in the Basilica . . .'

'And yet he was killed.' Alison's voice was cool.

'Yes,' agreed Anita flatly.

'And this girl – the one who had the convenient fit?' asked Larche.

'She's being questioned. I don't know whether she was in collusion with the assassin or not, but I believe someone paid good money to have Eduardo assassinated – and I'm not sure we need look so far afield.' Anita sounded hesitant.

'What are you driving at, Anita?' said Larche softly.

'I'm wondering – just wondering – if Eduardo's assassination was not after all some kind of major political act – but a local one.' She glanced rather sharply at Alison. 'I realize it doesn't fit in with your international hired assassin theory, but maybe that's why Eduardo wanted you here, Marius.

Perhaps he wanted you to investigate something delicate – maybe something that, like me, he was only a little suspicious of. Clearly we both underestimated the depth of feeling.' She hesitated. 'You see, he wanted to do his bit for Catalonia – for the coastline here. It's been raped by tourism and the fishing industry has been practically wiped out, but Eduardo believed the industry could be revived. The old port, Sebastia, has been with us forever on the southern tip of the island, but it was ruined, derelict. Fifteen years ago Eduardo brought in a man called Lorenzo from the mainland to run the fleet. He was – still is – an odd character – very inward, even hostile – but he and Eduardo had one common concern: to start the fishing up again and make it economically viable.'

'And is it?' asked Larche.

'There are thirty boats at Sebastia now – all of them making a profit.'

'Has this revival spread to the mainland?' asked Alison.

'Not really. They still prefer to make money from the tourists; it's easier to do that than take to the water at all times of the year, sometimes for a poor catch. But in Sebastia they feel differently; the fish are brought home every night, shipped to the mainland and taken to Barcelona in refrigerated trucks.'

'Paid for by Eduardo?'

'By the Tomas Trust – yes.'

'Did Señor Tomas offer to *help* them restart fishing on the mainland?' said Alison, pursuing her train of thought. 'Perhaps they were jealous of Sebastia, felt *they* needed practical assistance, not just an example to follow.'

'Certainly he did.'

'And?'

'All they did was sneer. They would accept nothing from him and they created slanderous rumours about Sebastia – that it was a brothel, that Lorenzo – and we as a family – were implicated and –'

'So he *was* hated there,' interrupted Larche. 'Hated for starting a fishing industry.'

'Hated more perhaps for employing Lorenzo.' Anita was

looking out of the window at the large swimming pool on the terrace behind them.

'Why?'

'I've never been sure. He had some kind of reputation – or had done something bad over there.'

'Did Eduardo know?'

'I've no idea.'

'But you were close . . .'

'Yes. Not about Lorenzo, though. I didn't want to speak about him to Eduardo.'

'Why not?'

'I just didn't like him. He had his business arrangements with my husband – and for some reason this caused the most dreadful outrage on the mainland. I never got to the bottom of it because I didn't want to. Neither did I think it was particularly important at the time. Now I can see that I was mistaken and that's why it's very fortuitous that you have arrived here, Marius.'

'Couldn't Calvino –'

'He won't take me seriously. He's got to get quick results, you see, and he doesn't think all this is relevant.'

Larche's heart sank. Anita had always been so detached, so coolly independent. He realized she was deeply distressed, but even so he'd never thought she would lean on him to this extent.

4

The sighing of the ocean below, the rhythmic sound of the cicadas and the faint early evening light produced an atmosphere of presentiment in the big, airy, slightly bleak room.

Alison Rowe spoke softly and cautiously. 'So could we be thinking about a personal vendetta, something small-scale?'

Anita nodded her head impatiently. 'For some months now, Eduardo has been pushing through a programme for more Catalan independence. He wanted to construct local government, create Catalonian autonomy, give more grants to local culture.'

'And *that's* enough to provoke an assassination?' asked Larche unbelievingly.

'You have to appreciate that Catalan identity was totally suppressed by Franco and many people still feel that Catalonia should be kept in its place. I know there was . . . well, suspicion, that Eduardo had long-term plans for some kind of home rule. So you can see there are three broad strands: the far-flung political assassination theory that the police favour, and the two I've offered you – the seemingly incomprehensible mainland hatred and those who are against Catalan nationalism.'

'And which do you favour?' asked Alison.

'It's hard for me to say this because I have no evidence whatsoever, but I've always been worried about Lorenzo and the power he exerts in Sebastia. The men are afraid of him there – and I don't know why. It's an aura, a feeling – nothing more – and I realize you cannot investigate feelings, Marius.'

'The letters – the threatening letters. Were there many of them?' he asked.

'Oh yes. They came almost every day.'

'And the calls?'

'Two or three times a day.'

'My God – Eduardo never told me they were this prolific.' Larche turned to Alison Rowe in concern.

'No, I don't suppose Eduardo wanted to admit the scale of it, even to himself. He was so depressed; thought they'd never stop. And of course I'm often away performing.' She paused. 'They, whoever it was, always seemed to know exactly where he was – in Madrid, or here, or wherever.'

'But what did he do about it?' asked Larche.

'Took them to the Cesid – and to the police – but they couldn't trace them. They were posted in different places; there seemed to be no pattern. Girona, Barcelona, Port Bou, Palamos – dozens of different towns. The letters were typed on different machines, sometimes typewriters, sometimes word processors.'

'And the calls?'

'They were even worse, of course.'

'The voice?'

'It was distorted – obviously a tape recording.' She shuddered, her calm temporarily broken again. 'Horrible – like a mechanical voice but with hate and loathing in it.'

'Were the calls recorded?'

'Yes.'

'Do you have the tapes?'

'Yes.' For a moment she didn't move. 'I'll go and get them.'

She walked quickly and elegantly to the desk, her small body totally controlled in its movements. Alison watched her in fascination. She had several of Anita Tomas's CDs at home. She played like an angel.

Anita returned with a pile of papers and a tape and threw them on to the floor as if she couldn't bear to touch them. They fanned out untidily and were of varying sizes, composed of no more than one line. Larche went down on his knees, skimming the papers and handing a few up to Alison to read.

WE'RE GOING TO KILL YOU
YOU'LL DIE

SOON YOU'LL DIE
IT WON'T BE LONG NOW
DEATH WILL BE A RELIEF
YOU'LL NEVER KNOW WHEN YOUR DEATH IS COMING
IT'S GOING TO BE VIOLENT
DAYS NOT WEEKS

They went on and on, neatly typed, almost childish in their melodrama. But to get them so regularly every day must have been very hard, thought Alison. A grinding regularity, relentlessly threatening with every post.

'Can we hear the tape?' asked Larche.

'Yes.' Anita handed it to him abruptly. 'But if you'll excuse me, I'll go into another room for a few minutes. I can't bear to listen to it.'

'Of course. Would you rather I took it away somewhere?'

'When you've finished. Yes.' She looked at him expressionlessly. 'I'm just going to have a word with Bernard Morrison. He gives me . . . at least some temporary comfort. I shan't be long.' Anita Tomas walked hurriedly out of the room, her dark silk dress rustling slightly, and leaving behind a faint trace of delicately scented herbal cologne. What's under that frosted exterior, wondered Alison. Does she have any fire in her? Alison suspected she did – but had kept it all for Eduardo. She glanced across at Larche, wondering if he was thinking the same way. Alison decided that he was.

Larche walked slowly over to the cassette deck with the tape and paused. 'What did you think of her?' he asked softly.

'Difficult to say what's going on under all that reserve,' said Alison slowly. 'She seems obsessed by this local Lorenzo business without knowing much – if anything – about him.'

'Intuition?'

'Do we go on that?'

'Sometimes.'

'Do you know what her relationship with Eduardo was like?'

'He was devoted to her and she to him. Perhaps more so – I never had any doubts about that. They were often here together.

67

There is one thing I remember Eduardo telling me a few years ago. He said that she'd been abused as a child – by her father, I think – and that she found it difficult to show emotion – except to him.'

'That's quite a confidence – even for old friends.'

'Yes,' Larche admitted, 'it was. We were both pretty drunk when he told me.'

'I see.' She paused and then asked him, 'You think he was telling the truth?'

'There was no reason for him not to,' replied Larche. 'I didn't tell you any of this before, as I wanted you to meet her first – form your own conclusions.'

She nodded, accepting what he had said. 'You don't think it's odd that she's got this painter man here – at a time like this?'

'Not especially. I think it proves my point – that she loved Eduardo almost obsessively. Now she's having him recreated, on canvas.' There was a long pause and then Larche said, 'I'm very happy you're working on this case with me.'

'Thank you,' she replied with genuine pleasure. 'The same applies to me, but I have to say I feel a bit of a fraud.'

'Why?'

'This Hooper business. I'm out here on a wild-goose chase. It's obvious that he's not here – not on Molino. It would be impossible with this massive police presence – despite the security risk of Sebastia. I should be making enquiries in Barcelona. I don't even believe he had anything to *do* with this assassination.'

She was about to continue when Marius said, 'Stay on the island at least for tonight.'

'All right then – just tonight. But I really feel irrelevant.'

Marius Larche put the tape in the deck and they both steeled themselves.

'You will die. You will die. You will die. You will die. You will die.' The rasping metallic voice, horribly distorted, continued relentlessly. There was something else in the robot-like sound that for a while Larche couldn't identify. Then he suddenly realized that it was as if something or someone was bubbling

68

with electronic laughter. It was a terrifying sound, and to hear it so many times a day would have been appalling. Hurriedly he clicked the machine silent.

Alison shuddered. 'God – that's fiendish. It sounds like Bugs Bunny mixed up in an air compressor. And what's more, there's so much hatred in it – and a sort of sarcastic hatred. Do you know what I mean?'

'Yes,' said Larche slowly and painfully, 'I know exactly what you mean. It's been deliberately – psychologically designed to torment. To torture.' He took the tape out and put it in his attaché case. 'Filthy stuff,' he said in disgust.

'And unlikely to have been created by a local?' Alison ventured.

'I wouldn't like to say.'

They heard her footsteps coming back and stood up, waiting awkwardly as if they were children caught out at a smutty game.

Anita Tomas was as composed as before. 'You've heard the filth?' she asked as automatically as if she was ordering a cocktail.

They nodded. 'It's terrible,' Larche said simply.

'Yes, particularly when it couldn't be stopped. It nearly drove Eduardo insane.' She paused. 'We changed the number many times – but we couldn't always have our calls intercepted. So it proves that it must have been someone who knew what was happening.'

'And Calvino agrees?' asked Larche.

'Yes – even Calvino agrees,' she replied with a wry smile.

'Of course he wasn't . . . very much on the island,' said Alison.

'Oh no – he wasn't.'

'Then . . .'

'He got the letters and heard the tapes in Madrid – even in hotels – once at a house party.'

Larche was clearly shaken. 'That means it's got to be someone very close to him, surely?'

'There are many people physically close to my husband, Marius; servants, secretaries, bodyguards, researchers – the list is very long. Many people knew his movements, his exact whereabouts.'

Larche started to say something and then stopped. Alison watched him curiously, sensing a tension in him that he was trying to disperse.

'Anita – I need to know about the rest of the family. Are they all here on Molino?'

'Yes, they're here. No doubt you'll want to speak to them.'

Larche pulled out a piece of paper from his attaché case. 'We'd like to talk to the family first, if we may. Your son Salvador . . .'

'Is that necessary? He's only fifteen.' But her tone of voice was resigned, as if she was only making a token protest.

'I'm sorry.'

'Very well, but please be gentle with him. He and his father were very close.'

'We shall be gentle with everyone. Then I'd like to talk to Father Blasco Tomas. Is he here or at the monastery?'

'He's here,' she replied flatly.

'Jacinto and Maria?'

'They are here too.'

'And some members of his personal staff – Carlos Mendes, the bodyguard who was with him at the time of the assassination. Then there's his secretary, Julia Descartes, and his research assistant, Damien Alba.'

She nodded. 'They're all on the island, being questioned by Calvino and his people.' She smiled rather automatically. 'I'm sure they won't mind a second round – and we may be joined by Bishop Carlos later.'

'Eduardo told me that Father Miguel had been an adviser to Franco and was now occupying a similar position with the King,' said Larche.

'Yes, but when you say adviser, you must mean spiritual adviser.'

'Or an informant,' said Larche bleakly.

'Informant?' Anita stared at him in some bewilderment. 'What do you mean, informant?'

Larche's voice took on a slightly lecturing note. 'Surely in

Franco's time, the Church was a much more influential part of the state mechanism. It was powerful, it kept the people in order – so no doubt Father Miguel was able to pass on to Franco what was happening in the institution of the Catholic Church, the emotional temperature, the dissidence and so on. I believe he was doing something similar for the King, and I gather he was also keeping the Tomas family informed of what the Head of State was thinking. After all, you are one of the most powerful religious families in Spain. Eduardo's father was a minister in Franco's government, and he was a minister in the King's.'

There was a short silence, during which Alison looked at Larche with renewed interest. His sudden authority, his firmness, his frankness considerably surprised her. Up until now she had seen him as slightly hesitant, very charming but rather lugubrious. Now he had suddenly revealed that there was substance under the urbanity. Glancing across at Anita Tomas she noticed that she too had been surprised and was now at a loss for words.

'I feel the word "informant" is a little off-target,' she said, recovering her poise after a fractional hesitation.

'How would you describe him?'

'As an old and trusted friend who had influence in high places,' she replied quickly.

'And received information from high places?' Larche was relentless.

She smiled bleakly. 'I don't want to make any further comment.'

To Alison, frost seemed to hover in the warm Mediterranean air.

Larche nodded gravely, as if this was her right. 'Who *could* I talk to who knew Father Miguel well?'

'Bishop Carlos.'

'Isn't he an old family friend too?' asked Larche gently.

'Yes, he is. But unlike Father Miguel he has *no* influence in high places. No doubt you will remember the Bishop had a disagreement with the Pope some years ago.'

'Yes,' replied Larche, 'I remember.'

'Carlos was the Bishop of this diocese for some twenty years;

71

he is much respected. Of course he's retired now. Like Blasco he was once a Benedictine – but he left when he defied the Pope.'

'He lives on Fuego?'

'He was born there.'

'And Father Miguel?'

'He, too, was a Benedictine – and was also born on Fuego.'

Larche nodded and then looked out towards the darkening sea. 'We won't bother you with any more questions now.'

'I'll arrange accommodation for you here – for as long as you need.' Anita sounded brisk and formal. 'There is a guest house in the small valley behind us.' She paused. 'I want this ghastly business cleared up. It *has* to be. I want you to have full access to everyone.'

'I think we have that,' said Larche. 'Perhaps everyone could be available for interview tomorrow.'

'I will make sure they are.'

'And Calvino?'

'What about him?'

'Are you satisfied with the way he's conducting this investigation?'

'Yes. I am satisfied. But somehow, when someone is in a less obviously official capacity, people are inclined to open up more.' She looked at Larche as if he was a favoured pupil.

'Yes, I think that's true.' Larche turned to Alison. 'Will you stay?'

'Yes,' she replied stiltedly.

'Eduardo told me that you suffered your own personal tragedy last year,' Anita said to Larche rather regally. 'Your father . . .'

Larche nodded.

'I am very sorry.'

He bowed acknowledgement.

'I'll have you shown to the guest house. Paco will look after you. Thank you for coming.' She gave them a token smile.

The audience is over, thought Alison, and she largely ignored me – which is understandable enough. She obviously thinks, like me, that I'm on a total wild-goose chase. All Anita Tomas wants is Larche; he has the contacts and the authority to find out who killed the man that she loved with such intensity. Alison

72

suppressed a shudder as she wondered what this obsessive woman would do to her husband's killer if she ever confronted him.

'There is something else,' Larche was saying.

'Yes?'

'Your painter. Bernard Morrison. I would like to talk to him as well. He spent a large amount of time with Eduardo. They may have talked; something of interest might arise from those conversations if he can recall them.'

'I'll alert him,' Anita said, walking towards the door where she pressed a bell. 'I do hope you'll be comfortable in the guest house,' she added blandly, and this time the dismissal was unmistakable.

'God, how she loved him,' said Larche when they were out of earshot.

'She frightens me,' replied Alison.

5

The guest house was a smaller replica of the main building, with its own pool and more sculptures that depicted mythical creatures – the unicorn, the centaur and the hydra. Twilight was now stealing over the island, the cicadas were insistent and there was no wind to break the stillness that embraced Molino. Even the waves made no sound.

'Anyone else here?' asked Larche of Paco, the old servant who had brought them across.

'The painter fellow, but I doubt if you'll see him. He's spending the evening with Señora Tomas.'

'Obviously the paintings will help her,' said Alison.

'Yes.' Paco was clearly the most loyal of retainers. 'Thank God for the paintings; it will keep her busy, absorbed, giving instructions. She was devoted to Señor Tomas, you know. Utterly devoted. I can't think what she'll do without him.'

He showed them the lavishly furnished rooms, each with a marble bath and gold taps, extravagant but stylish, with Dali prints on the walls, and then departed, walking slowly away, still clearly stunned by his employer's murder.

When he had gone Larche said quietly, 'He doesn't know what's hit him.'

'Neither does anyone around here,' replied Alison.

Marius Larche lay on his canopied bed, absently surveyed the room, and then rang Monique at Letoric and found her subdued and depressed. She made no attempt to conceal the reason and came to the point immediately.

'I've seen some of your old sketches . . .'

'Yes?' He sounded puzzled.

'Your pictures of Jean-Pierre.'

'They've all been destroyed,' he said sharply, a feeling of nausea sweeping over him. He rose to his feet and stood rigidly by the side of the bed.

'No – there're several of them here.' Her voice was steady. Quiet.

'God . . .'

'It was Estelle – Estelle who found them.'

'The bitch – she's done this deliberately. They don't mean anything – they're from the past.'

Larche thought he heard her give a half-sob – or had it just been a quick intake of breath?

'I'll have to get rid of her,' he said abruptly, knowing that he was blaming the servant for the master's aberrations.

'I wouldn't.' Her tone was dismissive now but he guessed what she was thinking and feeling. 'Anyway, who else would you get to look after the place?'

Larche sighed, knowing she was right and that he was making the situation much worse. Confused feelings of guilt and self-doubt coursed through him.

'I don't think she wants the place changed, or even anyone else to live in it since your mother went into the home. She certainly doesn't want me around.'

'Those pictures . . .' began Larche again. He knew there was nothing he could say, but he didn't want to let the subject drop.

'It's *all right*.' She was having to reassure him now.

'Obviously it's not. Please destroy them and we must talk about it all when I get home. It's a conversation that's very long overdue.'

'Marius,' she insisted, 'I understand. It's all in the past.'

'Surely you expect it to happen again?' he said, unable to keep melodrama out of his voice.

'No, you know I don't. I trust you, Marius. I trust you. Please don't let's talk about this any more. It's my fault – I shouldn't have brought it up. It's just not important. How are you getting on? This dreadful assassination is all over the media here.'

Larche knew how childishly he had been behaving and replied rather grumpily, 'It's very confusing –' Then he stopped himself. 'Look, I love you. I love you so much.'

'I love you, Marius. Stop worrying. We can sort all this out.'

The call ended unsatisfactorily; both realised how frightened and defensive they had been, but neither was really prepared to openly admit as much.

Larche returned to the bed, but he couldn't relax and restlessly got up again and went to the window. The front of the house was in shadow. There was a smooth lawn on which a hose was playing; mosquitoes swarmed in a cloud at one end, while the lights of the Tomas house illuminated a small strip at the other. Dimly he could hear the sound of a cello. The music permeated the twilight, its full, mournful notes reaching out to him, filling his mind with a feeling of space – a clarity he had not experienced for a long time.

Larche moved away from the open window and lay back amidst the vastness of his bed. The clarity remained, and he felt that as long as the cello played his thoughts about Monique and himself were spare and concise – not clouded as they had been before by guilt and evasion.

He knew how profoundly he loved her but he also knew how afraid she was, afraid that he would be unfaithful to her – with a man. Over the first year of his marriage he had felt little temptation and his sexual life with Monique had been rich and tender and fulfilling, but there was always that unspoken danger lying under the surface: in his own case the possibility of temptation; in hers the uncertainty of never being sure if her love was enough for him.

His mind shied away from his obsessive problem, and he began to take a mental inventory of his surroundings. The room was furnished as lavishly as the sitting-room of the main house. Natural wood had been used; he wasn't entirely sure what it was, but it gave off a slightly sweet aroma that was satisfying. Rugs were scattered over the tiled floor, and the room was dominated by the magnificent four-poster bed, its damask hangings depicting sea-serpents in a jade sea.

Larche's thoughts turned to Alison Rowe. He admired her assertiveness and guessed that she must have fought hard to attain her present position. His experience of high-ranking British policemen had not been good; compared with their more civilized French counterparts he had found them brutish and manipulative and he was well aware of their sexist attitude to women.

She must be made of good stuff, he thought. There was something else about her that appealed to him; was it her single-mindedness, her obvious vulnerability, the fact that he was sure she had driven herself too hard and too long? Perhaps this ill-defined hunt for her assassin would be a catharsis. Larche closed his eyes against another much more buried thought that was tunnelling its way up from deep in his subconscious: there was something about Alison that attracted him – not only mentally but physically as well. The idea shocked him but it refused to go away.

Alison Rowe had gone for a walk to watch the night creep over the Mediterranean from a small beach that she had discovered to the west of the house. The sea was very calm, the dark sky clear and a pale crescent moon hung over the island. Alison felt much less troubled, although she knew it was probably only a temporary reprieve, and she was surprised to find she was able to think about Hooper with a new objectivity. For years she had buried the obscenity of what he had done to her, trying to enclose him in a sealed compartment in her mind. What did she really think about him, now that she was forced to confront his shadowy image? Was there hatred in her? Alison doubted that. Was there bitterness? Not really that either. The effect he had on her was so deeply degrading that even now she was quite unable to admit it, even to herself.

Gradually the weary permanence of her thoughts about Hooper began to ease as Marius Larche's face swam into her mind. Instinctively she knew he was troubled too. There was a hesitancy about him, a ruefulness that was subtle and elusive. At first he had seemed too laid back to have much authority, but when authority was demanded it came – and came quickly. She felt she had a good working relationship with him and didn't find him patronizing. What was more, he clearly respected her opinion and Alison didn't feel she had to battle against him as she had to with her English colleagues. Larche had taken her seriously, at face value; a Mediterranean man, how infinitely preferable to the Nordic type – mean of spirit, sharp in competition, insecurely looking over their shoulders, breathing in the thin, cold air of a sterile country, well past its imperial prime.

Alison sat down on the warm sand and stared into the gleaming, ebbing sea, now gently moving under the crescent moon. Quite suddenly, without procrastination, without even much surprise at actually having made one at last, she came to a decision. She would stop competing and marry Tom, and she would do her best to banish a little more each day the grim and all-pervasive shadow of Hooper and his invasion into her dreams. A sense of exquisite happiness instantly invaded her; for the first time in years she felt at peace.

Paco arrived to tell Marius Larche that dinner would be served in the guest house at nine. Looking at his watch, Larche saw that it was eight and he would have time for a leisurely shower. Then the telephone rang. It was Calvino.

'How did you get on with Señora Tomas?'

'I've read the letters and heard the tape. She was very co-operative.'

'She was devoted to her husband.'

'That's what everyone keeps telling me.'

'Do you doubt it?'

'I usually doubt everybody and everything in a case like this, but I have no reason to suppose she wasn't.' There was a short silence then Larche continued. 'Look, I want to spend tomorrow interviewing.' He read him the list. 'Alison Rowe will join me.'

'They should all be around. But do you want one of my men to give them a ring – say, early tomorrow morning?'

'That would be most helpful.' There was a hint of surprise in Larche's voice; he hadn't expected Calvino to be so co-operative.

Calvino took the point. 'The more we pool our knowledge . . .'

'I shall definitely do that.'

'You think you'll get through them all in a day?'

'I shall try. Suppose we have dinner tomorrow night – about nine?'

'That would be a pleasure.' There was another short silence. 'Did you think that Anita Tomas was holding anything back?'

'It's impossible to say.'

'Nothing obvious?'

'She was clearly horrified by the letters – even more so by the tapes. I mean – they *are* horrifying. I couldn't pin-point anything but I'll talk to her again when I've seen everybody else.'

'I'm glad you're here, Señor Larche. I feel I need all the help I can get.'

'Why's that?'

'*She's* been on to my boss.'

'She?'

'Who else but Señora Tomas. Do you not understand what a powerful woman she is, Señor Larche?' His voice rose.

'Yes – I think I do,' replied Larche slowly, conscious that Calvino was beginning to work himself into a frenzy.

'She says I'm not listening to her, not achieving results.'

'He's only been dead two days.' Larche paused. 'Where is he going to be buried?'

'At Empuries – where the Olympic flame was brought ashore last year.'

'That's a good place,' Larche replied quietly.

'Yes.' Calvino was impatient now. 'I have just two days before the funeral, señor; it's not long enough. She wants to see some action by then.'

'And if not?'

'I could be replaced.'

79

'Just like that?'

'Yes, señor,' said Calvino unhappily. 'Just like that.'

'Can she *really* have you replaced in this high-handed manner?' Larche was incredulous. 'I was told the Spanish government were looking for quick results but surely –'

'I assure you she can,' Calvino cut in. 'I have been very thorough in my enquiries – so has my whole investigating team – but I would appreciate pooling information, particularly as you are something of a family friend.'

'I'll keep you in the picture,' promised Larche.

'Come over to the mainland tomorrow night,' urged Calvino. 'Meet me at the Coll. It's a restaurant just off the main square. You can't miss it.'

'Very well.'

'And by the way, will you be bringing your colleague – the one who is searching for the assassin?'

'Of course.'

'What do you think of this assassin theory – this Hooper business?'

'I don't think anything at the moment,' replied Larche, wondering how much longer Calvino was going to detain him with his insecurity, 'but I'm sure I'll have more to tell you tomorrow night.'

Calvino rang off regretfully, as if the mere sound of Larche's voice was reassuring to him.

Larche undressed and stood in the shower. It looks as if I'm suddenly becoming invaluable, he thought cynically.

Alison Rowe was also in the shower, thinking about Hooper again. Now that she had made her traumatic decision to leave the force she was discovering a new objectivity. Hooper's face was etched into her consciousness and she was entirely confident that she would be able to identify him if the occasion demanded, but the occasion also seemed extremely remote. Alison allowed his face to slide into her mind. She would know his smile anywhere but it was impossible to describe – impossible even to draw. No identikit picture could possibly do justice to it. The full lips, the smile, the lustful pleasure – she knew for a certainty she would never forget him.

For some years she had wondered why Hooper hadn't come to her – had never tried to kill her – for she was certain that he was aware that she could identify him. That moment of realization had been a two-way experience; she was sure of it. Did he have a wife and children? Was he a loner? What kind of sexual identity, sexual desires did he have? Was he crazy or was he calculating? Who was he? Her thoughts ran on and she knew there was little she could do to check them. That was what was so depressing about the state of her emotions. Hooper had made them his own.

Dinner was on a small candle-lit terrace overlooking the pool. At first, Larche thought it might only be for him and Alison and he felt a rush of adrenalin, but then he saw a third place had been laid and the elation was replaced by disappointment.

Larche sipped a gin and tonic and watched a firefly flicker amongst some bougainvillaea that bordered the pool. He could smell the scent of rosemary and a tiny breeze, as slight as the firefly's light, cooled the warm air.

The crescent moon hung over the small valley in which the guest house lay; bare rock and small stunted bushes littered the rugged ascent to the main house. On the right, sheer cliffs soared above him but on the left, the rock fell gently away to the sea, which resembled a sheet of barely rippling silk. Small islands dotted the dark, winking expanse of water and Larche could just make out the mass of iridescent lights that marked the mainland. The silence was absolute, its cushion so intense that he started badly, twisting round abruptly when he heard the soft voice.

'Excuse me.'

The man was standing in the shadows, tall, very thin, with a bald pate which shone pallidly, caught by the wan rays of the moon. Then he stepped into the candle-light and Larche could see him more clearly. The features were beaky, untanned, but even so Larche was struck by the unmistakable likeness to Eduardo. He was wearing dark grey trousers and a loose cotton top of a similar colour; a large wooden cross dangled from a heavy chain around his neck.

'I'm sorry to have startled you. My name is Blasco. Blasco Tomas. You will be Detective Chief Inspector Larche? I don't think we met on any of your previous visits.'

'No.'

'I have to admit I'm hungry – despite everything.' Blasco rubbed his hands together rather awkwardly and Larche noticed that they were swollen and disfigured with what he took to be arthritis. 'The food here is very good, and the wine. I look forward to coming home occasionally; in fact I have to say that I make excuses to come. But this time . . .' He made a rather hopeless gesture. 'I wish I could say I had lost my appetite, but I always eat large quantities of food when I'm depressed.' He spoke slowly and easily in English and his eyes never left Larche's for a moment.

'I'm hungry too,' Larche replied quietly.

'Are you making progress?' The question was asked abruptly and Blasco's fingers shook. With an effort, he made them steady again, but his body language clearly stated how uneasy he was.

Paco appeared with a pastis. He obviously knew exactly what Blasco preferred. Larche waited for him to disappear as silently as he had come before answering the question.

'I've only just arrived.' He didn't want to put Blasco at his ease – nor did he wish to make him unduly defensive. Somehow Larche needed to strike a balance of detachment.

'I'm very sorry. Of course I've heard about you . . .' He paused and then spoke more positively. 'If there's *anything* you can do to discover the identity of my brother's murderer –' He paused again and continued with difficulty. 'We were close despite our different callings and I loved him dearly.'

'I shall do my best,' Larche replied. 'I have to say I feel I let Eduardo down very badly.' Again he was confessing, he thought, this time appropriately enough to a priest.

'I've discussed all that with Anita,' said Blasco. 'We both consider you have nothing to blame yourself for.' He changed the

82

subject rather quickly. 'Are you finding that rather desperate man Calvino co-operative?'

'Yes. But what do you mean, desperate?'

'Well, I would imagine his head will be on the chopping block if he doesn't find a positive lead very quickly.'

'He said that himself.'

'My sister-in-law is particularly ... powerful, in terms of chopping blocks.' Blasco sipped his Pernod and smiled at Larche rather as if he was sharing a deeper confidence than the one he was offering. 'When would you like to see me?' There was a cautious eagerness to his question, as if he was anxious to prove how co-operative he was going to be.

'Tomorrow – one of Calvino's men is arranging a schedule.'

Blasco looked surprised. 'He *is* being helpful. I had a very long session with him, but I'm afraid he didn't find me particularly illuminating. I can't for the life of me think of anyone who would kill my brother – either politically or socially.' There was a long pause which Larche didn't attempt to interrupt, then Blasco continued as he had hoped he would. 'My brother was a man of integrity – unlike most politicians – and he tried to carry out his duties in as Christian a way as possible. He was a great humanist – and he cared very much for the Spanish people ...'

This is becoming a eulogy, thought Larche. What was more, he was certain that Blasco's homily was protective. There was something about its intensity that was too powerful – almost too commanding.

'... both in terms of the population at large, and locals here.'

'What was the attitude of the locals to your brother?'

'They've given him nothing but trouble ever since he restored the fishing industry at Sebastia, but that's quite understandable. They are narrow, ill-educated people and they don't like change.' He sounded impassioned but still protective. Then Larche noticed that Blasco had begun to speak more casually, as if he had realized how artificial he was sounding. 'Tourism is a well-established business here now and they've got used to it. Most of them didn't want to go back to the old ways; they've largely been forgotten – and besides, it's much easier to bleed tourists than earn a living by fishing.'

'Would someone have killed him because of that?'

'I don't think so. I mean, it does seem an inadequate reason for such a drastic step.'

Does it, wondered Larche. Maybe someone stood to lose everything in Sebastia.

Blasco stood up as Alison Rowe came out on to the terrace. She was wearing a pale blue print dress, dark blue stockings and a jade necklace – a combination that made her look slightly austere.

'Blasco Tomas – Alison Rowe.' They shook hands and Paco brought in a first course of poached truffles. But it was not until they were into the second – Lobster Newburg – that Larche felt able to draw Blasco out even further on the subject of the island, Sebastia and the suspicious hostility of those on the mainland.

'As Anita has no doubt told you,' he began, 'much of the old life of the Costa has been destroyed by tourism. When you go to Sebastia, all you'll see is a simple fishing village, but in the harbour there are thirty boats. They're bringing home big catches now and they have modern equipment. That's the industry my brother made, and he was prepared to extend it to the mainland.' He was beginning to sound defensive again.

'But why don't they want it?' asked Alison, sipping the good white Chablis that had been served with the lobster. 'The tourist trade's falling off in the European recession, and isn't the King trying to restore the environment, to drive everything up-market?'

Blasco nodded. 'Yes, but I understand their reluctance. At least, I understand it to some extent.'

'What extent?' asked Larche quickly.

'Eduardo appointed a manager in Sebastia to oversee the fleet and handle the distribution of its catch. He's rather a controversial fellow unfortunately.'

'What's the matter with him?' asked Alison.

'He drives the fishermen too hard, insists they go out in all weathers.'

'And was that Eduardo's wish?' asked Larche.

'He was hardly ever here – and he believed in hard work. Lorenzo simply said he worked the men hard and Eduardo accepted it. But it's more than that: Lorenzo dominates the village; he's all-powerful. The fishermen are afraid of him, and so are their families. There are no unions involved; he can sack a man on the spot, deprive him of both his home and his livelihood, so as you can see – he's a force to be reckoned with.'

'Don't they have any protection against him?' asked Alison. 'I mean – it seems so out of character for your brother to have treated them in this way.'

'I just feel he had a blind spot about Lorenzo. Eduardo hardly had the common touch. In fact he was downright feudal.' Blasco paused.

'In what way?' prompted Larche.

Blasco looked reluctant and then plunged into speech. 'Well, the fishermen of Sebastia had to mortgage their cottages with Eduardo in return for the family trust's financial assistance in providing modern equipment. Eduardo was always the businessman.' Blasco paused uneasily. 'He wanted people to be responsible – to understand and comply with the work ethic.'

'That would have been understandably feudal,' said Alison Rowe, thinking of her own background, 'but it doesn't account for Eduardo's letting his servant run amok.'

Blasco bowed acknowledgement.

'Why did Eduardo let Lorenzo get away with it?' asked Larche, mystified.

Blasco shrugged. 'I don't know. I appealed to Eduardo time and time again, but he wouldn't listen. For some reason Lorenzo could do no wrong.'

'What does that imply?' interpolated Alison. 'That he had some kind of hold over Eduardo?'

'I don't know.' Blasco drank some more wine. 'I just don't know.' There was something so despairing about the way he bent over his glass that both Alison Rowe and Marius Larche felt an onrush of pity for him.

'Did you tell Calvino all this?' asked Larche very gently.

'Oh yes. He's already seen Lorenzo, but I don't know if he came to any conclusion.' He paused. 'You must remember I don't come to Molino very often – and anyway, I see things differently. My two brothers and their wives – even my nephew Salvador – they are people who revel in power and influence. Eduardo lived for politics; Anita for her music; Jacinto and Maria for pleasure and excitement. Even Salvador is ambitious. To what end I don't know but I can feel it in him. It was the same when we were children: the powerful, privileged family; the love of power. It wasn't as if it was all bad; Eduardo, as I've already told you, was in general a power for good, as far as any politician can be. But I didn't want any of it. I'd always had a desire for the contemplative life. At first I wanted to be a priest and then I visited Fuego and knew that I wanted to join the community there – knew that that was what I wanted to do with my life. It all seemed gloriously simple at one time, but of course it's been very hard.'

'Do you spend all your time on Fuego?' asked Larche.

'No, I'm sent where I'm needed. I'm a qualified teacher so I've occasionally worked in schools, and very often amongst the destitute in Barcelona and Girona. In between I return to the island – to Fuego – both to seek spiritual replenishment and to help the community.'

Paco came in to clear the plates away and to place cheese and fruit on the table with more wine. When he had gone, Blasco said, 'I've talked of myself and my own family, but I know nothing about either of you. Tell me about yourselves.'

Much to their own surprise Marius Larche and Alison Rowe found themselves telling him. Blasco was a good listener and clearly had a gift for drawing people out. Nevertheless, they both gave carefully edited versions of their lives, wondering at the same time if he suspected there was more.

Alison told them about her home, her relationship with her father, her struggle to succeed as a woman in the British police force and, glancingly, the greater struggle back from the physical shock and pain that Hooper had given her. She did not, however, mention the fire in the family home, the vengeful gardener and the mental scars of the shooting.

86

Larche described the murder of his father, the subsequent murders in St Esprit, and the unmasking of Alain, but he naturally said nothing of Jean-Pierre.

Blasco listened as Larche had never seen anyone listen before, and he and Alison found themselves talking well into the night, not being self-indulgent but with genuine, if edited, feelings of confession and renewal. In Larche's case he felt a catharsis, and knew that he wanted to speak to Blasco again, this time alone. Gradually, as he half listened to Alison, he realized that he wanted to tell Blasco more, that he wanted to touch on his own personal dilemma, that despite his loyalty to Monique he had a right to, for Blasco was a holy man, a monk, could have been a priest – *was* a kind of priest to whom he could, should confess.

Larche relaxed as the good wine went down, and he observed Blasco listening to Alison intently, with gentle concentration. It was a considerable ability to be such a good listener, he thought.

Eventually, after coffee and an ethereal local liqueur, they parted, bid each other goodnight and went to bed.

But Larche found sleep impossible; he spent hours tossing and turning, oblivious of the case, of the tragedy, even of Monique. He just couldn't get Alison Rowe out of his mind, and eventually his gathering erection forced him out of bed to wander restlessly to the window and then back to the four-poster, where his desire continued to grow. This is ridiculous, he thought. I've never felt this way in my life before. What was so special about this British policewoman? What had she finally awakened in him?

Eventually Larche drifted into a light sleep, dreaming that Monique was watching him make love to Alison Rowe while Anita Tomas's cello accompanied their gyrations. Monique pleaded with him to stop as she sat on the edge of the bed with her head in her hands, but her entreaties were ignored.

'Haven't I had to bear enough?' she cried, but rather than

87

leaving the room, she pushed him aside and began to caress Alison Rowe.

Larche groaned, waking to find himself lying on his back, his erection gone but no sign of the climax he had shared. Instead, he was shivering and the sweat lay cold on his chest. Sometime later, he heard a noise outside the window and sat up, his head throbbing and his mouth dry. Wasn't that a door being lightly shut?

Hurrying to the window, Larche looked out into the moonlit garden and saw Alison Rowe walking slowly past the statue of a centaur.

'God! You terrified me!'

'I'm sorry.'

Larche had followed her on to the rocks that overlooked the Medes, the lazy swell rolling up to the reef without vigour, combing them with a lethargic sheet of water.

'I don't think it's wise to walk about on your own at night.'

'No. No, of course not.' She decided not to be annoyed or patronized. 'It wasn't very clever, but I couldn't sleep,' she explained. 'I found the bedroom oppressive. I mean – it's very luxurious but claustrophobic somehow. I had a job to open the window.'

'Do you normally have difficulty sleeping?'

'Off and on – yes, as a matter of fact, I do,' she admitted. 'Ever since I was shot by Hooper. The months after I came out of hospital were pretty bad. I've been better recently but sometimes . . .'

'Particularly since he's emerged again?' suggested Larche gently.

'Yes – I find it very difficult playing this role. Although I'm sure he's miles from here, maybe not even in Barcelona. But it's not that – I feel him inside. Do you know what I mean?'

'Yes.'

'It's a dreadful feeling.'

'Do you dream about him?'

'Yes,' she said slowly.

'Do you want to tell me about the dreams?' Larche was very hesitant now and his question was followed by a long silence.

'I dream that he's screwing me,' she said at last, her voice stilted, restrained.

Larche said nothing.

'Have I shocked you?'

'No – no, of course you haven't. Do you . . . have the dream a lot?'

'I do at the moment.' She looked up at him, and in the shadowed moonlight Larche could see that her eyes were bright with disgust and anger. 'It's so fucking revolting.'

'Have you had any help?'

'A shrink? Yes – but she didn't do me any good.' Alison looked down at the gently moving sea. 'In fact I thought about Hooper more after I'd seen her than I did before.' She laughed. 'Thank you psychiatry.'

'Are you – do you have a boy-friend?'

'Yes. Tom. I'm thinking of packing in this damn job and marrying him.'

Larche felt the pain of his need for her acutely, its intensity a shock; he had not expected to feel physical desire for more than one woman. Monique had been difficult enough. 'What's stopping you?' he said coolly.

Alison hesitated. 'I used to pretend to myself it was because of the job, but the real problem is that – every time I go to bed with Tom . . .'

'Hooper comes between the sheets too?'

'It's horrendous.' A single tear ran down her cheek and Alison angrily wiped it away. 'Goddamn it! Why am I telling you all this?'

'You don't have to. Shall I go away?'

'No. Please stay. It's just that – I'm being so unprofessional.'

Larche shrugged. 'You can't be on duty all the time. Besides, if you don't talk about these things . . .' He let his voice fade away. 'Have you spoken to Tom?'

'No.'

'Wouldn't that help?'

'I feel so ashamed,' she said bitterly. 'It's all so bloody squalid.'

Larche looked at Alison Rowe in her jeans and sweater. If anyone was being squalid, it was himself, for he knew he was about to take advantage of her.

'But it's good to tell someone,' she continued. 'Specially now. I suppose once I get back to London, maybe these – feelings – the dreams will lessen.' She paused and then said quickly, 'I hope you don't mind me telling you. The point is – I think I can. You're very sympathetic, monsieur.'

'Please call me Marius. I'm glad that you can confide in me. I think we work well together and –' His words were coming too fast but she didn't seem to notice. Larche slowed himself up. 'I want you to go on talking to me about this dream. Maybe that will drive him out.'

'We're on a case,' she said blankly.

'And the case involves you.' He was calmer now. 'You're part of the whole dark business.'

'Hooper may be irrelevant.'

'Certainly. But you're not.' Larche reached out and touched her shoulder, watching the outline of her legs against the rock, the erotic charge inside him making him want to take her now.

'Thank you.' She took his hand very briefly and her touch was soft and cool. 'I'm not going to be a liability.'

'Why should you be?'

'There have been enough confessionals,' she muttered.

For a moment Larche was thrown and then quickly marshalled his thoughts. 'You mean . . .'

'Eduardo.'

'Yes – but I doubt if he was confessing at the time. Father Miguel had asked him to come.'

'Do you have any ideas?' she asked.

'Not yet. Not until we've started interviewing. But I'm still more inclined to the political assassination theory than the internal problems – even if Eduardo did have some kind of brothel on his doorstep.'

'With a built-in concierge?' she reminded him.

'Lorenzo's obviously an unsavoury and manipulative character but nothing points to him. Maybe there's someone in Sebastia who resents being under Lorenzo's yoke sufficiently to kill Eduardo, but it would have been easier to kill Lorenzo – it all seems a bit far-fetched.'

'So we come full circle,' said Alison.

'To Hooper? We might do.' Suddenly Larche knew he couldn't be with her much longer without doing something stupid – something that he would very much regret. 'We'd better get back.' He yawned artificially. 'I'll be good for nothing tomorrow.'

'I'm sorry I woke you.' She stood up and they began to clamber away from the slippery rocks with their strong smell of seaweed, leaving the black velvet of the Mediterranean gently nudging at the reef.

'I wasn't sleeping too well myself. I feel better for the fresh air. But what about you? Will you sleep now?'

'I don't know. Hopefully. It was being shut into that damn room with Hooper. I couldn't get him out of my mind unless I left.'

'Is he still in your bed?'

'Maybe.'

'If I come in – will he go?' Larche's voice was trembling so much that he only just managed to get the words out, but she didn't seem to notice.

'Maybe he would.' She sounded like a delighted child. 'But we'd have to be careful – make sure Paco doesn't see us.' Alison suddenly pulled herself together and laughed uneasily. 'I mean – it wouldn't do for us both to be seen in one bedroom. Unprofessionalism again.'

'I only want to exorcize your demon lover,' said Larche, hardly knowing what he was saying, his heart pounding and his sexual adrenalin rising to a height he had only known in his encounters with Jean-Pierre. He fought for control but failed, the cold sweat of mixed desire and fear on his back. 'Let's hurry,' he said, conscious that his voice was shaking even more now. Surely she must have noticed.

But Alison just smiled and continued to climb lithely over

the slippery black rocks. Larche had the alarming but exultant vision of tearing off her clothes and rising and falling on the canopied bed that he was sure she had in her room. He stumbled and almost fell, cursing and feeling ridiculous.

'Are you all right?' A cloud passed across the moon, blotting out her features, leaving only her disembodied voice. He was surprised to find how strong and clear it was, unlike her body, scarred inside and out by that anonymous bastard Hooper. Damn him, he thought fiercely – this dark shadow of an assassin who had touched and tainted her very soul.

They walked stealthily back into the guest house, surreptitiously closed the door and climbed the stairs to the bedrooms. Once inside, Alison switched on a small lamp on the dressing table and flooded the space with soft, muted light.

As he had suspected, the room was almost identical to his own. Alison sat on one of the two Regency chairs that faced each other across a low table with Larche in the other. He felt they were at something of an impasse. Then, rather uncertainly, he remembered the so-called avuncular reason for his visit.

'Do you want to talk about what happened?' he asked. 'I mean – when Hooper shot you.'

Alison shook her head. 'No – it's pretty hazy anyway.'

'Can I make love to you?' Larche spoke the words slowly, amazed at the simplicity of getting them out. After he had said them, he felt as if he was in shock.

Alison stared back at him very calmly, her features composed. There was no trace of any surprise. 'I thought you might say that,' she said.

'Did you?' He was alarmed now, wondering if she was going to laugh at him.

'I think we both felt that – down by the rocks.'

'You too?'

'I don't know why.' She paused. 'I mean – I didn't feel directly I met you that I was going to . . . to want to . . .'

'I'm glad,' said Larche simply. He got up and walked over to her, taking both of her hands and pulling her up. 'If we make love, will that help you exorcize Hooper? Will you think about what *we* did – and not fantasize about him?'

'I don't know. But that's not the reason I want to do it with you.'

'What about Tom?' asked Larche.

'I love him.'

'I love Monique,' said Larche. 'We haven't been married very long.'

'Then perhaps you should think again,' she replied gently, warily.

'No.'

'You're sure?'

'Quite sure.' He hesitated uncertainly, nervous about asking her the same question. Then he said abruptly, 'What about you?'

'I'd like to have sex with you, providing you don't think me . . .'

'Unprofessional?' He smiled for the first time, amazed but delighted by her bluntness – her miraculous acceptance of it all. 'You mustn't keep saying that.'

She began to lead him towards the bed. They were both trembling slightly.

'I'm getting boring, am I?' There was a slight tartness to her voice.

'Something like that.'

'Will I be boring if I screw the arse off you?'

The hardening took hold and suddenly Larche couldn't fence and cut and parry any longer. They fell on the bed, thrashing, making little muffled noises of desire, pulling clumsily at each other's clothes but somehow getting them off.

'I'm hot for this,' she muttered, biting his ear and running her hands over his body.

'Sebastia isn't in it,' grunted Larche as they rolled and entwined on the generously sized bed.

Alison laughed as they grappled. 'Bedroom farce,' she whispered. 'Isn't that something you French specialize in?'

'Not farce,' replied Larche, battling not to come to a climax too quickly. 'Bedrooms, yes.'

* * *

After it was over, they lay naked side by side, looking up at the painted stuccoed ceiling.

'That was good,' she breathed.

'I think it was wonderful. Don't let's say much about Tom and Monique. Don't let's say that we love them and this is just a one-night stand.'

'It must be,' she replied. 'You know it must be.'

He did but didn't want to say so. 'Do you mind if I tell you something?'

'Another confession?'

'I suppose so. It's just that . . .' Larche hesitated and then felt compelled to continue. 'I've never felt this way about a woman – the way I feel about you. The physical way.'

'Why?' she asked bluntly.

'Because – ever since I was a child – I thought I was gay. I had a number of affairs with men – although affair is somewhat glorifying the event. Then I met Monique and I genuinely love her. But not physically. Not exactly. I never loved the men. But you – I feel so physically drawn to you, physically excited by you. It's incredible.'

'And the sex? Did that let you down?'

'No. It was wonderful, but I know how selfish I'm being – and I'm sorry.' He winced, knowing he sounded hypocritical.

'Don't be. You're a very good lover, Marius. I enjoyed what we did very much.'

'Tom?'

'He's a good lover too, but he's not here on the island, and I needed this now.'

'Because you think Hooper's on the island – in spirit?'

'Maybe in fact. Who knows? But it wasn't just that. I needed this, Marius, and not to shore me up. I was drawn to you so much.'

'Just physically?' he asked.

'More than that. But there isn't a future.' She stroked his chest.

'No.' He tried to sound sure. Would he feel differently about Monique now? Would he be able to stop forcing himself, to feel physical as well as spiritual love for her? In the end, wasn't the

94

latter more important, more binding? But what did Monique think? They made love regularly – she had never indicated she found what they did unsatisfactory.

'Do you want me again?' asked Alison. 'I want you.'

Back in his own room, Larche lay between the cool sheets, and slept dreamlessly for the little that remained of the night. He woke the next morning completely refreshed – mentally as well as physically. Clear, luminous Mediterranean light stole through the half-open shutters and from somewhere he could smell the aroma of good, strong coffee. For a while he lay on his back, contemplating the powerful events of last night, the miracle of what he had felt for a woman for the first time at forty-eight years old.

After a while he turned to the bedside phone and dialled the number of the Château Letoric. 'Did you sleep?' he asked.

'Not very well. I feel Estelle's hostility to me. I'm going to see your mother today which will annoy her even more.' Monique's voice was low and depressed.

'I doubt if Mother will recognize you,' he said, desperately trying to sound casual yet concerned.

'I'm not sure that she recognizes Estelle.'

'Don't ever tell her that,' cautioned Larche.

'I won't. How's it going out there?'

'With great difficulty.' He tried to think of something honest to say to her, and failed. Instead he floundered, casting clumsily about. 'I met a very unusual man last night – a monk – Eduardo's brother. He had this extraordinary ability to listen.' He had wanted to say something profound to her, something unaffected by last night.

'He sounds interesting,' replied Monique rather wearily. Then she asked impatiently, 'When are you coming back?'

'I can't say. Not yet. I know you can't wait to get away from Letoric.' He inwardly resented the fact that she couldn't assert herself over the recalcitrant Estelle.

'I'm missing you, Marius.' Her voice was bleak. 'Is something the matter? You sound most peculiar.'

'It's just the strain of it all.' He was on his guard at once. 'I'm missing *you*,' Larche added gently.

'Despite your British police lady?' But she was laughing.

'Despite her.' Larche spoke calmly.

'Do you get on with her all right?' said Monique curiously. 'You don't say much about her.'

'Yes, she's a nice person.'

'Absence doesn't always make the heart grow fonder. You can't take it for granted,' she said, and laughed to take the sting out of the comment. 'I always seem to need reassurance,' she added quickly, almost angrily. 'Especially with Estelle's disapproving face around.'

Larche tried to be more positive, to imagine that there was life outside Molino and it included Monique. 'Look – we don't have to restore Letoric. Let it rot – and Estelle with it.'

'She'll be all right if you're here.'

'And when I'm not? I'm going to get rid of her,' he said and then wondered if he was overdoing it.

'You can't do that – she's a family retainer.'

'She's a menace.'

'Estelle can't help it – she really can't. She sees me as an interloper.'

'You're the mistress of the house, not her.'

'God, how can you be so feudal? That's what comes of owning a château – however run-down.'

'I'll phone you tonight in Lyon.' Larche looked at his watch, wanting to end the conversation.

'OK. Goodbye, darling. Take care of yourself.'

'And you.'

He put the receiver down gently and got off the bed. Going over to the windows he pushed the shutters open, desperately needing fresh air. But all he smelt – or seemed to smell – was fetid Mediterranean ozone.

'*Buenos dias.*'

'Oh – good morning.'

Alison Rowe stood in bright eight o'clock sunshine, staring

out to sea. She had returned to the same cove she had visited the night before, not sure now of the resolution she had made there. Their love-making had been very special, and although Alison was entirely certain that she was not in love with Marius Larche, she also knew that she wanted him again – wanted him badly. Mixed feelings of guilt came and went but the central overruling desire remained. She needed Larche – and she was sure that he needed her. Then to her surprise, her thoughts were interrupted by Blasco Tomas, jogging across the sand towards her, looking slightly incongruous in a grey jogging track suit with a blue flash down one side. He laughed as she examined his appearance with interest.

'Aren't monks allowed to jog?'

'Of course.'

'And wear jogging suits?'

'Why not?' She laughed too, easily confident of their relationship.

'I've always kept myself fit.'

'I try to,' said Alison, wondering how artificially bright she sounded, 'but there's not a lot of time. I play squash regularly, but I don't think I could fit in a jogging programme.'

'Surely a police officer needs to be able to chase the villains?'

'Not when you're in my position. I just push pieces of paper round a desk.'

'You look well on it,' he said, smiling. 'In fact you look radiant.'

'Well, I made a decision last night.'

'What was that?' Blasco asked gently. 'If it's not confidential.'

'I decided to leave the police force and get married, and have children.' Alison wanted to affirm the commitment.

Blasco clapped his hands and opened his arms. Without thinking she ran into them and they hugged each other. 'May God bless you,' he said. 'May God bless you.'

Alison slowly broke away from him, feeling uneasy. It had seemed the most natural thing in the world to run into his arms and receive his blessing, but now all she felt was increased guilt.

'Will you have a paddle?' said Blasco unexpectedly. 'It's the kind of activity monks are allowed to do – better than jogging and sweating anyway.'

They stood knee-deep in the cool Mediterranean, looking out towards the islands that sparkled with crystal sunshine. A few early sailing boats skimmed the emerald surface and gulls wheeled and dived in the wake of an outgoing fishing boat.

'I'm sorry.' Alison shivered suddenly. 'I'm behaving like a child. You're mourning your brother's death and I'm just going on about myself. Please forgive me.'

'There's nothing to forgive.' His legs were brown and slender under his rolled-up track suit trousers. He must have been about forty-six but he had the legs of a much younger man, she thought. 'I loved Eduardo very deeply – as a brother and as a man. He had great power of personality – of influence. He had achieved most of what he set out to achieve. I know he didn't want to become Prime Minister. And he was proud of the model fishing fleet he had created here – the way he had revived an old and failing industry.'

'Was he a good Catholic?'

Blasco paused. 'I wouldn't say he was that. But then, who is?'

'Are you?'

'I try. And fail.'

He turned to look back up the cove and the silenced automatic pistol fired again and again. Blasco moved forward protestingly a few feet, the ragged holes opening in his chest and forehead. Then he pitched forward.

Glancing at his watch Marius Larche saw that there was just time to take a quick stroll on the cliffs and then return for breakfast.

As he ran lightly down the stairs, he met Paco who looked more rheumy-eyed and mottled than ever.

'When will you require breakfast, señor?'

'Half eight? I thought I'd just take a quick stroll.'

'Very well, señor. Your colleague is also walking.'

'Ah.'

'And Father Tomas followed soon after.'

'Tomas?'

'Father Blasco Tomas.'

'Ah – well, maybe I'll catch them up.' He had an odd, unsettling feeling of anxiety. 'Do you know which way they went?'

'Over towards the sea – I think to the cove.'

'Just over there?'

'Yes, señor.'

Feeling childishly excluded, Larche hurried over the rocks, climbing up the valley and then down towards the flickering cobalt blue of the ocean.

Within seconds he was sweating, and looking up he saw the sun was already high in the sky, a red, hazy orb which was nevertheless already generating a substantial heat. It's going to be blazing hot, he thought miserably, not a day for sitting indoors conducting interviews. I'll use the terrace, he decided, as he scrambled down the warm boulders to the lapping water, but all the time he was really thinking about Alison Rowe's body and of how their love-making had changed him. On the one hand Larche felt elated, and on the other confused and apprehensive.

The cove was tiny and bounded by long fingers of sinewy rock that ran out into the breeze-stirred sea. Again, as last night, he was struck by the silence of the island; there was not even the cry of a bird to break the flat calm of air and water. Then he saw them – dozens of gulls perched on the ledges of the cliff, staring down at the narrow strip of beach.

Suddenly, one of their number detached itself from the cliff face and fluttered down to a great slab lying on the sand, half in and half out of the sea. Slab? It didn't quite look like rock. It was softer, less substantial. Puzzled, Marius Larche stared down at the unrecognizable object. Then, with a little gasp, he began to run.

6

Alison Rowe and Blasco Tomas lay together, face down on the beach, their heads almost dug into the sand. Spreadeagled, half in, half out of the water, they lay still while the tiny waves licked at the great pools of crimson liquid flowing from their shattered bodies. Pulp, brains and other matter protruded and already a cloud of black flies hovered over the whole shambles.

'God!' Marius Larche sank to his knees beside them, shaking all over, making little noises of combined fear and revulsion. 'Please God – no.' The shock was incredible; the nausea overwhelming. He shut his eyes, looked again at the carnage and the dark blood and was sick all over the fine white sand.

Larche went on retching until he could retch no more. Then, very shakily, he stood up and moved closer to the bodies, horribly aware that the cloud of black flies had thickened. At once he noticed that their hands were interlocked, and as he bent down to touch Alison Rowe's arm he found that it was still warm.

By now he was sweating so profusely that it was as if he was running a fever; every limb of his body seemed to be immobile and his head throbbed with searing pain. Hot tears sprang to his eyes and he clenched his fists tightly, looking up at the mocking heat of the burning sun. Then he cried out with rage and horror and despair, the sound ringing and echoing over the cove, frightening the seabirds into flight above him, their cries combining with his, rending the air with primeval force.

'Holy Mother!'

Calvino was suddenly standing beside him without Larche

having even noticed his arrival. He was wearing a white suit with sweat patches under the arms and he wore no tie.

'Holy Mother!' He repeated the phrase and then looked, mesmerized, at the bodies.

'You found them?' he said at length, raising his numbed eyes to Larche.

'Yes . . .'

'No one must leave the island,' said Calvino more calmly. 'No one. Whoever did this is still here! God in heaven – we have the island secured and this happens. How?'

'Get the fuck off your arse. We've got to find whoever did this. We've got to find them now!'

Calvino went across to Larche and grabbed his arm. 'Steady – you must be steady.'

'I am.' He tried to control himself, to make his body steel, to pray for some blessed anaesthetizing of the senses. But none came – and the shock waves continued to roll through him, while he thought again and again of how they had made love last night and then someone had shot away so much of her head.

'Someone's been sick,' said Calvino.

'I have.'

Calvino turned and spoke sharply into his portable radio, giving rapid, precise instructions in Spanish. Larche stared at him in silence, noticing that his hands were shaking and there was a daub of spittle on his chin; beyond him he could see a fishing boat, moving slowly and silently towards the cove, its engine cut, drifting towards the beach.

Still issuing instructions into the radio, Calvino hardly looked up. The prow of the boat bumped on the sand and came to a halt, and Larche could just make out amongst the flaking blue paint the name *El Santos*. Then someone emerged from the wheelhouse. The man was small, slightly built, and looked almost like a boy until he jumped into the water and began to wade ashore. Then Larche could see that he was in his forties, had a stubbled chin and a square, deeply tanned face with delicate features.

The man's sudden appearance seemed unreal, as if he was

some kind of mythical figure emerging from the sea. 'God in heaven!' he said to Calvino.

'There's been a massacre here,' Calvino replied unnecessarily. 'A bloody massacre.'

'That's Blasco.' The man's face was working. 'Who's the woman?'

'A British police officer.'

'The one who's after this –' His accent was guttural.

'Who is this?' broke in Larche.

'Lorenzo Solana,' said Calvino. 'This is Detective Chief Inspector Larche of Interpol.'

They nodded at each other and then looked down again at what lay on the sand. Alison. Alison Rowe, thought Larche. He remembered the pale blue dress she had worn at dinner last night, the dark blue stockings, the necklace at the throat – the good, healing sex they had had. Why had she gone for that walk with Blasco? Was it just a coincidence – the two of them going to the same cove and deciding spontaneously to take a stroll together? And did the killer come across them by chance, or was it all planned in some way that he couldn't even begin to think about?

The questions rattled around in his head as he also dimly registered that this slight man was the infamous Lorenzo, the slave-driver, the much-hated tyrant. He stared down at Alison Rowe's shattered head. Could this Lorenzo have had something to do with it? Why had he brought his boat in here? The questions intensified in his mind and were then interrupted as a helicopter suddenly chattered into view.

The machine landed on a flat area of headland above them. With its rotors still gusting a flurried wind, half a dozen uniformed Spanish policemen disembarked and with guns in their hands began to scramble down to the beach and along the line of rocks that flanked the cove. Above them another helicopter appeared, bleeping and flashing, mechanical instructions clattering away, radios buzzing, lights winking – all the paraphernalia of modern technology.

The ragged wind from the hovering helicopter's blades caught Alison Rowe's blouse, making it flap on her cooling body.

Lorenzo took Larche's arm. 'Get in the boat,' he yelled over the roar of the blades. 'We'll go up the coast – see if we can head him off.'

Needing action – any kind of action – Larche followed Lorenzo on board and joined him in the wheelhouse as he steered the *El Santos* out of the cove, away from the penetrating noise, and headed for the open sea.

'Take this.' Lorenzo produced a flask.

'What is it?'

'Brandy.'

'No –'

'Drink – you're in shock.' With one hand on the wheel, Lorenzo rammed the flask into Larche's hand. He took a swig and then another and the fire surged through his body. As he handed it back, he could smell the brilliantine on Lorenzo's dark thatch of hair. It smelt good – herbs and a thick scent, almost like marzipan.

The fishing boat was nosing along past the towering cliffs of Molino now, staying close inshore as the swell carried them right up to the seaweed-hung rocks. The water was a greeny-grey and it made a hollow gushing sound as it slapped against the cliffs and occasionally foamed into shallow caves.

'Could anyone hide here?' asked Larche hesitantly.

'Difficult. There's no access except by boat really, but maybe – someone who was fit and was prepared to take one hell of a risk.'

Was Hooper here? The thought flashed into Larche's mind. Would he really have been prepared to take such a risk? To kill them both – almost a leisurely act on an island seething with policemen. And what was he, Marius Larche, doing out in this damned boat? He ought to have stayed with Alison, making sure they didn't hurt her – didn't hurt her any more.

'We'll go as far as the village,' Lorenzo said.

He's like a cat at the wheel, thought Larche, desperately trying to distract his thoughts, supple and pliant. Slightly crouched, with muscular shoulders and that mop of luxuriant dark hair, he looked magnificent, but there was a coarseness to him as well; the skin on his neck was dry and tough, sun-baked.

'Here is Sebastia,' said Lorenzo suddenly.

The place was not what he had imagined. There was a natural harbour with a low stone wall and a sandy beach, but it was not shambling and sleepy. Two long jetties ran down either wall and a crane stood on a small quayside with drying and storage sheds in harsh new concrete just below it.

'We'll go back along the coast.' Lorenzo turned and smiled at him. His eyes were gentle and his white teeth gleamed against his tan. 'There will be hell to pay now. The Minister for Home Affairs murdered in Franco's mausoleum along with a priest, and now his brother – a monk – and a police lady shot dead on Molino with the island swarming with security men.'

Determined not to feed his melodrama, Larche didn't reply.

When the *El Santos* returned to the cove, the beach was full of police and plainclothes security men. The bodies had been covered. Anita Tomas was standing beside them with three companions. The first two, a man and a woman, were extremely elegant. The man was tall, willowy and had smooth brown hair tied back into a pigtail. He wore a white tennis shirt and bermuda shorts while at his neck were a number of gold chains and there were bracelets on his deeply tanned arms. The woman was taller, extremely thin, and her long, narrow face was framed by silky black hair. She wore a cotton skirt and a patterned top. The man, who bore some slight resemblance to Eduardo and Blasco, was crying and the woman was comforting him.

'Are they Jacinto and Maria?'

'That's them!' There was a scoffing note in Lorenzo's voice. 'And there's Salvador.' Instantly, Larche could detect a softer tone.

The boy was beautiful as he stared expressionlessly out to sea. He wasn't very tall and looked even younger than his fifteen years, his dark eyes enormous in a delicately cut oval face.

The sun burnt down fiercely on them all while a group of policemen searched beach and rocks on their hands and knees.

A man with a small case, possibly a doctor, was standing talking to Calvino.

Then Lorenzo whistled.

'Now what?' asked Larche.

'Here comes Bishop Carlos. He'll get things moving, if anyone can!'

The Bishop was tall but with a substantial paunch. His face, narrow and aquiline, was chalk white, without a hint of a tan, and his linen suit, although clearly expensive, seemed to emphasize his pallid appearance. Larche watched him walk across to Anita. Rather surprisingly for someone so reserved, she flung her arms round him. Jacinto, Maria and Salvador also converged on him, and Larche had the surreal idea that they were all going to try and embrace the Bishop as well.

Whether it was the brandy or the horror of it all or a combination of the two Larche had no idea, but he felt light-headed and indecisive as he jumped awkwardly from the prow of the fishing boat on to the sand below.

'I think you should organize a press black-out,' said Larche to Calvino as he approached him, his face grim and expressionless.

'That's impossible,' he replied irritably. 'Besides, I don't think it's going to take too long to run our man to earth.' He looked down at the draped corpses. 'I think we both underestimated the assassin theory.'

'You think that Hooper is here – on the island?'

'Yes.'

'But how could he have got through your security net?'

'God knows. But every fishing boat that comes in and out of the harbour is very thoroughly searched.' He paused. 'I also allowed the Bishop here; he insisted on coming and I agreed.'

'His presence is necessary?' asked Larche.

'He knew Blasco as well as he knows the rest of the family; he could be very helpful.'

'Could anyone have left the island?' asked Larche abruptly.

'No.'

'You're sure about that?'

'Absolutely.' Calvino drew Larche aside and spoke to him

quietly. 'You know the problems I'm up against. We will work together – very closely. I've organized a detailed search of the island and I have reinforcements coming in by helicopter. In fact there will be over two hundred officers on Molino by lunchtime. I've also told all the remaining family you'll want to see them and they're going back to the house – including Bishop Carlos.'

'I must talk to London,' said Larche. 'Lorenzo took me down the coast searching. I don't know why I went – I should have been here on the phone.'

'We all do things instantaneously in shock. Use the phone in the house all you like – it's at your disposal . . .' Calvino paused. 'I ignored this damned assassin business. I was looking for links here on the island, or something political outside. I was sure we had the place well protected, although there seemed little chance of another killing. After all, it was Eduardo Tomas who was receiving the death threats. Now I discover we've let someone slip through, unless they were here already. But who on Molino would commit a crime of this magnitude?'

Larche touched his shoulder. Calvino was being highly efficient but he couldn't stand him talking any longer. 'Look, you carry on with the hunt and I'll conduct the interviews. I'd like to talk to this Lorenzo character as well, and then there's the painter – Morrison. How many others are on the island?'

'There's twelve house staff. Police and security are all billeted in tents near Sebastia – originally forty-two in all – and then there are the fishing families. About a hundred, maybe more. Everyone has identity papers.' Sweat poured down Calvino's forehead as the heat intensified. 'But I'll run more checks. We've got an operation base in the canvas village. Forget about the mainland tonight and come over to me as soon as you're through.'

'I'm Morrison,' said an untidy-looking middle-aged man as Larche walked up the beach towards the house. 'You're from Interpol, aren't you?'

Larche nodded irritably, not ready for him yet, but Morrison proffered his hand, almost socially, as if they were meeting at a drinks party and were wondering how long they would have to talk together.

'I gather your colleague has been murdered – along with Blasco.' He spoke slowly, his voice hesitant, almost as if he was fumbling for the right tone.

'Yes.' Larche was terse.

'Do you want to speak to me now? Out here?' His eyes were slightly bloodshot and his hair was tousled. 'Feel a bit muzzy – I've only just got up,' he said apologetically.

Larche stared at him without replying and there was an awkward silence.

'There's a cool place, a little herb garden, over there. I found it the other night. Shall I lead the way?'

'Very well.' Larche recoiled slightly. Morrison's breath reeked of stale alcohol, and as the painter shambled in front of him – a bear of a man, dishevelled and exuding body odour – Larche wondered how this untidy individual could possibly have spent so long with the elegant and fastidious Anita Tomas. Then Alison Rowe's body swam into his mind again and he shivered feverishly, feeling inert, sure that he should be doing something else, like hunting down the assassin. But Larche knew that professionally he was not equipped for that kind of job and there were others who were. There was no alternative but to begin his questioning and routinely pursue his usual course like an automaton. But first he must get through to Heycroft. 'Look,' he told Morrison brusquely, 'you go and settle yourself in your herb garden. I'll join you in a few minutes when I've made some telephone calls from the guest house. I won't be long.'

On the way to the guest house Larche ran into Calvino again. This time he was accompanied by a couple of Spanish detectives who were giving urgent instructions into walkie-talkies.

'I was looking for you.' Calvino sounded reproachful.

'I'm sorry – I'm not functioning properly,' admitted Larche. 'I've got to phone Lyon and then London.'

'Yes, I understand. I'm arranging to have all the people you need to interview gathered in the house. Will Tomas's study be convenient?'

'Fine.'

'I've arranged for the old servant, Paco, to bring you food.'

'I shan't need any,' Larche snapped. How could the man be so damned insensitive? He would have liked a drink, though.

'You may later,' Calvino fussed. 'And of course if there's anything else you need –'

'I'll ask Paco.'

'You have been through a dreadful experience, señor. Are you sure you wouldn't wish to rest before –'

'No, thank you,' Larche cut in savagely and Calvino quickly consulted a scrap of scribbled paper.

'You may wish to see Señora Tomas again; then there's Jacinto and Maria Tomas, Salvador Tomas – the immediate family. Bishop Carlos, of course, and then Eduardo's personal staff – his bodyguard Carlos Mendes, his researcher Damien Alba and his secretary Julia Descartes.'

And they're all locked up together, thought Larche – just like the Agatha Christie house-party that he had been joking about with Alison Rowe as the police boat had taken them towards Molino. The powerful and the lowly people – all penned up together by a panicky Calvino. Alison Rowe – he had known her for well under twenty-four hours but felt he had known her for ever, and the fact that she was dead, butchered, was unbelievable. Their love-making last night had been the most special, the most erotic, the most memorable he had ever experienced in his life. Alison had unfettered Larche from his strait-jacket of control and had given him a new and all too brief sensation of complete liberation. Now it was over.

'What about Lorenzo?' Larche remembered, conscious that Calvino was staring at him expectantly.

'I hadn't forgotten. I thought we'd both go over to Sebastia when you've finished. Unless you'd rather go alone, of course.'

'No,' replied Larche. 'We'll go together.'

* * *

He managed to get through to Heycroft, although it was an extremely bad line, full of static and echo.

'*What* did you say about Alison?' His voice was incredulous.

'She's been shot.'

'Shot? What are the extent of her injuries and who –'

'She's dead,' he said flatly.

'God . . .' Heycroft couldn't assimilate the fact for some time and even after Larche had repeated the information he still asked, amidst the crackle, 'Look – are you sure about this?'

'Yes – I've seen her,' Larche yelled down the telephone.

'This is dreadful. Dreadful. How the hell did it happen? Who did it?' The static cleared slightly.

Larche sought for control. 'I don't know who did it. She was found in a cove on the island of Molino – along with another member of the Tomas family. A monk. Blasco Tomas. He's dead too.'

'Hooper?'

'I don't know.'

'You don't *know*?' shouted Heycroft furiously.

'There's a rigorous search going on here. No one's allowed on or off the island.'

'If it *is* Hooper, then he's still *on* the damned island.'

'Certainly no one has been allowed to leave,' Larche repeated. But as he was trying to communicate with Heycroft, he suddenly remembered Lorenzo and his fishing boat. If that was motoring round the coast of Molino some time after the killings then there must have been many others around the harbour of Sebastia. Had the assassin escaped that way? Would Calvino have realized this? Surely he must have done. And what about Bishop Carlos? Who had brought him to Molino? With an effort, Larche switched his attention back to Heycroft.

'I'll have to get on to her father,' Heycroft was saying. 'And there's a boy-friend – a lawyer.'

'Yes,' replied Larche.

'A dreadful tragedy,' floundered Heycroft, clearly not anxious to end the call. 'I never imagined for a moment he would actually come for her like this.'

'We don't know that he did,' said Larche drily. 'There

are many other possibilities in this case. They're all being investigated.'

'It's incredible.' His voice shook. 'Two deaths in the Tomas family in days. And now Alison.' He continued in similar vein for another few minutes and only rang off after he had enquired about her corpse and its removal. Larche promised to ring him again later that day, keeping him posted with developments, but as he put the phone down, he wasn't sure that he was going to have time to give Heycroft the luxury of communication.

Larche then dialled Monique's number in Lyon. It rang and rang until he almost gave up, but just as he was about to put the phone down, she answered blearily.

'Monique.'

'Darling – I'm sorry. I was asleep; it was a long journey, or it seemed one. Are you all right?'

'I'm fine.'

'What's happened?' She immediately detected a different tone to his voice.

'Alison Rowe has been murdered – with another member of the Tomas family.'

There was a silence before she could find the words to reply. 'That's just . . . just appalling. Is this assassin involved?'

'No one knows. There'll be a full investigation, of course, and it puts a completely different complexion on the other killings. I shouldn't really be making this call, but I had to let you know I'll probably be on the island for longer than we thought.'

'That poor, poor girl. Are *you* safe?'

'Of course. There's a massive police presence here now; they're bringing them in by the helicopter load. Look, I've got to go. I'll ring as soon as I can.'

'Keep safe.'

'I will. God bless you, my darling.' Larche rang off and stood staring down at the phone. Morrison – the thought roared into his mind like a spring tide, flooding his consciousness, even dislodging Alison Rowe for a brief period. My God – had his mind been asleep all this time? Morrison was the only newcomer to the island. Could *he* be Hooper? Then Larche's logic rebelled against the idea which must be – had to be utterly

110

ludicrous. His credentials had been vouched for by the family and could be verified all the way down the line. The man was an eminent painter with an international reputation and it was doubtful that he could also be an assassin. How strange shock is, Larche thought. There's almost an hallucinatory effect to it.

The little herb garden was shaded by cypresses and redolent with the scent of rosemary, marjoram and thyme. A small fountain in the shape of the head of a cherub with the water spurting from its mouth gushed gently in the centre, flooding into a tiled pond with the spread wings of an angel at the bottom. Wisteria crept up the back balcony of the Palladian house and somewhere there was a bird singing.

Morrison was sitting hunched on a wooden seat by the fountain, his hands stuck in the pockets of a paint-stained overall. His head was sunk on to his chest and his eyes were closed.

'Monsieur Morrison.'

He jerked awake, turning eyes of clear and lustrous grey on him. He must have been good-looking once, thought Larche, underneath all that flab and hair. He sat down heavily beside him, and there was a long silence.

'I'm very sorry about your colleague,' said Morrison uneasily.

'Yes.'

'I'm not sure if the killer will still be on the island,' he continued. 'He's probably long since gone, despite the security screen.'

Larche wasn't interested in the speculation. Instead he asked, 'You spent some time with Eduardo Tomas. Did you know he was receiving death threats?'

'Yes,' replied Morrison quietly. 'He told me.'

'Was he afraid?'

'Very.'

'He took them absolutely seriously?'

'Absolutely.'

'Did he talk about who might be responsible?'

'No. But he told me some other things. Painting a portrait is as intimate a process as being held hostage; you get to know your subject very well. What is more, the subject will often tell you a good deal – will tell you about personal matters.'

Another confessional, thought Larche – the air is thick with them. But he wasn't so sure about Morrison's high-flown images. Maybe having his portrait painted was more akin to a visit to the hairdresser for someone like Eduardo. 'So what did you learn?' he asked, trying not to sound patronizing.

'Blasco made Eduardo very uncomfortable . . .'

The unexpected comment took Larche by surprise.

'What exactly does that mean?' he asked sharply.

'Eduardo led me to believe he wasn't a favourite brother.'

'Go on.' Larche was impatient. 'What was the context?'

'We were talking about marriage.'

'Oh?'

'His and Anita's. Then he suddenly said that he had always been close to his brothers – perhaps too close – and that Jacinto was compatible but Blasco was not. He didn't say why and then he changed the subject abruptly.'

'How many sittings did you have with Eduardo?'

'About six hours – broken up into three sessions.'

'Is that long enough?'

'It never is.' He had a deep, rather pleasantly resonant voice which made him sound almost too confident. 'But all my subjects are busy, distinguished people.'

'Should I have heard of you?' asked Larche, irritated by Morrison's air of self-satisfaction.

'Well, I like to think I'm well known, but there's always the grim possibility of someone not recognizing my name.'

Larche deliberately let another long silence develop. Eventually, Morrison was discomforted enough to break it.

'Did you know that Anita Tomas has commissioned me again?'

'Yes. Did Eduardo strike you as a loving husband?'

'He wasn't in the same league as Anita,' said Morrison slowly. 'She's obsessed with him and goes on about him endlessly – to me, at least. He's become an icon. I think that's why she

112

commissioned me again, so she could talk while I paint.' He grinned. 'I'm the real painter therapist.'

Larche looked at him with considerable distaste. 'You haven't answered my question,' he said abruptly.

'He struck me as a philanderer.' Morrison smiled, quietly conscious of what appeared to be a calculated time-bomb, almost pleased to have made the detonation.

'How did you make that out?' Larche said evenly, determined not to seem surprised. Gradually he was becoming more and more aware of the impression Morrison liked to give – that of confidant to the rich and famous. Delighted to be mixed up in such a ritzy murder case, he was already planning how he was going to sell his account to the nearest tabloid. He's a bastard, thought Larche, and a manipulative one at that.

'Eduardo Tomas was gay,' said Morrison.

Larche felt a surge of fury, and registered fleetingly that this time the shock was not masked by any hallucinatory qualities. So this was the kind of gossip Morrison was going to spread. To Larche, Eduardo had been the epitome of Spanish macho heterosexuality; no vibrations of homosexuality had ever reached him. Surely he would have known.

'How can you be so certain of this?' he asked him, annoyed that he was clearly displaying his dislike.

Morrison sighed. 'In my studio I have a sculpture of a shepherd boy which was made by Richard Crakey. It's sensuous, beautiful, delightful – Eduardo couldn't keep his eyes off it.'

'Is that all?' Larche was scathing.

'No – but it was enough for me at the time. I thought I'd prove it to myself a little more, however.' He paused reflectively. 'I've a very attractive model who's gay. On the second session I got him to drop by.'

'Why?'

'To satisfy my curiosity – which it certainly did.'

'Is that all?'

'What other motive would I have?'

'You didn't by any chance want to blackmail Eduardo Tomas?'

'That's outrageous,' said Morrison calmly. He didn't seem thrown in the least.

'Nevertheless, I'm asking you if that was in your mind,' Larche persisted.

'No.' For the first time Larche detected a spark of anger. 'I had no intention of that kind, and unless you withdraw the imputation I'll have to phone my lawyer.'

Larche's anger increased; he could almost have hit Morrison for his smug pomposity. Then he pulled himself together. It was essential to find out why Morrison was telling him all this. 'I withdraw it,' he said briefly and rubbed a stem of rosemary through his fingers. 'Was he escorted by a bodyguard when he came to your studio?' he added, trying another tack.

'Yes – a guy called Mendes.'

'He was with you all the time?'

'Yes, and there were a couple of others outside. He was well looked after.'

Larche could see the Mediterranean from the herb garden. On the horizon there was a dark cluster of fishing vessels and a solitary boat further inshore, cruising up and down the coast. It could have been Lorenzo, still searching. Then, like the black specks of seabirds, came more helicopters from the mainland. Larche's gaze returned to Morrison.

'Monsieur, your allegations about Eduardo Tomas are very serious.'

'I realize that,' replied Morrison quietly. He seemed to be rather downcast now, as if he had been caught out showing off.

'Suppose you were *right* – would Anita know?' said Larche, testing the supposition, hoping to catch Morrison off-guard again.

'I've no idea. I told you, she's besotted with Eduardo – talks about him all the time as a lover, friend, counsellor. They're both from up-market families and they met quite young. Now she's in her fifties. If she did have any suspicions, she would have blotted them out years ago, don't you think? Like Eduardo – *because* of Eduardo – Anita Tomas has spoken to me very frankly. I'm sure she's usually much more reserved. During dinner last night she even told me how much she disliked that Lorenzo character – the one with the boat.'

114

'Why?' Larche had the feeling that Morrison was now spilling out information rather than calculatedly proffering it as he had when he initiated the interview. Did he have him rattled?

'Because Eduardo allowed him to run Sebastia as he liked – as callously and insensitively as he liked.'

'Is there a connection?'

'What do you mean?' Morrison stared at him and Larche felt another surge of irritation.

'Between Eduardo and Lorenzo. A sexual one? Is that why Eduardo let Lorenzo do as he liked?'

'There could have been. Look – you're not going to tell Anita what I've been telling you, are you?'

He was definitely rattled now. Larche smiled, knowing Morrison would realize why he was smiling. The professional artist, the portrait painter who no doubt specialized in flattering his subjects, was getting insecure, wondering if his confidences were going to rebound on him. How could he even for one wild moment have wondered if this vain aspiring socialite was an international assassin? 'Anything you say to me is in complete confidence,' Larche reassured him with some satisfaction. Clearly his tactics were working.

'Anita loved Eduardo very deeply – more deeply than perhaps you realize.' Morrison looked away. 'Anyway, the point is she seems to think he's some kind of saint, so I'm sure she doesn't suspect anything about his . . . other sexual desires. This painting of him in the house – it's all she's hanging on to. Don't you see – it's as if I can re-create him.'

'And can you?'

Morrison scrabbled in his paint-stained overalls and produced a crumpled colour photograph. 'This is a photograph of the portrait that's being flown over from London. Judge for yourself.'

Larche took the photograph and despite himself was immediately impressed. It was not just a good likeness; the spirit of the man he had known, his elegance, his suavity, his dominance, his sense of his own importance, his distinction – all were there. It had soul. This was more than any official portrait of the official Eduardo.

115

'That's good,' replied Larche reluctantly as he returned the photograph.

'Thank you.' Morrison was watching him with some amusement, conscious he had scored a point.

'And you intend to replicate that – here on Molino?'

'Not replicate. But it'll be another likeness.'

'Where will you paint him?'

'In Sebastia.'

Larche paused. 'I see.'

'After all, he had produced a small economic miracle on his own patch,' Morrison continued. 'Maybe Anita considers this is how she would like to remember him – rather than for the work of more national importance he has achieved for Spain.'

'What are you trying to tell me?' Larche spoke softly.

'Nothing more. I'm simply savouring a possible irony.'

'Let's be very clear about your allegations.'

'Not allegations, monsieur. Just observations. But I *am* trying to assist the police with their enquiries – as we say in England. And in the light of a double killing . . .' His voice petered out but Larche detected a return to his old confidence.

'Very well – you think that a gay Eduardo had a sexual relationship with the unpopular Lorenzo and placed him in a position of power which he abuses.'

'Possibly.'

'So what are you suggesting? A disgruntled fisherman outwitted his bodyguards, hired an epileptic whore to create a diversion, shot Eduardo and Miguel – and then a few days later managed to avoid the security here and make another double killing?' Larche still couldn't bring himself to mention her name. 'It doesn't seem very likely, does it?' he said savagely.

'I'm not saying that.'

'Well, what *are* you saying?'

'Just that Eduardo was very proud of what he had done – and that's why Anita wants me to paint him there.'

'Did he talk about Lorenzo during your sessions?'

'He talked about why he had hired him,' said Morrison quietly.

'Oh?'

116

'Yes. He had heard about what a driving force the man was on the mainland. How determined and relentless – and ruthless he was.'

Larche thought about Lorenzo. He hadn't exactly come across that way to him, but then he had been in shock. 'What was his occupation?'

'He had a boatyard at Rosas. Specialising in servicing and upgrading motor cruisers and yachts. Apparently he had some very rich clients.'

'So he's not a simple fisherman?' said Larche.

'Not exactly. And there's something else even more significant that Anita told me.'

'Well?'

'Lorenzo was going to be sacked.'

Larche was puzzled. She had betrayed some emotion yesterday but would she really pour her heart out like this to Morrison? That was the strangest part of the affair so far. 'Why was Lorenzo being dismissed?'

'Anita had finally persuaded Eduardo that he had to go – that he was making the lives of the fishing community of Sebastia impossible. Apparently she had been so worried about him that she had asked Father Miguel to look into his background.'

'What did she suspect?'

'I don't know, but I do know she also consulted Blasco.'

'Why should these priests have something on him?' asked Larche impatiently.

'She told me Lorenzo was once a novice in Blasco's community.'

'How long for?'

'As a youngster. Then he left.'

'Under a cloud?'

'No – unless you think losing your faith puts you under a cloud.' Morrison shrugged. 'I've only got the barest of details, but I suppose it's possible Father Miguel called Eduardo to the Valley of the Fallen to tell him something he had discovered about Lorenzo.'

'Couldn't he have told him on the phone?'

'Apparently not. There's something else Anita told me.'

'What?'

'They were seen together.'

'Miguel and Lorenzo?'

'Yes.'

'Where?'

'In Sebastia.'

'Get on with it,' demanded Larche. He was petulantly angry now. Here was Morrison, arriving on Molino at the same time as he had, and gaining everything when he had gained nothing – if he was to be believed, that is. What else had Anita Tomas spilled out in her unlikely tête-à-tête? And why hadn't she told him any of this?

'Maybe Lorenzo was blackmailing him?' Morrison suggested.

'And what's *your* opinion of Lorenzo?'

'Oh – he's just rough trade, that's all,' he replied dismissively.

'For God's sake –' Larche began, but Morrison was suddenly indignant.

'I'm trying to help you. Anita loved Eduardo as much as any woman could. She hated and despised Lorenzo for what he was,' he concluded melodramatically.

'*What* was he?' snapped Larche.

'A bully. A despot. Someone she knew spread misery.'

'Maybe Lorenzo was just a good businessman, getting some lazy fishermen off their arses.'

'I think he went further than that.'

'But *how much* further?'

Morrison shrugged.

'Are you telling me everything she's told you?' said Larche sharply. 'Because if not you'll be committing a serious offence.'

Morrison regarded Larche steadily. 'I'm telling you *everything* she told me. I'm actually trying to be helpful – just in case you hadn't noticed.'

'And she had no idea of the gay connection?' said Larche irritably. 'If indeed it exists.'

'It exists all right.' Morrison was indignant. 'I can assure you of that. And if she did know she's fooled me and I think I'm pretty perceptive – in that direction at least.'

'One final point,' said Larche abruptly.

'Yes?'

'Did she like Blasco?'

'I suspect not. I think she felt he knew things about Eduardo she didn't want to know.'

'So . . . so you have theories about why Blasco was killed?' he asked, slightly contemptuously.

'Maybe he knew too much.'

'About Lorenzo?'

'I don't know. But I'm sure it was Blasco they were after. Your colleague must have witnessed something she shouldn't, or someone.'

Larche rose to his feet. 'Thank you.' His voice was neutral. 'Please keep our discussion to yourself, as I will – and I'll be getting back to you.' He paused. 'From your conversations with Eduardo – and Anita – are you sure you have no other idea who this killer or killers could be?'

'No. Anyway, surely a good deal of the information I've given you points to Lorenzo.' He spoke very slowly, as if he was trying to end the interview on the note of the concerned citizen who was willingly sharing views with the police.

'And does Anita feel that too?'

'I don't know, but I *do* know how much she despises and abhors him. You will, of course, be very discreet about what I've said to you?' He sounded edgy again.

'I've already told you that,' replied Larche, looking at him with contempt.

As Larche walked across to the house, Calvino arrived, his air of authority considerably increased.

'Have you found anybody?' Larche's voice was peremptory.

'No. We're concentrating on interviewing people in Sebastia at the moment but I've got a squad combing the island. Who were you talking to?' he asked curiously.

'Morrison. He's delighted to be in the thick of such a tragedy. Personally I find him revolting.' Larche paused. 'Have you heard his extraordinary allegations?'

'Oh yes.' Calvino looked at Larche unwaveringly as if he was testing him, wondering if his anger was going to make him too emotional. 'What did you think of them?'

'He's a poseur with an eye to a quick buck, that's all.'

'Exactly my own conclusions.' Calvino beamed at him.

'But is there anything in it?' asked Larche. 'I've known Tomas for years and never noticed anything.'

'There have been rumours – locally, that is. Nothing more. They were never picked up by the media.' Calvino shrugged.

'You can bet they will be now,' said Larche cynically.

'I'm not sure Morrison'll have the guts to go through with it.' Calvino looked doubtful.

'Anyone who could ingratiate themselves into a household and then sell it out must be a bastard,' Larche snapped with considerable feeling.

There was a short pause, broken eventually by Larche, this time more hesitantly. 'He's the only newcomer on the island, unless you find anyone in Sebastia. For a moment I wondered . . .'

'If he was Hooper? We've checked his credentials all the way but you're welcome to rerun the system –'

'No. At least, not at the moment. Revolting as he is, Morrison's an unlikely suspect. And he knows it – so that's why he buttonholed me.' Larche sighed, knowing he was becoming obsessed with his dislike for the predatory painter.

'Señor – we're going to move the bodies,' said Calvino awkwardly.

'Where to?'

'A mortuary on the mainland. I wondered . . . I wondered if you would like to be with your colleague for the last time.'

Once you peel away the skins, thought Larche, there are quite a few layers of sensitivity to Calvino which it had taken the crisis to bring out. He had changed from a wary colleague to a much warmer companion.

'Thank you. I would like that.'

'I'll ask my people to stand away.'

Larche nodded and followed Calvino back to the cove, feeling that he would barely be able to cope with seeing her again.

* * *

The sun was very high in the sky now and there was a white heat haze over the sea that, apart from a slight swell, was unruffled. A few uniformed Guardia Civil stood on the edge of the wiry grass above the sand but they withdrew as Marius Larche walked alone to the two black polythene covered humps on the beach. A police motor boat thundered past and above him, near to the sinewy cliffs, a helicopter chattered. Apart from their temporary intrusions, he was alone.

When he lifted the sheeting, he saw they had turned Alison Rowe over. Most of her forehead and one of her eyes had been blown away into a tangled, pulpy mess, but below that, the rest of her face was intact and completely unblemished. Looking around him to ensure he was unobserved, he bent over and kissed the dead lips. They were cold now, despite the heat of the sun, and they felt like cardboard. He knew that rigor mortis was setting in but when he took her hand, the skin was still soft and felt slightly moist.

'Alison,' he whispered.

He stayed with her for about ten minutes, kneeling on the hot sand and thinking over last night. Sometimes he stroked her wrist and once or twice he brought it to his lips. He didn't care if he was being watched but guessed that Calvino had instructed his men to be discreet and that he was really alone, except for the gulls and cormorants and oyster catchers that either hovered in the air above him, or stood on the beach, watching him with beady eyes. The swell sighed on the sand, but there was no wind and the stillness was such that Larche felt as if he was completely cut off from any sensation or memory or human contact – other than that of Alison Rowe.

Did he get you in the end, he wondered, a dull rage seizing him. He'd kill the cunt with his bare hands if he found him. Then his anger transferred, not to Calvino but to the dullards who were actually conducting the search. There must be one careless fool – maybe more – who had missed Hooper, and even now he was no doubt hiding out somewhere, an animal not at bay but audaciously deriding them all. He remembered instances in his own career when a minion had slipped up, plunging him into disaster.

But Larche's anger was short-lived as he turned again to Alison, holding her hand for the last time, stroking it gently, tears welling into his eyes but being blinked back before they fell. 'Thank you,' he whispered and pulled the black sheeting over her shattered head. He walked away over the smooth sand without looking back. The rage returned as he went but this time it was like a hard, painful ball resting somewhere in the pit of his stomach. He'd get the bastard. Somehow. At the same time, he thought of Morrison and his publicity-hungry cravings. He'd get him too, if he could.

'Do you want to see the others now?' asked Calvino, meeting Larche on the path back to the house. He had his radio in his hand and had obviously been giving instructions to what Larche felt was a too laid-back-looking group of plainclothes policemen.

'Yes.'

'Who would you want to start with?'

'Jacinto. But I'd like to check out Alison Rowe's room first.'

'We've already done that, but you're welcome to take a look.'

'I'm not suggesting that –' began Larche.

'I know you're not,' cut in Calvino, looking at him with a mixture of compassion and intelligent comprehension. 'Do what you want to do – in your own time.'

'You're being very good to me.'

'I want you to go on running your back-up system,' said Calvino. 'It's invaluable – an asset I wouldn't normally have.'

'Thank you, again. Send Jacinto in, say, ten minutes?'

'Of course.'

Larche strode on, that hard ball of rage and despair growing inside him.

* * *

122

Alison Rowe's room revealed nothing. She had even made her own bed and there were no signs of undue hurry. Her few personal possessions – the new Margaret Drabble, a packet of boiled sweets – were neatly placed, and after a few minutes Larche realized that there was nothing here for him to see or discover.

Returning to his room and looking at his watch, Larche decided to lie on his bed and try to unwind a little, for he knew if he didn't his temper would very likely break out during the interviews. Trying to ease the tension was very difficult, for in his mind's eye all he could see was the shattered head of Alison Rowe who had given him so much and who had been so summarily removed by – who? Hooper at last? Somehow it seemed very unlikely. There was still no hard evidence that Hooper was even in Barcelona. That left the field open to someone else – someone here on the island whose target was the Tomas family. Had they taken shelter in Sebastia? Well, it was up to Calvino and his new reinforced army to run them to earth. His own role was on a like-to-like basis. Perhaps he would only discover what Calvino had already uncovered, but there was always the chance that he might pick up a nuance here and there not recognizable to Calvino. Also there was a possibility that they would be more open with him. Then he remembered how much Anita had told Morrison – and felt instantly depressed. Like-to-like? What rubbish had he been thinking? People only confided because they wanted to.

These reflections eventually calmed him. At least Alison made me realize I had *some* kind of sexual identity, he thought. He tried to think of Monique's body but could only see Alison Rowe's. Gradually his rage began to smoulder again, until he felt choked, half stifled by the shock and pain.

As Larche rose from the bed he caught sight of the envelope. It was poking out from under the bureau and an electric charge of excitement filled him as he saw the unfamiliar handwriting. His stomach churning, he quickly scanned the contents. The letter was from Alison Rowe. She had probably pushed it under his door early that morning and it had slid on the bare boards until it was almost hidden under the bureau.

Dear Marius,

I wanted to thank you for what happened and what we did together. I don't love you nor do you love me. I have Tom and you have Monique and they exist in a separate world to the one we inhabited a few hours ago. But we did something special – very special for me and I hope it was for you. I'm just going out for a walk. I'll see you at breakfast.

With love and thanks, Alison

The tears flooded down Larche's face as he put the letter into his wallet. While she was amongst the rocks and wild flowers, while she was talking to that gentle and civilized monk, someone had come and butchered them both. Was it the same person who had so skilfully assassinated Eduardo and Father Miguel, or was it someone else? And that person – those people . . . He beat at the wall with his fist in fury and deepest frustration – he had to find out the meaning of it all before they killed again. But what he really wanted to do was to hunt down this last assassin and kill him with his own bare hands.

Larche followed Paco into the cool, gloomy interior of the house.

'I thought you might care to use Señor Tomas's study, señor. Will you need a tape recorder?'

'Yes.'

'Good, señor. I've already put one in there with a supply of paper and pens.'

'That's most efficient.' Larche was hardly listening to the old man. He was wondering again how a person as shallow as Bernard Morrison had managed to achieve such an intimate relationship with Anita Tomas in so short a time. Was it just his proximity when she was in such a vulnerable, emotional state, or was there some particular reason why she had confided in Morrison?

'I heard of the terrible tragedy in the cove this morning.' Paco's worn-out voice broke into his thoughts.

Larche put a hand on his stick-like wrist. 'Everything's under control. We seem to have half the Spanish police force on the island.'

'Yes, señor.' He paused and then rattled on. 'It was bad enough to have lost Señor Eduardo, but Father Blasco as well – he was such a very good man. Many times he has given me his blessing. Then there's your own colleague. Such a –'

'Yes,' interrupted Larche, unable to take any more. 'I'll just go and sit quietly in the study. Is there any coffee?'

'I'll have some brought immediately.'

'I would like to see Jacinto first.'

Paco inclined his head and went slowly away.

A persistent fly buzzed against the window-pane and there was a smell of pine furniture polish. The room was more of an art gallery than a study, with pictures – impressionist, expressionist, surreal and abstract – taking up most of the space on three walls, whilst densely packed shelves of books filled the other. The volumes were mainly to do with law and the constitution, but there was quite a large section on history and sociology. Larche studied them for a while and then returned to the desk to sip the scalding hot coffee that Paco had just silently brought in.

Gradually, the sheltering numbness withdrew and Larche saw Alison Rowe as he had first seen her at Sant Pere de Rodes and then last night. He now felt responsible for her death. He should have kept her beside him – not let her go wandering off. Then he sighed, sickened by his own childishness. How could he possibly have protected her? Yet again he thought of how she had been, how she had looked, what she had worn last night, what they had done together, and the pain stirred in his chest as if a hand was roughly squeezing his heart.

Part Two

7

Jacinto Tomas opened the door without knocking and surveyed Marius Larche with a kind of weary tolerance. He had changed and was wearing dark blue jeans and an open-necked white shirt. Deeply tanned with long brown hair, he was slighter and shorter than his two brothers and probably about five years younger. He had a crucifix at his neck, a number of expensive-looking rings on his fingers and an even greater number of bracelets on his thin, wiry wrists, but rather than giving any impression of foppishness, he had an aura of toughness and efficiency, expertise and resourcefulness. He would know how to sail a boat, thought Larche, skin-dive, wind-surf, water-ski. He would play tennis well, golf expertly. What was beyond this first impression, he wondered. He didn't think Jacinto was just a playboy, he was more like a wealthy machine. But there was something else – a hesitancy that didn't quite fit the macho image.

'Monsieur Larche.' The voice wasn't right either. He had expected more authority but it was in the minor key – almost disgruntled. Perhaps it's just a combination of shock and grief, thought Larche. They shook hands and sat down at a highly polished round table that had nothing on it but an antique lamp. The surface reflected their faces rather disconcertingly.

'You must accept my condolences,' murmured Larche. 'A double tragedy.'

'I'm very sorry about your colleague,' Jacinto responded automatically.

'As you can see, a full-scale search is being carried out.'

'Yes, but I fear the killer will have disappeared. He must have planned an escape route.'

'Did *you* see anybody?' Larche spoke sharply, irritated by the calm implication of police incompetence.

'No.' Jacinto paused. 'Are you co-ordinating the hunt?'

'That's Calvino's job.'

'So what is *your* job?' he asked quietly.

'I've been drafted in by Interpol to assist on the case – and you may also be aware that Eduardo wanted me here. Unfortunately I came too late to help him, although I'm sure I couldn't have prevented what happened.'

'I'm sure you couldn't,' Jacinto agreed rather too quickly. 'Well – I've told everything I know to Calvino, but I'm quite prepared to start again.'

Larche nodded, detecting the hint of smooth patronage but deciding to ignore it; he didn't want to turn this into a hostile encounter.

'Did Calvino brief you?' He sounded even more patronizing now.

'He didn't have enough time, in the circumstances, so we shall have to start again. I gather you and your wife run a diving school in Estartit?' A conventional interrogation wouldn't work with these people, he thought. They're too used to wielding power.

'Yes.'

'Is that successful?'

'It's a living. I'm a marine archaeologist by profession.'

'Yes?' he said encouragingly – but Jacinto remained silent. 'Do you have any . . . views on these killings?'

'Father Miguel knew the identity of Eduardo's killer – I'm sure of that,' he said with unexpected certainty, but Larche also thought he detected a hint of unease.

'Why?'

'He was an old family retainer who dabbled in secrets – a priest with dirty hands, soiled by the power games he played. I've told all this to Calvino anyway.'

'Is there anything you haven't told Señor Calvino?' asked Larche, using a sharper tone. 'Is there anything you held back? Because if there is, you'll find yourself in a very serious position.'

Jacinto's face was suddenly dark with anger, as if a servant had been unexpectedly impertinent, and for a long while there was silence. Larche felt a certain triumph; instinctively he knew he'd been right to go in for the attack. He'd shatter this arrogant façade if he could but all he had to go on was the gut feeling that Jacinto was, in some way, agitated. Was that because he was the last surviving brother? Did he fear for his own life? Or was there something else?

'There is something,' Jacinto admitted, with at least a display of reluctance.

'Why did you withhold information?' snapped Larche, trying to unsettle him.

'Because Blasco was alive.' His voice was quietly reflective.

'What bearing does that have on it?'

There was another silence, much shorter this time. 'I'll tell you,' he said gently.

'Let me ask you a question first,' cut in Larche, still trying to throw him off balance.

'Yes?' Jacinto replied impatiently, as if someone had raised a hand in a large audience.

'Did you love Eduardo?'

'Very much.'

'And Blasco?'

'Not at all.' He smiled, as if pleased with his own demonstration of decisive honesty.

'Why?'

'Because he was a conniving bastard – and I'm glad he's dead.'

'Will you explain?' Larche felt a sense of unreality – first Morrison's revelations, and now this. He also sensed that the interview was slipping out of control.

'Eduardo has been weak and he paid for it,' he said at length.

'What did he do?' asked Larche encouragingly.

'He was very self-indulgent,' replied Jacinto austerely.

'Was he a homosexual?'

131

'Yes. Blasco found out and told Bishop Carlos.'

'And you consider that conniving?' Larche felt not just shock but considerable alarm. How in God's name had Eduardo concealed all this so successfully? Was it possible?

'Well, that was bad enough.' Jacinto looked away.

'There's more?'

'Yes.'

'Are you going to tell me?' There was a long silence, then Larche tried another tack. 'Did Anita know about Eduardo's homosexuality?'

'It was kept from her.' Jacinto appeared to be very confident now.

'I *said* – did she know?' Larche insisted.

'I'm sure she didn't. Anita is a very strange lady. None of us really knows her – not even after all these years. She has this capacity to compartmentalize and she never bothers with anything she doesn't want to know about.' There was a pause and then Jacinto said unexpectedly, 'I don't have any money. The diving school just about breaks even, so Maria and I – we're leeches on Molino and all that it stands for.' He laughed as if making a pleasant little joke, but there was bitterness behind the laugh.

'It's as bad as that?'

'Yes. Last year I made a major archaeological find – just outside Ampurias. About a mile out to sea there's a galley – a Roman galley which has been preserved in a cavern on the reef.'

'Treasure trove?'

'She could have been.' The bitterness increased slightly.

'What went wrong?'

'Blasco,' replied Jacinto. 'He's been a pain in the arse all my life.'

'How was he involved?' asked Larche mildly.

'Eduardo and I formed a family trust; the ship would yield up a significant reward and Maria and I would be very comfortably off for the rest of our lives.'

'It all sounds very reasonable.' Larche was guarded.

'It wasn't – it was a fiddle. And Blasco found out and reported on Eduardo again, this time to the Catalonian Archaeological Department. Now the state has taken her over and we won't get a peseta.'

'I see.' Larche paused. 'So you think Blasco really had it in for Eduardo.'

'He'd do anything to score off him.'

'Why?'

'Because he was in love with Anita – years before he became a monk.'

The bombshell was perfectly timed and Larche was shocked. There were so many things about the Tomas family that he just hadn't known. 'And what were *her* feelings?' he prompted, anxious not to interrupt Jacinto's flow.

'They were engaged – until Eduardo came along. Blasco has hated him ever since.'

'You told Calvino none of this?'

'Blasco was alive,' replied Jacinto impatiently. 'I didn't want to voice my suspicions – however much I disliked him.'

Is he telling the truth, wondered Larche. Or is he manipulating me? He decided to become more aggressive again. 'Well, come on, what are you suggesting about Blasco?'

'I had no evidence of any kind about Blasco's possible involvement with Eduardo's death – and I still haven't. I would have been a complete fool to have said *anything* to Calvino.'

'But you are saying it to me now,' Larche reminded him.

Jacinto looked down at the highly polished table. 'It wasn't just Eduardo he hated.'

'Who else?'

'He hated me.'

'But why?'

'Because I told him what a bastard he was – repeatedly. Particularly when we were kids.'

'Are you afraid?' asked Larche.

'Of the assassin? Sure. I value my life, Monsieur Larche, despite the fact that it's become such a bloody mess.'

'When did that bloody mess begin?' asked Larche hesitantly.

'It began when I was a kid. Want to hear about it?' He grinned at Larche challengingly.

'If it's relevant.'

'Oh it is, monsieur. It's extremely relevant. You're probably aware that the Tomas family's position in Spanish politics goes back a very long way. My father was Franco's private secretary, my grandfather a diplomat and on my mother's side the men were also diplomats and the women society hostesses. Both sides of the family were devout Catholics, bastions of Rome, much loved for their respectability, their moral clarity.' He spoke with heavy irony. 'And, above all, their moral leadership, now more essential than ever in a country still emerging from the shadow of Franco – from a peasant society.' His voice had taken on a slightly hectoring tone. 'Hence our relationship with Bishop Carlos and Father Miguel. The Catholic faith was very central to us as a family. Blasco even became a monk.'

Larche almost told him that he knew Lorenzo had been there too, but at the last moment bit the comment back. Instead he asked curiously, 'Is Anita devout?'

'Yes. Very.' Jacinto suddenly radiated tension. 'She too comes from a very distinguished Spanish family, but this time connected with the arts – mainly with music. Her father was a conductor, her mother a pianist, her sister a singer and, of course, Anita's career as a cellist must be very well known to you.'

'I've never heard her on the platform,' admitted Larche, trying to relax Jacinto a little, 'but I've listened to her recordings. I was also privileged to overhear her practising last night. She is an exquisite musician.'

'Yes, she is, but she has had problems.'

'In her childhood. Yes – I heard.'

'How well did you know Eduardo? I've seen you at some of our house-parties.' He was only slightly curious.

'I knew him at the Sorbonne, but not so much recently. And I never knew the family well. They were just shadowy figures here – and in Madrid.'

'I can imagine that. Eduardo rarely let anyone into the circle.'

'There was no reason to,' said Larche.

Jacinto shrugged. 'Somewhat predictably, we were three lonely little boys.'

'Lonely little rich boys,' corrected Larche.

'The rich part didn't help. We didn't go to school – only university. Eduardo to the Sorbonne, as you know, Blasco to Cadaques – the community – and I went to Valencia. But from the age of five to sixteen, we had tutors.'

'Yes, I remember Eduardo telling me. But he also said that you had friends to stay.' He noticed with interest that Jacinto's tension seemed to have vanished. He definitely finds long monologues therapeutic, Larche thought wryly, wondering how relevant all these recollections actually were.

'Other children of the rich and famous, as the Americans would say. So stimulation largely depended on the tutors.' He paused. 'They were a mixed bag and naturally we gave them hell. Some stood it and others didn't, but none of them stayed long. Eduardo was charming and devious, Blasco was articulate and erudite and I – I was the little boy. Cheeky – never missing a trick.'

'Insufferable,' said Larche.

'You really mean that, don't you?' Jacinto smiled for the first time.

'Carry on.' Larche hardened up slightly, not wanting Jacinto to feel that he was being too helpful and emollient.

'Well, tutor-baiting was all the fun we had in life, or put it like this – it gave us a *raison d'être*, and companionship.'

'Did you get on together – you three little rich boys?'

'Do three ever get on? It was boring, baiting each other. In the end we fought each other to a standstill.'

'So – then it was time to "get the tutor"?'

'Very much so. Until Gabriel arrived. He was American but Spanish-speaking. He was also very tough. For once, too tough for us. Gabriel made our lives as much hell as we had made the other tutors'. As we two tried ineffectively to make his.'

'We two?'

'Me and Blasco.'

'And Eduardo?'

'He got on with him well.'

'Was he gay?' said Larche bluntly.

'No, I'm quite sure he wasn't, but he definitely got a kick out of violence. He had a local girl and used to knock her around. Her parents suspected him but she was too terrified to tell them. Eduardo knew, though.'

'How?' asked Larche carefully, not wanting to interrupt but anxious to show Jacinto how interested he was.

'He photographed Gabriel doing it.'

'But *why*? Why should he creep around photographing the man? He was a bit young to be interested in sadism.' Once again Larche wondered if he was being set up. Was there some kind of conspiracy here to sidetrack him? 'And why are you telling me all this?' he asked quietly.

'Because you should understand what Eduardo was really like, what had formed him. Even then he was highly manipulative, determined to be one up, but at least he didn't have Blasco's long-term vindictiveness.' Jacinto paused; there was a note of relish in his voice as he continued and Larche sensed that he was almost beginning to enjoy himself. 'For as long as I can remember Eduardo was a survivor. Gabriel made us work like hell – we hated him for it, but Eduardo never suffered to the extent that Blasco and I did. Of course we all got very good results and our parents were delighted, but we still hated him.'

'Did Eduardo manipulate his way out of his school work?'

'He didn't have to. He was clever and always found the lessons easy. One thing I'll never forget though – we all had the chance to go for a week's skiing in Andorra. Well, it was better than being stuck on the island even if we *did* have to go with Gabriel. But Eduardo picked us off one by one, set us up so that we couldn't go.' Jacinto paused, his eyes intent on the past. 'He fixed Blasco so that it looked as if he'd been bullying Gabriel's dog – a little dachshund that I think he loved more than anything else in the world. And he fixed me by making it look as if I'd torn up an important essay of Blasco's. It was all very clever indeed –' He laughed. 'I can find it funny now but not then. Not then. Naturally we didn't go skiing.'

'But Eduardo did.'

'Of course.'

'But why did he want to go?'

'He didn't, particularly,' said Jacinto. 'All he wanted to do was to get away from the island, and us. He wanted to be special. And he succeeded.' Jacinto smiled.

'Did Blasco hate you both?'

'He was always so irritatingly *good* – even then. But I'm sure he did underneath. And of course when we grew up Blasco had other reasons for loathing Eduardo. Like Anita, for instance.'

'And do you think Eduardo remained manipulative?'

'He became a politician, didn't he?' There was a sneer in Jacinto's voice.

'How would you assess his character – as a man?' asked Larche casually.

'He was constrained. Like he was in a cage of correctness. What he really wanted, increasingly wanted, lay outside. By employing Lorenzo I believe Eduardo reached out for what he wanted.'

I wonder how relevant all this has been, thought Larche wryly. We seem to have wandered right away from the main point. 'I can understand that family life was pretty good hell, but do you have any theories about the connection between these killings?'

'No.' Jacinto was very positive. 'I can't see who could have carried out all this butchery.'

'Lorenzo?'

'Not clever enough.'

'The Church?'

'I'd give you the same answer. When Blasco was alive I had my suspicions, but now he's dead I'm sure it's much more likely to be a political assassination.'

'Eduardo – yes. But Blasco? He wasn't political.'

'Maybe he knew something he shouldn't have done – who wrote those poisonous letters, for instance.'

'That means the assassin's on the island,' said Larche sharply.

'Or was – I wouldn't rely too heavily on Calvino's security system.'

Larche tried another tack. 'What about Sebastia? Did that mean something to you when you were a child?'

'It meant a lot to all of us – in different ways.' Jacinto eagerly

137

grasped the opportunity for more analysis of his childhood. 'To me it was freedom. Of course, at that stage it was very run down, but there were a few boats left, a few families. We were forbidden to play with the children there, but I did have a friend – Pedro – a secret friend because my parents and Gabriel would have been very angry if they knew Pedro and I played together.'

'What did you do?'

'Nothing much. Swim. Stroll around. Gawp at girls. What do other adolescent boys do? There were a few pinball machines in the bar but I didn't dare go in there in case I was recognized and taken home. We used to dive and fish off the rocks – it's a beautiful cove. Sebastia was very important to me; it represented a freedom that I never had – not until I went to Valencia, anyway. When I take groups of people diving off the rocks now I often remember those days with Pedro.'

'Do you still see him?'

'We've lost touch. He went to the mainland looking for work and he's probably moved a long way away now. I liked him though – he was a bird-watcher too.' Jacinto's whole face lit up with genuine enthusiasm. 'We used to watch the gulls and cormorants and Pedro taught me to identify all the different species. In the end I bought a pair of binoculars and we'd share them, watch the gulls soaring. God, how I envied them. I was trapped on Molino – so damn trapped. This house, the buildings, a mile or so of rocky coast – that's all we had. The occasional trip, a visit abroad, always with a tutor and servants. You've no idea what a suffocating life it was – and how endless it seemed.'

'Why *were* you so cut off? Surely your parents realized how bad all this was for you?'

Jacinto shrugged. 'We were the ruling classes, weren't we? We were being trained for public duty. Eduardo was the only success. I became a playboy, Blasco a monk –'

'You're not a playboy,' said Larche. 'You're a marine archaeologist.'

'Much good may it do me.'

Larche was silent, aware of the renewed bitterness in Jacinto's voice. What kind of people had the Tomas parents been? Didn't they realize that by imprisoning their children they had done such appalling psychological damage to them? 'What was Eduardo's reaction to Sebastia?' he said evenly. 'Did he yearn for the freedom it represented – just like you did?'

'Not in the same way. Not as a child. As I told you, Sebastia was forbidden fruit. I think he was frightened. Anyway, he never ventured in.'

'And Blasco?'

'It was against his principles.' Jacinto laughed.

'His religious principles?'

'Yes.'

'But why?'

'Well, it wasn't a brothel in the Tomas back yard as people like to imply, but it was a village of looser morals than Blasco, a good Catholic, would like – as many other villages are. So he gave it a wide berth, and stayed within the safety of his cage.'

'Do you think Eduardo loved either of you?'

For a long time Jacinto said nothing, then he spoke slowly. 'Do you love your fellow prisoners? Did three lonely little rich boys, waiting to do their duty in high places, love each other?' He was silent again. Then he said impatiently, 'Why ask me? How would I know? I love my wife, and I'll love my children if we ever get round to having them, but I won't have them here – not on Molino. I want us all to be together where I feel free too.'

Larche nodded.

'I know every rock, every stone, every blade of grass on this island. Maybe I even counted the gulls.' He rose to his feet. 'Do you need me any more?'

'Do you have any idea who killed your brothers? If so, you *must* tell me. And if you're still withholding information . . .'

Jacinto shrugged. 'I told you – it must have been an outsider. There's no one capable of killing them here.'

Larche decided not to take him up on this; he needed to complete all the interviews first and then analyse the results. Also, Jacinto's image of the three lonely boys who tormented each other had made Eduardo's study oppressive. 'Very well

– that'll be enough for now.' Jacinto walked towards the door. 'Oh, by the way . . .'

'Yes?'

'What happened to Gabriel?'

'He's back in Boston – in his sixties now and teaching in a private school. We exchange greetings. Occasionally.' He hovered by the door. 'Am I free to leave the island?'

Larche shook his head. 'No. Incidentally, do you have an opinion on the telephone calls Eduardo received? And the letters?'

'Political terrorism.' He spoke with considerable authority and Larche believed that his conviction was genuine. 'You have to follow that line, monsieur.'

'And Blasco knew who it was?'

'He knew something.'

'You wouldn't like to hazard a guess as to what he told Father Miguel?'

'I wish I could.'

'Blasco didn't expect to die,' mused Larche. 'He didn't strike me as someone who felt he was in danger because of what he knew.'

'How can you be sure of that?' asked Jacinto reasonably.

'Experience. Experience and . . . intuition.'

'I didn't think policemen were allowed to have that.' There was a hint of a sneer in the smooth voice. 'So, I'm trapped on the island again, am I? Unable to leave until given permission. Do you think I killed them, monsieur? Is it me you are wondering about?' Jacinto smiled. 'Have I made myself a prime suspect?'

Larche met his eyes and then looked away, for he could see the yearning of the prisoner there. 'Everyone is a suspect here,' he replied formally.

Before Larche left the confinement of Eduardo Tomas's study he dialled a number in Lyon and spoke to Chalon, his second-in-command there.

'Philippe –'

'How goes it?' The voice on the other end sounded relieved, as if Larche had been out of contact too long.

'It's a nightmare.'

'Any progress?'

'Everyone here is anxious to confess, but not to the killing. They're convinced we're dealing with an assassin. My point is: maybe, but in that case, who hired him?'

'This Hooper the British are obsessed with? But where is he? Do you reckon he's got off the island?'

'I'm not convinced he was *on* it – yet,' said Larche, and realized that he was having difficulty feeling convinced about anything at the moment. It was good to talk to Philippe though. Good to reach a friend on the outside.

'What kind of show are the Spanish putting up?'

'Formidable. They've come in by the helicopter load, and there were plenty here before that.'

'But not enough of them to prevent a double murder.'

'Clearly not. Calvino is shit scared.'

'What's he like?'

'He's good, but understandably nervous. Anita Tomas is trying to get rid of him. I like his style though; he's thorough and he doesn't flap.'

Chalon laughed unfeelingly. 'So it's all power and influence stuff. I told you it would be like that. What about the Tomas family? Any chinks in the armour?'

'Their armour's shot through and through. Full of old jealousies and repressions. Jacinto Tomas gave a pretty graphic description of a hellish childhood, but it didn't get me much further. Still – they're telling me more than they told poor old Calvino. That's because of the last two killings,' he added quickly. He liked Calvino and didn't want to put him down.

'Isn't Jacinto a golden person? He's always in *Hola* magazine.' Chalon was clearly intrigued.

'Yes, I suppose he is a golden person, but he also struck me as bitter but possibly honest. I rather liked him.'

'And did you like her? Anita?'

'Yes. There's something magnificent about her complete adoration of Eduardo.'

'And was it reciprocated?'

'In a way – but it looks as if he could have been a closet gay with some local outlets.'

Chalon whistled. 'Does that have any bearing?'

'I don't know. The assassin theory's still big.'

'I suppose because it's convenient.'

'Yes.'

Larche was fond of Chalon. He had been his number two for nearly ten years now and they had always got on well. Chalon was an antiques expert and quite often, while working on a case, they would unwind by trawling antique shops whilst still meditating upon clues and solutions, debating this and that suspect. Chalon was a brutal cynic, mentally much tougher than Larche, married with two grown-up daughters whom he adored. Predictably he considered they had married badly and was always complaining about their husbands. But then Chalon would complain about anyone his beloved daughters married.

'I've also been talking to Bernard Morrison,' said Larche.

'The British portrait painter?'

'I confess I hadn't heard of him. What's he like?'

'He's very good.'

They both laughed. Then Larche broke it to him. 'He's here – on the island.'

'Good God.'

'Did you know he was painting Eduardo?'

'No.'

'I thought you read *Hola* magazine.'

'Not cover to cover.'

'Anyway, Anita Tomas has asked Morrison to stay on – and paint Eduardo at home. Posthumously.'

'I see. That sounds understandable. I suppose the widow's hanging on to every shred of comfort and if Morrison can bring her husband back to life on canvas in his own home . . .' His voice trailed away and then picked up again. 'I'm sure it's the kind of crazy stunt my Isobelle would pull if anything happened to me. And what would Monique do?'

'Hopefully not have me nailed up on the wall.'

'What's Morrison like?'

'He's a conniving bastard.' Larche relished the sentence.

'Is he now? In what way?'

'He's obviously delighted to be so close to the horrors – and I reckon he'll sell the story to the tabloids as soon as he possibly can.'

'Sounds a delightful character.'

'I'd like you to check him out again – just for luck.'

'Are you saying you suspect him of being the assassin?'

'I realize it's a long shot . . .'

'I should say so,' replied Chalon with feeling.

'I just want to check that the man on this island who says he's Bernard Morrison really *is* Bernard Morrison.'

'Give me his description then.'

Larche gave him a very detailed one, deliberately ignoring his unspoken amusement.

'I'll get back to you. Give me the number you're on now.' Larche gave him the number and then Chalon said, 'What are you expecting next?'

'What do you mean?'

'If the assassin's on the island – do you expect more carnage?'

'Please God, no,' said Larche.

When he had hung up Marius Larche continued sitting quietly, letting ideas run through his mind. There was no doubt that the Tomas family were split – had been split and festering for years. If only he could see through it all, get a definite lead, for there seemed plenty of motives. All he needed was intuition – a quality that he normally relied on but which seemed to have been shocked out of his psyche by the killings. He remembered the Demarche case where, strolling through an antique market with Chalon, he had simply recalled the look on the grandmother's face as she gazed down at her poisoned daughter's body. He had subconsciously recognized satisfaction, not grief, in those eyes. Larche shared the intuitive recognition with his colleague and weeks later, after an intensive enquiry, the grandmother was arrested.

Larche was about to walk out into the herb garden to talk to

Maria Tomas when Calvino appeared, looking slightly dazed. There was perspiration standing out on his forehead and a strange smile – a curious mixture of satisfaction and doubt – hovered on his lips. 'It's all over,' he said. 'We've got our assassin.'

'What?' Larche gazed at him uncomprehendingly. 'What the hell are you talking about?'

Calvino was staring at him, gabbling slightly. 'He's Irish. You'd better come with me now.'

'But where did you find him?'

'In Sebastia.'

'What has he said?' Larche was incredulous.

'Nothing,' replied Calvino. 'He's dead.'

8

Calvino drove Larche the quarter of a mile to Sebastia in a small, rather battered jeep. As he drove, Calvino's mood changed; the doubts and lack of confidence faded and he allowed his satisfaction at this unexpected turn of events to have full rein.

'The affair could be over,' he said. 'Thank God.'

'You say the man is dead?' Larche spoke incredulously. 'How did this happen?'

'He shot himself in the head – and then fell from the cliff. At least, that's the way it looks at the moment. He's not recognizable.'

'How convenient,' muttered Larche. There was no doubt in his mind that this was all far too neat for comfort.

'What did you say?' Calvino yelled over the noisy engine.

'Who found him?' substituted Larche.

'Lorenzo – and some of the local boys. They called my men immediately.'

'And you say he's Irish?'

'There are papers on the body.' The jeep bounced crazily over the rough track and the dust rose above them, sending a hazy film up to the gathering harshness of the midday sun.

Larche's scepticism immediately increased and he felt he couldn't accept any of this. But what if he was wrong – and he was about to view Hooper's body? Hypothetically, who would have hired him? A politician? A terrorist organization? Or someone much nearer to home? Someone – or some people connected with the fishing industry or the more nefarious activities in Sebastia? Someone in this too close, too privileged, too carefully groomed family? The Church? The last thought came as a shock. What did he mean – the Church? Was it pushing even his imagination too far to conjecture that the Catholic Church itself might have hired Hooper to arrange for Eduardo's death? And Father Miguel's? Later to use their assassin to eliminate anyone else with dangerous knowledge? It was an intriguing and terrifying thought – one that he should dismiss immediately as wholly ludicrous. And yet, given the scenario of one of Spain's most powerful and influential Catholics, the Minister for Home Affairs himself, being exposed as a closet gay with his own home-made brothel on his doorstep, if such a scandal had broken the Catholic Church would have been deeply wounded – just as the government would have been. And now, what if the assassin really had been eliminated? What if Larche's suspicions about convenience turned out to be unfounded? Could a neat job of self-protection have been perpetrated, leaving Molino, the decimated Tomas family, the Church and Spain to return relatively undamaged to normal? After all, a professional assassin could always be explained away as part of the contemporary tapestry of life, but the philanderings of the eldest son of a distinguished Spanish family could not. Eduardo had been a leader, a moral example, a media icon. If he could get away with perceived immorality, then why couldn't the ordinary citizens of Spain?

The jeep skidded to a halt and Calvino broke into Larche's troubled thoughts. 'I would like to thank you, señor.'

'*Thank* me?' Larche was thrown.

'You have been most helpful.'

'Oh that – I should be grateful to you. I'm very much the intruder.'

'You are a friend of the family. You could have made life impossible for me.'

Larche got out of the jeep shakily, all his misgivings about such a neat ending returning. As a man, he liked Calvino. He didn't want to see him humiliated. 'We'd better go and see if it *is* our man.'

'My people are certain.'

'Nevertheless . . .'

But Calvino was not to be rattled by Larche, and his small,

plump frame exuded forced confidence as he sprang out of the jeep.

The crowd was standing beside a rocky headland that was covered in coarse grass and salty, stunted little pine trees that were all bent by the prevailing wind, huddled protectively into thickets. Two Range Rovers, another small jeep, and three helicopters were parked very close together, and over fifty uniformed and plainclothes police and security men stood around, looking elated, smoking, talking, laughing – rather as if they had all won a much-awaited prize. Larche could feel the atmosphere of relief, the running down of tension. He half expected to see bottles being passed round, drunkenness beginning – maybe even a bit of wild singing and dancing. Calvino's spirits, however, seemed diminished again as he moved through his triumphant forces like a disgraced general about to face a court martial.

Calvino walked up a rough flinty path that smelt of thyme and Larche found himself looking down at the sea. The wind had dropped again and the Mediterranean had a sluggish, rather oily look to it, the waves slapping the rocks petulantly. A flotilla of yachts were almost stationary some hundred yards away behind a ring of protective buoys, but just beneath the headland, pulled up on a narrow strip of shingle beach, were a couple of motor boats, and anchored just off the rocks, riding up and down on the swell, was Lorenzo's fishing boat.

The body lay on the beach, covered with some sheeting, just as, a few hours ago, Alison and Blasco had lain in another cove. Half a dozen men stood around it, talking and looking out to sea. Lorenzo and a few fishermen occupied the other part of the beach. They sat on the rocks, watching the police with interest, as if they were expecting them to do something dramatic. The fact that they had clearly been doing nothing at all didn't in any way diminish the fishermen's interest.

To Larche's surprise, Salvador Tomas was standing beside Lorenzo.

'Now what the hell's he doing there?' asked Larche of Calvino as they scrambled down the precipitous little path.

'Yes, I've already reprimanded him,' Calvino panted. 'He said that he couldn't stand being cooped up in the house and he'd just gone down to Sebastia for half an hour.'

'I see,' replied Larche disapprovingly.

'Then the body was found.'

'How?'

'The man was seen on the cliff by Lorenzo. Later, there was a shot – and he fell.'

'And what was Lorenzo doing here?'

'Cruising round the shore in his fishing boat.'

'How convenient,' said Larche again.

'The man had been there on the cliff for some time, according to Lorenzo,' said Calvino rather shortly.

'What was he up to?' snapped Larche. 'I mean – sunbathing? Bearing in mind a full-scale police hunt was on at the time?'

'He must have been hiding – and then came out to give himself up.' Catching Larche's sceptical gaze he added quickly, 'Presumably he thought better of it.'

'You mean, he decided to kill himself?'

'Or escape perhaps – until he realized he'd been spotted by Lorenzo.'

'Why didn't he wait until night?' asked Larche waspishly. 'To try and make an escape in broad daylight seems pitiful.'

Calvino smiled. 'He wouldn't have been able to get off the island at night. I had the coast patrolled by those two motor boats with searchlights mounted on them. Last night we covered every inch of the island from the sea, right up until dawn. It was only when it got light that I called off the boats – and then there was this discovery. Lorenzo was certainly persistent,' he added unwillingly.

'You organized your land and sea search teams well,' Larche said quickly, instinctively subscribing to Calvino's conspiracy of convenience. 'You'd have found him eventually.' But all the time he was thinking: this isn't right, it just isn't.

Calvino smiled at him gratefully, as if he needed his approbation. He's becoming increasingly uneasy, thought Larche with

some satisfaction. 'Thank you,' he said. 'I'll show you the body.'
He turned and led Larche towards the corpse. Calvino's men
drew back, relieved that something was happening at last, and
the fishermen's patient interest was finally rewarded. As Larche
followed Calvino, he glanced across at Salvador Tomas. The boy
immediately looked away but Lorenzo gave a half-wave and it
was Larche's turn to avert his eyes quickly. Then he wondered
irritably why he had.

The corpse wore loose cotton trousers and a singlet. His white
skin was reddened by the sun and a small, cheap money belt
was round his waist. He was totally unmarked up to his chest
which had a ragged tear in it so deep that Larche could see the
man's lungs. But if this was not riveting enough, the fact that his
head was partially shattered was far worse. Larche turned away
for a moment, bile rising in his throat at the recollection of the
earlier killings. Then he controlled himself and quickly turned
back, staring down at the ripped, raw gouts of bloodied flesh –
the obvious result of immense impact on the knife-sharp flinty
rocks which pierced the shingle of the cove.

'He has a passport – and an identity card.'

'In the name of . . .'

'Liam Mullen. Irish citizen.'

'You won't have had time to check him out –'

'Oh, but I have.' Calvino's triumph was slightly childish but
Larche didn't grudge him his moment; he was sure that he
wouldn't have many more. 'I made a phone call to the British
police. Forgive me for not interrupting you earlier.'

Larche nodded forgiveness.

'That was the alias being used by the man the British
secret service spotted at Gatwick. Their computer gave me
the information in ten minutes. I was very impressed.'

'Were you able to access Alison Rowe's description? Does it
tally with the body and the ID?'

'Yes.'

'And?'

'Well, it's a very general description, and you can see the state
of his face, but as far as it goes I think it fits him.' He sounded
slightly hesitant.

'Do you have any doubts?' asked Larche.

'I shall have,' replied Calvino. 'I always do in the fullness of time. But who *is* this man if he is not the assassin?' He pulled the sheeting back over the ravaged human remains.

There was a long pause while Larche thought again of the three poor little rich boys trapped on their island paradise. Had the seeds of disaster been sown long ago, back in that privileged, arid past? Calvino was still begging the question: if this indeed was the assassin, had he also killed Eduardo and Father Miguel – and, above all, who had hired him? 'Lorenzo,' he said to Calvino. 'Why was Lorenzo searching the coast? Why didn't he leave it to the police – there are enough of them?'

Summoned briskly by Calvino, Lorenzo moved slowly and gracefully over to them. His leathery features looked curiously young and Larche wondered just how old he really was. Mid-forties? Younger? Older? He was ageless and his movements were athletic, almost feline. Glancing across at Salvador, Larche could see that the boy was watching Lorenzo with a steady concentration. The heat was now intense – a shimmering wall that seemed to separate them from the sea.

As Lorenzo began to speak, Larche listened intently, trying to find a loophole in what he was saying.

'I was still patrolling up and down the coast with Juan, feeling shocked at what had happened to Blasco Tomas and your colleague.' He turned to Larche for the first time. 'I was sure as I could be that there was no one on the island and their assassin had somehow managed to escape. We had checked all the coves – all of them are shallow – and I went to take another look at this headland. I suddenly remembered that there was a small cave half-way up which was very inaccessible and I knew the police would have difficulty getting to it. I could have managed it if I hadn't been worried about the *El Santos*. I regret it now, but I delegated the job to Juan.'

'Surely he would have done what you told him?' interrupted Larche brusquely.

'Yes – but he was careless. The headland as you can see is very

150

difficult to climb. If someone had been clever and lain very still, it's likely that Juan would have failed to find him.'

'You really think he was up there then?' Larche's tone was challenging, but Lorenzo continued very calmly.

'I'm sure he was. We were motoring away from the headland when I looked back and saw a figure on the cliff. We turned about, and just as we reached the inlet I heard a shot and saw him falling to the beach.'

'OK,' said Calvino. 'We know the rest.'

'Can I see the documents?' asked Larche impatiently.

'Of course.'

Lorenzo returned slowly to Salvador and the group of fishermen.

Conscious that he had been rather patronizingly dismissed, Larche said, 'Thank you,' very distinctly, but Lorenzo didn't seem to hear. One of Calvino's aides produced a passport and identity card and Larche thumbed through them curiously. Both showed the same blurred photograph – of a man in his late thirties, with blond hair unfashionably long and a wide but indistinctive face. He could have been anyone – anyone who vaguely fitted Alison Rowe's description.

'There was something else,' said Calvino. He picked up the cellophane package from just behind the corpse. 'The gun is a Smith & Wesson automatic. All ten bullets were fired.'

'I see.'

'And there were nine entry wounds in the bodies of Blasco Tomas and Alison Rowe – five in Tomas and four in Rowe. This man blew away his face with the last remaining bullet and dropped the gun as he fell. It landed on the beach some distance from the body.'

'Lucky it didn't fall into the sea,' replied Larche and Calvino shrugged.

There was another long silence and it seemed to Larche as if everything around him had stopped in a kind of freeze-frame. For seconds it appeared that the ocean, the sky, the figure on the beach were all in suspended animation. Then the surging of the waves filled his ears again and the fleecy clouds once more travelled across the face of the blinding sun.

'I don't think that there can be many doubts left, señor.' Calvino sounded reproachful. 'It'll be just a question of clearing up the loose ends.' His voice trembled slightly as if he was now completely exhausted.

Larche felt deeply depressed. The end was neat, wrapped up and unsatisfactory. The press would be delighted that there had been such a dramatic conclusion to events, and for some days the coverage would be at a premium. Then the headlines would lessen, a few more facts would be relegated to the inside pages and on television and radio some small profiles might linger. But soon the Tomas story would be dead. Larche could see the whole scenario. And yet no motive for the killings had been established – only a probable assassin. The unanswerable questions ran through Larche's mind again. Why were Eduardo and Father Miguel killed in Madrid and then Blasco and Alison on Molino? If this Liam Mullen had been set up to kill them, or some of them, weren't the rest of the Tomas family in danger? And what about the letters and the telephone calls? Then, of course, there was the motive for the killings . . .

'Just a few loose ends,' agreed Larche. 'Like who hired the assassin?'

'I know that,' said Calvino defensively. 'There are many unanswered questions, but this man was on the run and hiding out. He killed himself when he knew the hunt was closing in and he has the right alias.' Calvino stretched his arms out in a gesture of entreaty. 'We have something to go on. Yes?'

'We have something,' agreed Larche. 'But I wouldn't want to go far on it.'

'I'll need to talk to my office,' said Larche.

'I'll have you run back,' said Calvino, signalling one of his men.

'I'll walk – if you don't mind.'

As he spoke, one of the radios crackled into life. Seconds later, Calvino said in a slightly injured tone, 'Paco says there's a call from Lyon for you at the house – from a man called Philippe Chalon.'

'My number two. Tell him I'll ring him back.'

Larche walked away over the pebbles and up the steep little path, feeling considerable disquiet. It was true that this corpse vaguely fitted a description but he knew that this was not enough – could never be enough – to close an investigation, and that Calvino was only trying to ease off the pressure he'd been under. As he paced his way back to the house Larche passed a crumbling dry stone wall to which a lizard clung. He paused to look at its mottled skin and then hurried more briskly on.

'We've checked out Morrison,' said Chalon on the telephone in Eduardo's study. 'He's absolutely bona fide and his house-keeper tells me he's on Molino at Anita Tomas's request. She described him in detail and I also checked with his secretary. Both descriptions tally exactly with the one you gave me. Any other questions?'

'Events have moved rather fast here, Philippe.' Briefly he outlined what had happened. 'There's no indication of who hired him – not at the moment anyway,' he added quickly. 'Nor am I convinced that he *was* the assassin.'

'Then who is he?' asked Chalon.

Larche didn't reply.

'Look – I don't work with a man for ten years without know-ing him,' Chalon persisted. 'What's really bothering you?'

'Nothing specific. It's just all too damned neat.'

'And?'

'Lucky.'

'Lucky? What do you mean by lucky?'

'It's all so convenient, isn't it? Lorenzo, the sighting of the man on the cliff, the shot, the fall – all such a coincidence.'

'So do you think it's a set-up?'

'Yes,' replied Larche slowly. 'I'm sure it is.'

'Why does this Calvino character believe in it, then? Is he some kind of arsehole?'

'No, he's a good man under pressure. He just wants a breathing space.'

153

'What are you going to do?'

'Stay on.'

'You haven't finished your interviews?'

'There are just two more people I'd like to talk to – Maria Tomas and Salvador, Eduardo's son. And perhaps I'll talk to Anita again.'

'Keep in touch then. And by the way . . .' Chalon paused.

'Yes?'

'Take care of yourself.'

Larche had just finished explaining the situation to Monique when there was a tap on the library door.

'I'll have to go,' he said softly into the phone. 'I'm sorry – someone's here.'

'I love you,' she whispered.

'I'll phone later if I get the chance.' He put the receiver down with some relief and turned to the door. 'Come in.' He was exhausted by his conversation with her, finding it impossible to be natural, to pretend that nothing had happened. It could only be guilt, he thought desperately. He couldn't be in love with Alison Rowe. How could he? A woman he had known for a few hours. But she had given him something so precious. Now he found himself gazing irresolutely at the old servant who was standing on the threshold like a grey shadow. 'Yes?'

'They are asking –'

'Who are?' snapped Larche, unnecessarily abrasive.

'Bishop Carlos – Señora Tomas. They are wondering if you still wish to speak to them – in the light of recent events?'

'Of course I do.'

'Thank you, señor. They are getting a little restless.'

The scene that met his eyes when Larche walked through into the long, elegant main room of the house resembled prison conditions with revolt about to surface. Outwardly, there was however a certain brooding restraint.

Bishop Carlos was thumbing through some papers, Anita

154

Tomas was reading *El Pais*, Julia Descartes and Carlos Mendes were playing cards, Maria Tomas was pouring herself a drink and Damien Alba was seemingly immersed in a detective story, sitting uncomfortably on a rigid-looking ultra-modern chair. Bernard Morrison, who seemed to be sketching the assembled company, looked up immediately. Jacinto and Salvador were disinterestedly watching the flickering images of the muted television set.

'You've heard what happened?' Larche asked.

'Calvino phoned,' Anita replied abruptly. As she spoke, the Bishop looked up and regarded Larche thoughtfully whilst Maria switched off the TV. Expectancy took over amongst the nervous company. 'So they've got the assassin – at last,' said Anita. For the first time she was human in her strange mixture of relief and anger. Her usual cold detachment seemed to have been temporarily jettisoned. 'I find it utterly incredible that there should have been such an enormous police presence – and he could have hidden in a cave all the while, waiting his opportunity. I shall be taking this up at the highest level. I've never been happy with Calvino,' she ended viciously.

'He penned us up here together like criminals,' Morrison muttered. 'What's going on?' His face was more apprehensive now and Larche felt a glow of pleasure.

'I'm sorry.' He spoke the words softly, watching the tense hostility towards him steal slowly over all their faces. 'Calvino has only been doing what he thinks is right. I consider he's handled the affair as well as anyone could –'

'I must disagree,' snapped Anita.

'But I'm not at all happy with the situation,' continued Larche.

'You mean you don't think he *is* the assassin?' asked Morrison.

'I don't know,' Larche replied quickly. 'They've found a gun and the right number of bullets has been fired from it, but there are too many loose ends.' He paused, watching his words spread the unease he had predicted. 'Far too many.'

The Bishop nodded somewhat absently, as if he was too confused to be anything else but slightly dismissive. Then he stood up. 'I agree,' he said. 'The police approach has been thoroughly amateur.'

'In my opinion Calvino and his team have been as thorough as they could be,' Larche retorted, determined to avoid the obvious scapegoating, 'but there are a large number of unanswered questions which I'm sure they're investigating.'

'Perhaps you could enumerate them for us?' asked Anita frostily.

'Very well.' Larche paused and then began to speak slowly and reflectively. 'The evidence does seem to suggest that this man might be Blasco and Alison's killer, but this brings us to the unanswered questions. For instance – what was the motive? Did this man also kill Eduardo and Father Miguel? Are the two sets of killings linked?'

'Presumably,' said Bishop Carlos softly.

'But what *is* the link? If it's the Tomas family, then you're all in danger. And what about the death threats?'

'Loose ends,' muttered Anita dismissively.

'Too many, wouldn't you say?' returned Larche, wondering why she was suddenly so accepting. Was it just a result she had been wanting – *any* result? Larche found it hard to believe. Surely she was too astute for that?

'The mere fact that this man was hiding here is bad enough,' Anita said brusquely, rearranging some ceramics on a side-table with irritable exactitude. 'Every section of this island should have been combed – and it obviously wasn't. I shall be taking legal action against the police.'

'What will happen now?' asked Bishop Carlos, trying to spike her anger, but Larche didn't reply. He noticed that the atmosphere had completely changed; they were no longer rebellious about being penned up, no longer anxious that the case should be rather unsatisfactorily closed. They were afraid – all of them, in varying degrees. It was clear to him that the corpse on the beach was no more than a distraction.

'I'm sure Señor Calvino will be talking to you and giving you all the details,' he said, conscious of their expectant eyes. 'And at the risk of being tedious, I must repeat that Señor Calvino and his team have been very thorough in their investigations so far.' Larche was determined that Calvino should not be pilloried.

'I'm afraid I must disagree with you.' Anita's voice was

cold and flat. 'But I see no point in arguing about it.' She stared at him challengingly but he didn't reply. 'I have to press on with the funeral arrangements,' she said at last. 'It gives me something to think about – occupied. I *need* to be kept occupied.' Anita's words were too emphatic, her tension obvious, but she was quick to regain control. 'He's going to be buried at Empuries,' she said aggressively to Larche, as if defying him to bureaucratically suggest otherwise. 'The King has given permission.'

Larche nodded, knowing that she was trying to deflect any more questions, to wrest a breathing space from him. Well – he had successfully wound them all up. Now he could let them off the hook for a while, give everyone a false sense of security. In Larche's experience this often resulted in someone tripping up. Empuries, he thought: someone had already told him before that Eduardo would be buried there and he had always liked the place – a magnificent Graeco-Roman archaeological site bordering the Mediterranean, the original harbour still intact. 'I don't think anyone has ever been buried there before,' he said quietly.

'No.' She glanced at him with angry pride. 'It's a first. Eduardo once told me he'd like to be buried near warm Roman stone – and he'll have his wish. The tomb is to overlook the sea under the shade of some cypress trees.'

'A singular honour,' murmured Bishop Carlos.

'A beautiful resting place.' Bernard Morrison would always sound false to Larche now and this time was no exception.

Larche nodded. 'That will be wonderful,' he said. 'Are you going to Empuries on your own?' he asked gently. He wanted to talk to her again – and to be off the island would be a good opportunity.

'I'm never alone. I shall have my security staff – headed by Señor Mendes here, in whom I have very great confidence.'

The man made her a little sheepish bow but Larche gave him no opportunity to speak. 'Of course. I was just wondering – if I could accompany you,' he said persuasively.

'Why would you want to do that?' She sounded more curious than anything else.

'I should like to see Eduardo's resting place – and perhaps talk some more with you. But I shall quite understand if you would prefer that I didn't.'

There was a short pause and then Anita said easily, 'You must come if you wish.' She stood up abruptly and turned to Mendes, Descartes and Alba. 'I would like to thank you now – although I will thank you again formally – for your loyalty and devotion to my husband over the years you've worked for him. I am deeply grateful – as I know he was.'

The three rose to their feet, muttering deprecating platitudes. Loyal servants, Larche thought, suitably and pleasantly rewarded. No doubt financial recompense would follow.

Anita was solicitous. 'Marius – you must rest. You look exhausted.'

'I shall take a siesta,' he assented.

'And then come here for dinner tonight. There'll just be Bishop Carlos and myself.'

'What about Mr Morrison?'

'I want to be alone, as I believe Greta Garbo once said.' Morrison smiled lazily up at Larche, putting away his sketchbook in the pocket of his overalls. 'I'll be painting tomorrow – and I'd like to have an early night.'

'So it will just be the three of us – if you'd like to come.'

'Yes, I'd be delighted. Thank you.'

'About ten.' She paused. 'Marius – I pray this discovery must be the end of it all, at least here on the island. I need Molino to be a sanctuary again.'

Larche saw the entreaty in her eyes. 'The question is,' he repeated, 'if that man *was* the assassin, then who in God's name employed him?'

Anita nodded. 'The investigation will take months, years – and might still end inconclusively.' She sighed. 'Perhaps I've been naïve. I was hoping for a quick solution; now I have to accept an inconclusive one.'

'There is *no* solution,' replied Larche. 'Not yet.'

His remark seemed to throw them all into uproar – except

158

for Anita who remained both cool and detached. A battery of questions began and he could see the fear in their eyes quite clearly now. They had expected a lull, but were now being plunged back into uncertainty.

'The point is,' said Jacinto sharply, cutting through the noise, 'are we expecting any more killings, monsieur?'

Before Larche could reply Maria Tomas spoke for the first time, her voice husky and uncertain, her face in shadow. 'Is there another assassin?' she breathed. 'Is there someone still on the island?'

'I think so.'

'Someone who is one of us?' asked Bishop Carlos, and there was a deep impenetrable silence.

'I want you to stay together,' replied Larche. 'Don't go anywhere alone.'

Larche walked back to the guest house, lay on his bed and reread Alison's note. His emotions seemed to have been anaesthetized and he could feel nothing. Worse still, Larche could no longer see her face in his mind's eye. Exhausted, he slept but woke an hour later, unrefreshed and tense. Trying to calm himself, he thought about the people he had interviewed. He had always found it useful during other investigations to sit back and quietly reassess each person he had spoken to, but here on Molino he was finding everyone difficult to discern.

There was Morrison – full of revelations but intent on personal gain. Was that all there was to the portrait painter? Anita, cool and remote and normally in control, now showing her emotions under the greatest stress. If only he could get closer to her, find out how she really felt. Had she always loved Eduardo so obsessively? Was she simply blind to his activities? Then there was Jacinto, full of bitterness with many rational explanations for his anger and sense of unfairness. What other thoughts did he harbour? How strong was his hatred? What about his wife?

Then of course there were the minions: servants and chauffeurs, bodyguards and secretaries. But Larche knew he would leave them to Calvino – look up his notes and rely on them for he was sure that he could. Besides, he couldn't afford the time; Larche was intuitively certain that in some unidentified way it was running out on him.

The motive behind Eduardo's murder could well be political, but was Blasco really murdered because he knew something? Couldn't the motive here have been personal? His mind churned away at the possibilities. Somehow Larche had a gut feeling that the roots of the killings, both on political and personal levels, went back a long way and he tried to consider carefully who were the main protagonists – both institutional and individual. On the one hand there was the government, the Church and the fishing industry; on the other there was Anita, Morrison, Bishop Carlos, Lorenzo, Jacinto or even Maria. It was quite a line-up from all points of view. And then there were the servants, unknown people from Sebastia – the range seemed to be infinite.

The surface of the pool, thought Larche, his mind turning over the confessions of the last few days, might be composed of the more predictable emotions that people for all their devious reasons wanted to show him. But underneath, in the primeval slime, were the real feelings that provided motive. That was where he needed to be.

Were the two sets of murders *necessarily* connected? Certainly it would be an enormous coincidence if they weren't. But perhaps the one could have triggered off the other.

Again he slept, and this time dreamed that he and Alison Rowe were walking across the lavender fields in Provence, heading for the hills. It was evening and all they could hear were the crickets, and from somewhere in the valley there was the steady drone of a tractor. They came to a stream and walked across it over stepping stones, holding on to each other and laughing, almost but not quite falling in. Later they wandered up the rocky slopes until they came to a plateau where they made love.

Larche woke sweating. He could see her very clearly now, hear her voice in his mind, see her smile, feel her lips, explore her body. He got out of bed shaking, the erotic experience

160

strong within him. Gradually his erection lessened and he went to the bathroom to splash water over his face. The shaking, however, continued and looking at his watch he saw that it was six. He turned the television on and watched the news, confident that the butchery would soon be faithfully recorded amidst massive speculation.

Part Three

9

In fact there was far less speculation than Larche had imagined. A large part of the newscast was given over to the latest sensational developments in the Tomas tragedy. 'We reported earlier that two more killings had taken place on the island home of Eduardo Tomas's family – his brother Blasco, a monk from the community on the island of Fuego some miles up the coast, and a British police officer, Detective Superintendent Alison Rowe. Their brutal murders, closely following the assassination of Eduardo Tomas and Father Miguel Fernandez in the Basilica of El Val de los Caidos, have shocked the nation. But now a further dramatic development has occurred; another body has been discovered – this time of an Irish citizen. The head of the police investigation team, Inspector Emilio Calvino, made this statement to our reporter Carmina Mandri.'

Calvino's figure, framed by the imposing frontage of the Tomas house, came sharply into focus as he spoke into the microphone. He looked calm, collected and entirely professional. Larche smiled. Good for him.

'We have discovered the body of a man – an Irish citizen – on the island,' said Calvino briskly.

'Does this mean that you have the assassin?' asked Carmina Mandri urgently. The camera came in for a close-up as Calvino said, 'I can't comment on that.'

'So the major threat against the Tomas family is over?'

'We are actively investigating the situation and directly we know something more positive I shall be holding another press conference.'

165

'So the family is still under protection?'

'Yes.'

'Are they safe?'

'Of course they are,' snapped Calvino authoritatively.

'Can you tell us the identity of this corpse?'

'I've told you, I can't make any further comment at this time. There will be another statement made later.'

Larche switched the television off abruptly and, with anguish in his heart, rose from the bed and slowly and reluctantly began to dress for dinner.

Minutes later, there was a knock on the door. Larche opened it irritably to find Salvador Tomas standing on the threshold. He looked older in the dying light and there was a sallowness under his tan that marked his pristine beauty.

'Yes?' Larche was curt.

'I want to speak with you, señor.'

'Now?'

'Please.'

'Come in then.'

The boy was wearing jeans and a floppy shirt with a wide collar. He licked his lips, cleared his throat, licked his lips again and then looked away.

'Do you want to sit down?' asked Larche, rather grudgingly trying to put him at his ease. He felt exhausted as well as extremely depressed and Salvador was filling the space he needed for objective thought about the case.

'No thanks.'

'Take your time then.'

'You are leaving Molino?'

'Not yet.'

'Are you still asking questions, señor?'

Larche smiled at him in weary encouragement. 'Yes, I'm still asking questions. I was going to talk to you tomorrow – but if you have something urgent to tell me . . .'

'I loved my father. He was a good man.' Salvador's voice shook. 'How do we know that assassin is genuine? How do we know it's not some kind of set-up?'

'You mean that this Irishman was imported here – with the

166

documentation and the gun and the neatly allocated missing bullets?'

'It's possible, isn't it?'

Yes, it was possible, thought Larche.

'You should go to Sebastia,' insisted Salvador. 'Talk to people there. Talk to the women. They hate him and all he stands for – all he's done.'

'Hate who?'

'Lorenzo Solana.'

'Him again.'

'He hated my father – knew he was going to sack him.'

'I realize the circumstances, but we have no evidence to suggest Lorenzo was in any way involved,' said Larche, deliberately dismissive.

'*Have* you questioned him?' Salvador spoke so childishly yet so fiercely that Larche could almost feel the force of his frustration.

'Calvino is in charge of the case,' replied Larche firmly. 'I'm simply backing him up.' He looked at Salvador speculatively, wondering if he would be able to push him into further angry confidences.

'You were invited here to make enquiries by my father.'

'This latest corpse has put a fresh complexion on everything,' replied Larche calmly. Then he tried another tack. 'By the way, I saw you with Lorenzo when you should have been waiting for me in the house. Why did you go off like that?'

'I wanted to feel his hatred – know that it's still burning.'

'Aren't you being rather melodramatic?'

'No.' Salvador was suddenly logical. 'Lorenzo's hatred for my father is as strong as my mother's love for him. They are both powerful people.'

'Yes.' Larche nodded acquiescence. He was listening very carefully now.

'Lorenzo could have set all this up to deflect attention away from himself.'

'How would he do it?'

'Find someone . . .'

'An Irishman?'

167

'Not necessarily. Anyone.'

'That could be proven.'

'Kill them and give them false papers. Supply the gun and fix the chambers.'

Larche nodded. 'So you went to Lorenzo. What did you do? Challenge him?'

'Nothing – I was too afraid,' he admitted and paused, frowning, his assurance evaporating.

'Why were you afraid?' asked Larche.

'He is still very angry.'

'Because he knows he has to go.'

'Yes.'

'Your mother hasn't mentioned that to me,' replied Larche. He decided to turn on the heat a little, frighten the boy out of this rather childishly aggressive mood. 'So let's get this quite clear. You are saying Lorenzo hired an assassin who went to the Valley of the Fallen, set up the epileptic girl and, while she was rolling on the floor and suitably distracting attention, assassinated your father and the priest.'

'It's possible,' Salvador replied doggedly, looking away from him.

'Why send the assassin all that way?'

'To kill Miguel too.'

'I see. And why should he want to do that?' Larche asked crisply.

'Because Miguel knew a lot about Lorenzo. Wanted to tell my father what a conniving bastard he was.'

'Didn't he know that already?'

'He blinded himself to it,' said Salvador, and Larche could detect the forced surety in his voice. 'Miguel was going to warn him again – tell him some of the terrible things Lorenzo's been doing . . .'

'Very well,' Larche continued briskly. 'So a few days later, Lorenzo then imports the assassin to Molino and this time he kills your uncle and my colleague. Why?'

'Because Blasco also has information on Lorenzo – and your colleague happened to be in his company.'

'A little too neat?'

168

'Not if you're desperate,' said Salvador angrily.

'Then this hired assassin conceals himself on an island full of policemen, evades a full-scale search, and eventually commits suicide.'

'That's the bit that's too neat, but perhaps Lorenzo killed him. He and Juan are the only witnesses,' Salvador continued blandly.

'And now he's ready to murder the rest of your family . . .' Larche let the note of derision creep into his voice.

'While he's around I'm afraid for my mother.'

'And you reckon Lorenzo has all this administrative ability, do you? You also believe that he could hire a sophisticated international assassin? He's just a fisherman!'

'He's more than that!'

'He used to run a boatyard. Not *much* more.'

'It was a boatyard with a difference. He fixed up boats for the rich and famous,' Salvador retorted quickly.

'And the odd assassin?'

There was a long silence during which Salvador seemed to lose some of his anger. Is he going to come clean, Larche wondered. There was very obviously something behind all this – but what? He decided to push him a little more.

'Look – why do you hate this Lorenzo so much? There must be a reason. Don't you think you can confide in me?' His voice hardened. 'If you don't, you're wasting my time.'

'People say my father was gay.' The words tumbled out and the boy wouldn't meet his eyes.

'What people?' Larche spoke very gently.

'Lorenzo.'

'He said that?'

'He mocked me. I tried to hit him, but he's too strong. He just pushed me on to the ground and they all laughed. All the men. The women looked on, but I could feel their hatred for him. He's a bastard!' Salvador was sweating with anger now. 'Saying those things. My father wasn't gay. He couldn't have been.' He switched his angry and confused gaze to Larche. 'You knew him well. He wasn't, was he?'

Larche didn't reply.

10

'Was he?' repeated Salvador impatiently.

Larche sighed. 'Not in my experience.'

'What have you heard?' He was aggressive again now, but his lower lip was trembling.

'A man like your father – a distinguished public figure, a politician – he would be surrounded by rumour.' Larche knew he still wanted to give Eduardo the benefit of the doubt, and by doing this he could well be playing the useful role of the devil's advocate – useful, that is, as regards Salvador. He still couldn't decide whether the boy was stringing him along or was genuinely terrified of all the implications. Something had made Salvador come to him like this, but his real reasons were far from clear.

Salvador looked at him in frustrated contempt. 'You mean you're not going to tell me, don't you?'

Larche caught the flicker of reserve in his eyes. 'Look,' he replied with sudden resolution, 'I think you're getting this all out of proportion.'

'You don't believe me?'

'I mean that I want time to think over what you've told me,' replied Larche. 'We'll talk again tomorrow, but I want you to tell me the truth.'

'I am.'

'Think about the truth.' Larche was curt. 'Sometimes it can be very elusive – even to ourselves.'

Bishop Carlos cut up his beef, adding another spoonful of the excellent meat sauce from the wide china bowl. He broke bread and dipped it in, transferring it to his mouth vigorously. 'I am praying this Irishman was the assassin, even if he was just a hired hand. At least it will give the investigation a bit more breathing space.'

Anita ate little, toying with some salad, glancing curiously at Larche from time to time as if she was going to ask him a question but was putting it off.

The three of them were sitting around a small, gilded table in the herb garden. The cicadas were calling, and dimly Larche could hear the beat of waves on the Molino rocks. A wind had risen, but in the sheltered garden the evening was mellow with the day's heat.

'His background has to be examined thoroughly before any conclusions can be reached,' said Larche dampeningly.

'And Calvino will be doing that?'

'His team will.'

'So your own role is diminished?' said Anita. 'You've been marginalized.' There was a sharpness in her voice he had not heard before.

'I always was.'

Anita didn't return his smile. 'So you will only be asking your questions here – on Molino?' she said impatiently.

'I'm only here at all courtesy of the Spanish police.'

'And my late husband,' she snapped.

'Yes, but if I want to make my relationship with the Spanish authorities work I have to be in fairly low profile, Anita. That doesn't mean to say I'm sitting on my backside.' Now it was his turn to be impatient.

She sighed. 'I know.' For the first time since Larche had arrived on Molino, he saw that she could be sorry. He was taken aback, not knowing what to make of this new discovery. 'I just feel . . . it's all so unsatisfactory, being kept away from information, not knowing what's going on. Do you know what I mean, Marius?'

'Yes,' he said. 'I know what you mean.'

She started to speak, hesitated and then began, 'I haven't had the opportunity to . . . say how deeply concerned I was about the death of your colleague.'

'Thank you.' Larche felt a dreadful lurch in the pit of his stomach and for a ghastly moment he wondered if he was going to cry. 'Of course – I hardly knew her,' he said hurriedly.

'Nevertheless,' said Bishop Carlos, 'it was an appalling tragedy.'

'Yes. She was a very good police officer.' Larche quickly changed the subject. 'I've just seen your son,' he said, turning back to Anita.

'Oh?' Her voice was neutral.

'He came to my room.'

'I see. What did he say to you?' She sounded only casually interested.

'He's convinced Lorenzo is implicated in all this. He has some wild theory that *he* hired the assassin.'

Anita shrugged. 'Salvador's hated him for a long time now.'

'Why?'

'Something happened – a long time ago.'

'Something you should have told me?'

'I don't think so. It has nothing to do with the case.'

'So why *does* he hate Lorenzo?' Larche was conscious of a slight tightening of tension in the atmosphere, and for a moment he had the wild thought that they were participants in some kind of mass conspiracy. He hurriedly dismissed the idea, wondering if this investigation would break him. As it was, Alison's face, her body, her voice continually invaded his mind, making deduction cloudy.

'He killed his dog. It was an accident – I'm quite sure of that – but Salvador doesn't agree.'

'What exactly happened?' Larche forced himself to concentrate and his head pounded with the effort.

'Lorenzo used to take Salvador out fishing –'

'You were happy with that?' he intervened.

'Not particularly. As you know, I've never liked the man.'

'So why did you let him go?'

'Eduardo was keen he should know the ways of the sea.' There was a slight sneer in her voice which Larche picked up immediately. This was the first time she had criticized Eduardo.

'You mean he thought Salvador should mix with the common people and absorb their folklore?'

Larche's irony made her frown regally. 'There's no need to be cynical, Marius,' she admonished. 'Eduardo had a narrow and élitist upbringing on this island, as I'm sure Jacinto told you. Neither of us wanted that for Salvador.'

'And the dog?' asked Larche.

'A much-loved pet called Asterix. Anyway, the poor creature got tangled up in the winch on the boat.'

Larche's headache increased. There was something about the insularity of this place that bred violence – even accidental violence.

'Salvador says Lorenzo killed the dog deliberately,' she continued. 'Of course that's ridiculous.'

'It does seem unlikely. How old was Salvador at the time?'

'Eleven.'

'Did he have any explanation?'

'He simply said they'd had some kind of argument and Lorenzo pushed Asterix into the winch.'

'Did anyone investigate this?'

'Eduardo.'

'What did he say?'

'That Lorenzo was terribly upset – that he'd warned Salvador not to let the dog go near the winch, but somehow Asterix did and got mixed up with it. I know it was horrible – a ghastly experience – but Eduardo was certain the whole incident was just a tragic accident.'

'And you? What did you think?'

'Yes,' Anita replied slowly, 'I thought it was an accident too. I don't like Lorenzo, but why should he do a terrible thing like that?'

'But Salvador didn't think so.'

'No.'

'And did he ever see Lorenzo again?'

'Not to my knowledge – at least not until he went to see him yesterday.'

'So you knew where he was going?' asked Larche slowly.

'Yes. I tried to stop him but he's very impetuous. Like

173

his father. He had this fixation that Lorenzo was somehow implicated – a ludicrous fixation.'

'Is it?' Bishop Carlos interrupted suddenly, wiping his plate with his bread. 'Anita – I'm not so sure that you didn't half believe Salvador yourself.'

'Perhaps I would have liked to,' she said, the old detachment returning, 'but can you imagine for one moment I would have allowed Salvador to go and see Lorenzo on his own if I thought he was involved? It's a ludicrous idea. Lorenzo is nothing; a little man who has become a nuisance and has already received a month's notice.' Anita concluded on a cold and derisory note. But she *has* been showing emotion, thought Larche. Maybe she regards that as a weakness. Would she ever agree to psychoanalysis, he wondered. But he knew that it would take an apocalypse to convince her that psychiatry could help.

'Salvador ran off before you could stop him,' demurred Bishop Carlos.

'I could have sent Jacinto after him.'

'But you didn't.'

'No, there was no point. We'd been cooped up together for a long time. I thought my son needed a break.' She looked challengingly at Larche but he said nothing. Then Anita snapped out, 'Lorenzo could never have had the power or the influence to employ an international assassin, and when the body of this Irishman was discovered I was even more certain that Lorenzo could have had nothing to do with it.'

'Sure enough to let Salvador off the leash?' Larche was insistent.

'Yes,' she replied firmly.

Larche turned to Bishop Carlos. 'I gather Lorenzo was a novice on Fuego.'

'For a short while.'

'Did you know him?'

'Not well.'

'But you must have formed *some* impressions of him?'

'He seemed very much an idealist.'

'What does that mean?'

174

'It means he was young and enthusiastically devout.' The Bishop's tone was enigmatic.

'Isn't that what he should have been?' asked Larche ingenuously.

'I would have wished him to have a little more discernment. Perhaps more doubts. But all this is very superficial; as I said, I hardly knew him. Father Gallo was in charge at Fuego. If you want to know more you should ask him.'

'Why did he leave the community?' asked Larche a little brusquely.

Bishop Carlos paused, reflecting for some time. Then he said, 'Father Gallo told me that Lorenzo lost his faith.'

Larche felt he could detect something uneasy in Bishop Carlos' manner and decided to press him. 'Did you follow it up yourself?'

'No,' said Bishop Carlos. 'I knew the Father would have talked it all through with him.'

'And there was nothing else?'

'No.'

'He is not . . . he had not been involved in any homosexual acts?' Larche heard himself sounding pompous and was conscious of Anita's eyes on him.

'Certainly not,' replied the Bishop authoritatively.

'You're sure?'

'Father Gallo would have told me.'

'You're quite sure he would?'

'Absolutely.' The Bishop looked offended and glared down at his empty plate.

'I don't think Lorenzo is a homosexual,' said Anita. 'But I do think he terrorized Sebastia with his bullying, his unreasonable demands, the way he lined his own pockets. Many of the villagers complained to me. Repeatedly.'

'And Eduardo? Didn't they complain to him too?'

'They gave it up because he wouldn't listen. You have to appreciate that despite everything Lorenzo got results, and Eduardo liked results.' She paused and then said abruptly, 'It was only in the last few weeks that he realized Sebastia would no longer tolerate him. Will you be talking to Lorenzo

175

yourself? Or are you going on Calvino's word?' Her voice was very smooth, but he detected a hint of malice.

'Yes, I will talk to him, perhaps more out of curiosity than anything else,' observed Larche mildly.

'Of course.' There was a long pause. 'He must accept his month's notice. I'm not keeping him.'

'And who will run the Sebastian fishing industry?'

'We'll find someone,' she replied with easy confidence.

The remainder of the meal continued with an unanimated discussion about the fishing industry in Sebastia, Eduardo's original hopes and how they had been fulfilled until Lorenzo became unpopular. The conversation was led by Anita, listened to by Larche and largely ignored by Bishop Carlos who ate cheese, sipped at a liqueur and almost fell asleep. Meanwhile, Larche came to the conclusion that he would walk over to Sebastia tonight. He had to see the place for himself at last.

Half an hour later Larche left the guest house again, feeling drowsy; the ornate bed had seemed more than welcoming but he was determined to keep going, partly because he didn't want to be alone and have his mind swamped with visions of Alison. Somehow he had to keep on his feet until there was some resolution of the case. He paused, feeling short of breath. The heat of the night had sharply increased and the velvet darkness was an oppressive wall through which he had to push himself. The cicadas had stopped singing and the silence was weighty, impenetrable – so much so that he gave a little whimper of anxiety as a voice whispered, 'Monsieur Larche?'

'Who's that?'

'Bishop Carlos.' His tall figure emerged from the shadows. 'I'd like a word. It won't take long.'

'Do you want to go inside or –'

'No.' The Bishop was sweating heavily. 'I lied to you.'

Larche was horrified. After all that had happened, a confession from almost anyone else on Molino would merely be surprising, but this admission from the eminent and seemingly courageous Bishop was yet another twist that set Larche's mind racing with conjecture. By his presence, by his knowledge of the family, perhaps by their need to confess, finding him so much easier to talk to than Calvino – Larche had definitely started something. The problem was that he was hard pressed to know exactly what to do with his scrambled information – how to fit its seemingly ever-changing pattern into something coherent.

'I had to,' Bishop Carlos was saying. 'Anita's feelings . . .' His voice petered out. 'There's a limit to even her self-control.'

'I agree.' Larche was quietly soothing. It seemed the only attitude to take. 'What do you want to tell me?' He shortened his pace to the Bishop's. The island's getting smaller, he thought illogically. Emotions have been fermenting too long, and now they've started to flood over the top of the well. He had to be up to this; he had to regain his objectivity to stand any chance of success.

'That there were . . . incidents . . . in the monastery on Fuego. That Lorenzo was asked to leave. He . . . did have a relationship with another man.'

'A monk?'

'Yes.'

'It was hushed up?'

Carlos smiled bitterly. 'Of course.'

'Who by?'

'Me. There was no need for scandal,' he added stolidly, but there was a profound sadness in his eyes.

'Is there anything else you want to tell me?'

'I believe you know there is. Don't play games with me, Monsieur Larche.'

'You mean Eduardo.'

'Yes.'

'And Salvador?' asked Larche tentatively.

'I'm very concerned for him. But of course – I haven't the slightest shred of evidence.'

'But you are sure about Eduardo and Lorenzo?'

There was no reply.

'Aren't you?' insisted Larche. 'A number of other people are.'

'Anita mustn't know. Ever.' His voice broke slightly.

'These things get around,' said Larche mercilessly. 'I should have thought they would have got around to her.'

'She was well protected from rumour.'

'By who?'

'Eduardo himself. Who else?'

'And you feel certain she doesn't guess – that everything was well covered up?'

'She very often talks to me and I have taken her confession. Believe me – I would have known.'

'But you don't agree with Salvador?'

'That Lorenzo is behind this? Of course not. It would be out of the question. The killings were far too sophisticated. Nevertheless, I had to let you know about Lorenzo – admit to you that I lied – but it mustn't go any further.'

'So what are you telling me?'

'I'm not telling you, I'm asking you. I want her protected. It's a sacred trust that I must take on for Eduardo.'

'Why shouldn't she know the truth?'

'It would kill her.'

Larche nodded. He was right. It was as simple as that. The walls of Anita's beseiged citadel of evasion were crumbling.

'You will be seeing Lorenzo?' Bishop Carlos seemed anxious.

'Yes.'

'When?'

'Tonight, perhaps. I'd like to have an informal chat.'

'You'll keep her out of it?'

'Yes.'

'She must never know.' Bishop Carlos was insistent. 'Anita is a good woman – a damaged woman – and she has lost so much. At least her memories must be kept intact.'

'So she has the perfect portrait of the perfect man?'

'She deserves that. You've no idea how much she has done for the Church – for charity. Anita Tomas is the most self-sacrificing person I know, and she must be supported.' He was very agitated now – agitated and insistent. Larche was sure that he had more to tell him.

'It's very big all this, isn't it?' he said. 'To hush up, I mean.'

'Yes, but so far it's been achieved. We just have to go on protecting her until the worst of all this is over.'

'You don't think Lorenzo will blackmail her.'

'No.'

'Why not?'

'Because he's already blackmailing me.'

Bishop Carlos looked steadily at Marius Larche in the claustrophobic blanket of darkness. 'No, monsieur, you're wrong. I'm entirely celibate.'

'But why should he be blackmailing you then?' Larche stared at him with incredulity.

'I have to protect Anita. He told me he would provide complete proof of the homosexual relationship he had with Eduardo – unless I paid him.'

'But you could be doing that for the rest of your life. Why didn't you go to the police?'

'I have come to you now, monsieur. You *must* keep him quiet.'

'How long has it been going on?' Larche was trying to adjust himself to this latest development.

'Since he had his notice.'

'Where's the money coming from?'

'Not from church funds, if you're thinking that. My aunt left all her money to me recently and it is my personal choice as to how it is spent.'

'How could you be so naïve?' said Larche furiously.

'This is not a situation I can easily live with, believe me,' the Bishop said stiffly. 'I would prefer to take a more clear-cut Christian stance than support a blackmailer.'

'You'd do all this for Anita?'

'Of course.' Larche couldn't see his expression in the darkness but his tension was almost tangible. 'But now I want you to intervene – to arrest him if necessary. Nevertheless, you have to reassure me that none of this will reach Anita.'

'I can't reassure you of that, Bishop. I wish I could, but it's impossible. I can try to keep everything discreet, but Calvino will have to know – of course.'

'If she's told it'll kill her.'

'I suppose you wish the assassin had struck him too,' observed Larche.

Bishop Carlos gazed at him expressionlessly. 'Such an idea would be totally against my Christian belief.'

Larche was silent.

'I have to trust you, monsieur. *Can* I do that?'

'You can trust me to do my best for her. That's all I can say.'

'I sincerely hope so, monsieur. You will only be perpetrating yet another tragedy if you can't protect her. If she discovered these things about Eduardo, I'm sure she would put an end to her life.'

'One other point,' said Larche, 'did you ever see Eduardo and Father Miguel together here on Molino?'

The Bishop looked surprised. 'Dozens of times. The last was an inconsequential visit. We talked about Lorenzo's brutality to the locals – that's all. I advised Eduardo to talk to him. Miguel was as concerned as I was but Eduardo took his usual blinkered view of the man. Said he was doing a good job under bad conditions and that he had a lot of provocation. There really wasn't any more to it than that; the conversation was most unsatisfactory.'

Larche left Bishop Carlos feeling thoroughly compromised. On the one hand he had tried to be reassuring and on the other to be honest. The combination was not an easy one and a surge of disgust at his own lack of resolution gripped him as he walked through the herb-scented valley along the flinty track towards Sebastia. The moon was bright and there was a balmy, musky feel to the Mediterranean night. The conversation he had had with the Bishop went round his mind in circles; the whole affair was like a vast cobweb with Lorenzo at its centre, and Eduardo and Father Miguel, Blasco and Alison were already dried and desiccated corpses at the far corners. Others had survived but become enslaved to the spider.

Trying to ease his nagging and oppressive thoughts, Larche looked down at the sea which seemed to be composed of sullen, liquid lead surging metallically on to the dark rocks.

There were tiny dots of phosphorous and the smell of rotting weed. There could be no doubt that Bishop Carlos had behaved with considerable foolishness – but also some astuteness. It was unlikely that all this secrecy was *just* for Anita's sake. The Tomas family's Catholic connection was so strong and so well known that clearly the Church was anxious for a quick solution and not too much investigation. Despite his denials Bishop Carlos was clearly certain that Lorenzo was the killer; he had gone out of his way to encourage Larche to check him out carefully, although how the Bishop thought he could be hushed up if accused of murder Larche couldn't imagine. Personally he was not at all sure that Lorenzo could provide him with a solution, but he was almost certain that Sebastia would – and that he should have gone there much, much earlier. As Larche walked on, however, he was certain of something else: he had not wanted to go to Sebastia.

As he reached the village, Larche could hear the sound of slow, bluesy jazz coming from the open door of what seemed to be the only bar – a one-storey building with a few San Miguel logos and a faded sign that he couldn't read. The café was in the middle of a small network of streets, and was built of grey, weathered stone. The surrounding dwellings were almost like caves, with narrow windows and flaking shutters, but even in the dark Larche could see that the little gardens were bright with bougainvillaea and pots of geraniums.

There was a small shop, a church with a rugged tower, flying buttresses and a porticoed door, and further down one of the streets he could just glimpse the quayside. The masts of the fishing boats rose and fell on the swell, protected by the harbour wall. Larche paused, hesitant now that he had come to Sebastia at last, looking around him, hoping to find time suspended for a while. There were a few motor scooters parked in the run-down cobbled square which smelt of fish and tar and was full of untidily coiled netting, broken-up boxes, and anonymous scrap iron and old tyres. Larche assumed that the quayside and its jetties must be neater, more representative of Eduardo's faith in Lorenzo's efficient management. Maybe the square represented the old Sebastia, the timeless order of circular activity, of merging days and nights, of the slow and casual putting to sea and returning.

With sudden decision, Larche turned and walked into the bar.

Despite the lateness of the hour, the place was crowded and the cigarette smoke was as thick as the jazz was loud. There was a long wooden counter at one end and solid-looking tables and chairs scattered around the remainder of the long, dark room.

Larche walked slowly over to the counter but no one looked up.

'I'll have a beer.'

'Yes, señor.'

He waited until the glass was brought over, gazing around him at the drinkers. There was no sign of Lorenzo.

'Thank you.' He gave the barman some pesetas. 'I wonder if you can help me?'

There was no response.

'I'm looking for Lorenzo Solana.'

'He's not here.'

'Where can I find him?'

'I don't know.'

'Who wants him?' asked a woman's voice and he wheeled round to see someone vaguely familiar who he couldn't immediately place. She had been sitting unseen at one of the tables and was slightly – more than slightly – drunk.

'The name's Larche.'

'Of course.'

'You are . . .'

'Don't you recognize me?'

'I'm afraid not.'

'My name is Maria. Maria Tomas.'

Larche stared at her in some amazement. Then suddenly he *did* recognize her, scruffy jeans, dirty top and all. What was she doing here? Slumming?

She read his thoughts with what appeared to be considerable amusement; she was certainly not in the least embarrassed. 'Surprised to find me here?'

'A little.'

'I enjoy coming. It's refreshing.'

'Yes?'

'I have friends. Fishermen. I enjoy listening to their stories – and they enjoy mine.'

'Your stories?'

'Tales of the rich and famous.'

'I'm sure they're most entertaining.' Larche paused, not knowing what to say. 'What would you ... will you have a drink?'

'Thank you. I'll have a scotch.'

While he was trying to attract the attention of the barman again she asked, 'Are you leaving Molino, monsieur?'

'Not yet.'

'Ah. So it's not over?'

'What's not over?'

'The investigation,' she said, having some difficulty with the word.

'It's moving into another phase.'

'The grey men who hired the assassin?'

'If they did,' he replied firmly.

'You mean – if the assassin's the assassin?'

'Something like that.' Larche relaxed slightly. It was rather refreshing to find one of the ever articulate Tomas family pissed out of her mind – or nearly out of her mind.

'So what are you doing here?' She lurched against him slightly and he smelt the musky perfume she was wearing. It was subtle but pervasive.

'Tying up a few loose ends.'

'That all?'

'That's all I'm telling you.' He smiled at her, wondering if it was worth trying to talk to her now. Unlike Jacinto, Salvador, and Bishop Carlos she clearly had no intention of making a confession, nor would she have been capable of that, but Larche was equally certain she could be useful.

'Will the security here ease up?' she asked, stumbling over the words.

'I'm sure it won't. There'll be round-the-clock protection for the family until there's some kind of resolution.'

'That could be a long time.'

'Yes, and you shouldn't be wandering about like this,' Larche added with a mock admonishment that rather disgusted him. 'I really mean that,' he added more sincerely.

Maria shrugged impatiently. 'I feel trapped enough on this damned coast without seeing this island as a prison as well.'

'It's always been like that for your husband, hasn't it?'

'He told you all about it, did he? The poor little rich boys saga,' she sneered rather more drunkenly.

'Jacinto told me how claustrophobic the island was for him and his two brothers.' Larche tried to maintain some kind of formality with her but it was no good and suddenly they both smiled at each other disarmingly, as if restraint was quite out of the question. Immediately he felt more relaxed and, for the first time in hours, much more equipped to cope with the situation.

'But think of the money,' she said.

'He wasn't worried about that.'

'He is now. He's worried that Eduardo may have changed his will.'

'Why should he have done that?' asked Larche in surprise but Maria only shrugged in a rather bleary way. 'And Blasco?' he asked. 'What would he have done if he'd been left any money?'

'He'll have left it to that bloody community in Fuego. He wouldn't leave it to anyone here and I'm sure you know why.'

'I gather he loved Anita, but Eduardo stepped in.'

'That's right. Never forgave him.' She drank her scotch in one gulp and asked for another which Larche rapidly bought for her. 'So he brooded in his monastic cell, cooking up scandals and consorting with that old Machiavellian Miguel.' She stumbled slightly over her words again.

'They plotted against him?'

184

'They didn't need to. Eduardo dug his own grave. Blasco and Miguel didn't realize how quickly, although Miguel tried to warn him.'

'Are you making an accusation?'

'Against Lorenzo?' She gave a peal of laughter. 'He wouldn't harm a fly.'

'Then what are you trying to tell me?'

She paused. 'Why *are* you here?'

'To see Lorenzo.'

'What for?'

'Just for a chat.'

'I'll take you.' She staggered slightly and clutched at the bar. 'Lorenzo and I are in business. Always have been. Good long time now.'

'Fishing?'

She laughed. 'The fishers of men. And women. We've got a nice little number going for us.'

'Señora.' Two men, old but purposeful, had come up while they were talking but neither Maria nor Larche had noticed.

'Oh, it's you.' She smiled perfunctorily. 'I want another scotch.'

'You must come with us.' The man was irritable, ignoring Larche, his eyes fixed on her in disapproval.

'I'm busy.'

'Immediately.' There was complete authority in the old man's tone – as if he was talking to a wayward and troublesome child who had already overstepped the boundaries of decorum.

'Hold on,' said Larche.

'Don't interfere, señor.' They had taken her arms now, one apiece, and she was struggling feebly.

'I'm talking to this lady.' Larche tried to intervene but he knew he had no chance.

'She's going to bed.'

'Here?'

'Why not?'

'Do you know who you're handling? That's Maria Tomas.'

'We know that.'

'You can't manhandle her.'

185

'It's for her own protection, señor. Please do not interfere. This is not your business.'

'Of course it is. I'm a police officer.'

'She's done nothing wrong.'

'I didn't say that.' He was shouting now and a sudden silence fell on the room. The jazz was switched off, everyone stopped talking but there was no tension in the tobacco-hazed air.

'Please, señor, don't make things difficult.'

'I wish to go on talking with her.'

'That's impossible.'

'We had a long talk,' said Maria happily. 'I like men's company. Specially here. It's only the women who think I'm a rich whore. Well – maybe I am.' She had stopped struggling and was leaning back luxuriously in the arms of the old men. 'Happy days. What about another drink?' She raised her voice and bawled, 'The drinks are on me, boys. Drink them up and let's have a bloody good fuck.'

The old man raised his eyes. 'You do not understand, señor.'

'How big's your prick, copper?' laughed Maria.

Larche sighed. 'I *do* understand,' he said. 'But could you tell me where I can find Lorenzo?'

As the old men led Maria away, a teenage boy edged his way forward, took Larche's arm and pointed to a door at the end of a long, whitewashed, stone-flagged corridor. Slowly, he walked down towards it, his steps seeming to ring out all too loudly on the hard surface. He knocked and there was a moment's pause until it was opened by a comfortable-looking middle-aged man with dark hair brushed back. He looked like his own father had some years before.

'Yes?'

'I've come to see Lorenzo.'

'Who are you?'

'Marius Larche.'

'Do you have an appointment?'

'He'll be expecting me,' he replied evasively, wondering if that would work.

'One minute.'

He walked back through a bleak, very functional ante-room

186

and knocked at another battered wooden door. Eventually this slowly opened and Lorenzo stood on the threshold, wearing shorts and smoking a Celtas. He was smiling. 'Señor Larche, what a pleasure.'

'I know it's late but I just wanted a few words,' he replied uneasily.

'Come in.'

Larche hurried self-consciously through into a large room whose surprisingly well-made furnishings included a double bed, a highly polished table, a couple of well-stocked bookcases and a drinks cabinet. The lighting was subdued and pleasantly intimate. Sitting on a long, low sofa was a young woman.

'It's good to see you.'

At close quarters Larche was chiefly aware of the bags under Lorenzo's eyes, his leathery skin, his wrinkled stomach. He was no more than an old lizard, probably dry and reptilian to the touch.

Lorenzo's eyes were on him questioningly. 'Well, señor? Have you come here for a purpose?'

'Just an unofficial chat.'

'You come at a very good time.'

'Oh?' Larche was suddenly on his guard; there was something smug in Lorenzo's proprietorial manner.

'Why not take a closer look at the lovely creature on the sofa? She was anxious to leave when she was told you were here. Just like her father – a little bashful, I'm afraid.' There was an edge of menace to his voice now.

Larche's gaze hypnotically returned to the sofa. He realized that he was not looking at a young woman at all. Dressed in a loose blue skirt and matching top, wearing a blonde wig, with heavy mascara and a pale lipstick, was Salvador Tomas.

There was a long, long silence during which Larche's mind grappled with what he saw. His first reaction was one of considerable anger.

'Why have you done this to him? It's obscene.'

'I've done nothing to him,' replied Lorenzo quietly and without emotion. 'He likes it this way.'

'Rubbish.' Larche turned to Salvador but the boy's eyes were expressionless, staring back at him without the arrogance or the defiance -- or even the guilt – that he had expected to find.

'You have to go,' muttered Salvador.

'I'm not going anywhere,' snarled Larche. 'You've got one hell of a lot of questions to answer.'

Lorenzo looked sharply at Salvador who slowly rose to his feet and then walked out.

'Wait . . .' But he had gone and Larche was left fuming.

'Listen.' Lorenzo was placating. 'I have things to say.'

'I wanted to talk to the boy.'

'You will find talking to me more profitable.'

'I'll be the judge of that.' Larche was still filled with a cold anger that made him want to lash out, kick over a table, do something violent, particularly to Lorenzo.

'Please sit down.'

'Just get on with it.'

In the end it was Lorenzo who sat down, the age blotches on his hands and arms making him oddly vulnerable.

'They're going to kill me.' His voice was wooden.

'They?' asked Larche. 'Who are *they*?'

'How the hell do I know?' he said evasively.

'Because you've withheld information?'

'There is something I have to tell you.' Lorenzo looked away.

'Why didn't you tell me before? Or tell Calvino?' Larche increased the pressure, wondering to what extent Lorenzo was calculatingly leading him on.

'I didn't have any evidence. I still don't. But I believe that those who killed Eduardo and Blasco and your colleague . . . are also going to kill me.'

'What makes you think that?'

'I've been . . . There's powerful people on Molino. I know a great deal about them.'

'I bet you do,' sneered Larche. 'It's your stock in trade, isn't it? Bullying, perversion – extortion?'

'Whatever you say about me, señor – it doesn't concern me in the least. I'm going to leave the island tonight.'

'No one's allowed to leave,' said Larche sharply. 'You'll be arrested.'

188

'I have my wits about me.' Lorenzo was quiet now, more in control of the situation. 'I know where to go to earth.'

Larche advanced on him threateningly, trying to keep his confidence intact. Suddenly he was beginning to lose his grip. Was Lorenzo genuinely afraid? Or was he simply winding him up? 'You're not going anywhere. This interview isn't finished yet.' Larche spoke softly but he was sure that the tension inside him was all too obvious. 'I'll have you arrested,' he continued, 'if you don't stop pissing me about.'

Lorenzo looked at him appraisingly and Larche had the impression that he was weighing him up, seeing where he could find a weakness. He's like that, thought Larche. A man who looked for weaknesses and found them. He had made a profession of it.

'If you tell me the truth I'll see you're protected,' he said.

'I'm not telling you anything.' Lorenzo shrugged with sullen challenge. 'I don't trust you – and I don't want to trust you.' For once he looked considerably shaken, and Larche became even more convinced that Lorenzo genuinely feared for his life – the only honest emotion he had expressed so far.

'Try me.' Larche sat down on the edge of the table. Lorenzo looked up at him warily and then began to speak softly and quickly, as if he had known exactly what he was going to say all the time.

'I was given a powerful position by a powerful man.'

'Did you abuse your position?' cut in Larche sharply.

'The people here were lazy. Eduardo wanted me to revive a dead industry – so I was tough. Very tough. It worked. But Eduardo wanted more of me than just running a fishing industry.'

'Immediately?' asked Larche.

Lorenzo shook his head. 'Eventually.'

'He had an affair with you?'

'Yes. But I procured for him too. It was not difficult – Sebastia always had a certain reputation.'

'I'm amazed that Eduardo's parents allowed such a situation to exist.' Larche was conscious of sounding pompous but Lorenzo didn't seem to notice.

'They all wanted something out of it,' he replied carefully. 'The rich must have outlets. Sebastia can be straight – or not, as the case may be.'

'So Eduardo paid for Sebastia's services? Your services?'

'He paid very well.'

'And Salvador? He's just a child. Did Eduardo know?'

'No.'

'Anita?'

'I'm sure she doesn't.'

'So how did it happen?'

'He came to me.'

'A young boy like that.'

'He wanted to learn.'

'And you taught him,' said Larche contemptuously.

'He didn't need any teaching.' The laugh in Lorenzo's voice was particularly unpleasant.

Larche had a new thought – one that he knew should have occurred to him earlier and had been obscured by his sense of outrage. 'Did you do this to Salvador because you had learnt to hate his father?'

Lorenzo grinned. 'The boy had a particular yearning . . .'

'Which you encouraged.'

He shrugged. 'You have to realize that our little Salvador has something of a father complex – as well as certain other problems. His own father was a remote figure – you and I are not.'

'You and I?' Larche repeated.

'You don't wish to be associated with me, señor? You don't wish to share a bond?'

'I would find that very distasteful,' replied Larche, trying to work out what he was getting at.

'Listen – he was drawn to me.'

'You brought out the deviant in him,' said Larche bluntly.

'That's why he hated me.' Lorenzo stared ahead woodenly for a moment. 'That's why he loved me as well. And he sees a father figure in you too, Señor Larche.'

'Rubbish.'

'He thinks you'll make it "all right" for him.'

'You hated Eduardo because he had finally been forced to sack you – after you'd been overreaching yourself for years,' said Larche, deliberately changing the subject, trying to divert his opponent from what he now considered was a well-thought-out script.

'I was very angry. But he was still more useful to me alive. I mean – I can be very persuasive. I'm not your killer, señor. I just don't have the necessary powers. But I'm afraid now. Very afraid.'

'I can see that.' Larche paused. 'Don't you have any more to tell me? So far you've told me nothing.' Was he going to confess – just like the others? It was bound to be a tissue of lies, but then weren't all the other confessions he had heard manipulative?

Lorenzo was silent. Then he began to speak very slowly, clearly, enunciating each word as if he was on the edge of some mental precipice. 'Those bastard priests . . .'

Are we still on the script, wondered Larche, or is something genuine about to creep in?

'I had a vocation – believe it or not.'

'Yes?'

'You didn't know I was called, did you?' Lorenzo seemed anxious to shock.

'To be a priest?' Larche's surprise, although feigned, was studiedly genuine.

'I might have gone to the seminary and taken Orders. But I would more likely have wanted to stay on in Fuego – in the community.'

'You? At Fuego?'

Lorenzo smiled. 'I've taken you by surprise, señor. Haven't I?'

'Yes – yes, you have,' he lied.

'But they threw me out.' His voice shook, but Larche couldn't work out whether all this was clumsy deception or at least an attempt at the truth.

'Why?'

'No reason.'

'There must have been one,' Larche encouraged.

'I was told I didn't have a vocation, but I'd set my heart on serving God.'

'You were very bitter?' Larche wondered if Lorenzo was actually levelling with him now. There was a conviction to all this – a lack of glibness that made him pay more attention.

'Señor – I was born in a small fishing village down the coast. My father left when I was a baby, my mother killed herself when I was ten. I went into an orphanage in Girona which was brutal and . . . I don't even want to think of what happened there. When I was old enough, fifteen, I left and went on the fishing boats and most nights I slept in a store room. I can tell you without self-pity that I had no one, señor, no one and nowhere to call my own.' He paused and looked across at Larche, as if he was trying to make up his mind whether to continue or not. Then he plunged on. 'Not only did I learn a good deal about the fishing industry but also about how to maximize its efficiency. That was easy; it was as lazily and incompetently run as the children's home. Then I saw her.'

'Saw who?' asked Larche, mystified.

'The Holy Mother.'

There was a wary silence while Larche wondered how to react.

'The Virgin Mary,' he repeated as if he had not been understood the first time. 'It was very early, a misty morning in late spring and there was no wind at all. The sea was utterly calm, señor, and Ivan had cut the engines while he put the nets down. But for some reason he didn't do it immediately. Instead he went into the wheelhouse and lit a cigarette – as if . . . as if he was going off-stage. Then I saw her – on the water, coming out of the mist. She was walking on a very, very slight swell and the mist closed in until all I could see was her. She had a cormorant in her hand and she drew the bird up so that it fluttered against her cheek. Then she smiled and spoke to me.'

Again he paused but Larche, who appeared to be concentrating intently, said nothing.

'She spoke to me. She told me to go to Fuego – that I had a calling. I was nineteen. When she went it was as if time had been suspended. Perhaps it was. Next day I went to Fuego and told the Abbot what had happened. I don't know whether he believed in what I had seen and heard, but I know he didn't doubt my sincerity. A few days later I brought over my few personal belongings and joined the community as a novice. A year later I took my first vows.' He lit a cigarette and stared reflectively at Larche. 'Do you believe me, señor?'

'Why should I do otherwise?' Larche replied easily. 'How long did you stay in the community?'

'Until I was told I had no vocation.'

'There was no other reason?'

'None that I know of.' Lorenzo was watching him steadily and Larche had the feeling that he was challenging him.

'Did you . . . did you not become . . . did you have a relationship with another brother?' He cursed himself for fumbling the words.

'Who told you that?' said Lorenzo quickly, but he didn't wait for a reply. 'People regard me here as some kind of devil's spawn.' He laughed. 'It amuses me.'

'But did you?'

'No, señor. How many times do I have to tell you? They made it clear that I had to leave, but I took my time. In the end Blasco Tomas gave me a contact in a boatyard in Rosas and I got a fetch and carry job. I did well – well enough to take responsibility and so I learnt a new trade.' He ground out his cigarette. 'Then I had two kinds of expertise, señor. Fishing and boat-building. But I had lost the centre of my life and I was so bitterly unhappy that I often thought of committing suicide. Then Blasco contacted me again.'

'He contacted you?' asked Larche in surprise.

'Yes. He introduced me to Eduardo. He wanted someone to help start up the fishing industry on Molino again and he thought I was the man. Eduardo agreed. I think he was right.'

Larche nodded slowly, the new realization creeping into his mind with traumatic stealth. So Blasco's hatred for his brother was that intense. It hardly seemed credible, but what he had done was to plant a time-bomb in the shape of lonely, damaged, rejected Lorenzo and stand aside to let events take their course. If this was true then Larche was appalled. Or was the statement part of Lorenzo's script? Nothing was what it seemed. For a minute he stared blankly at Lorenzo, his thoughts racing, then he was suddenly jerked back into the present. If Lorenzo was so afraid, why the hell had he waited for him to arrive? Why hadn't he gone to earth already, old fox that he undoubtedly was?

'Why are you still here?' he asked. 'Why haven't you bolted?'

'I knew you'd come here eventually. I wanted to tell you what had happened – why it had happened.' The glib statement was made as easily as Larche suspected it would be.

'That's what everyone's done. They've come to me – almost as they'd come to a priest – all with their carefully prepared confessionals.' Larche paused threateningly. 'Fortunately, I am able to be analytical. Perhaps a priest is that way too.'

Lorenzo smiled. 'The only difference is that you can hand out retribution. Maybe that's what they're all looking for.'

'I doubt it. Six Hail Marys are a little easier than a life sentence,' Larche observed.

Lorenzo shrugged. 'You'd be surprised how barren life is without the Church's approval, señor.'

11

Something stirred in a recess of Larche's mind. How all-consuming was this killer's obsessive hatred? Surely those killings must be the work of someone whose anger had been built up over such a long period that it had eventually become frenzy. What had Byron written? *Now hatred is by far the longest pleasure; men love in haste, but they detest at leisure.* And leisure had been an enforced pursuit in varying degrees for those that had lived on Molino. Anita, for instance, unless she spent the rest of her life touring, might have to face considerable periods of watching the Mediterranean. So would Lorenzo – wherever he tried to hide himself – for he would not be able to come out of hiding. Larche considered two important points. The first was that his investigation could well be getting somewhere at last. The second was that he was determined not to allow Lorenzo to leave Molino. He held too many secrets and Larche was determined to extract them from him.

'I've enjoyed the power I was given,' said Lorenzo quietly, breaking into his thoughts. 'Enjoyed it very much. But I didn't kill anyone, señor. Eduardo was far more useful to me alive.'

'And Blasco?' asked Larche gently.

'And Blasco.'

'Did you not feel he played some part in your dismissal from the community?'

'I'm sure he didn't.'

'You hate the Church, don't you?'

'For what they did? Yes, I hate them, but it's an old, dormant hatred.'

'Is it so dormant?'

Lorenzo looked at him with a sudden wariness and a rush of adrenalin flooded through Larche. 'I don't understand you,' he said guardedly.

'I think you do. Foolishly Bishop Carlos has been paying you to protect Anita's so-called ignorance of Eduardo's ... weaknesses. You must have been enjoying that.'

Lorenzo shrugged. 'I've been receiving financial gifts.'

'Calvino will arrest you for extortion,' said Larche quietly. 'On my evidence.'

'You've got no evidence.' Lorenzo was completely calm but Larche could detect the flicker of panic in his eyes. I can break him, he thought triumphantly. I can break him. Now.

'I assure you I have.'

'The Bishop – he can prove nothing.'

'He can testify against you. You'll be put away for a long time, Lorenzo – and it's going to be much worse than the orphanage.'

'Then I shall make public everything I know about Eduardo Tomas. It'll be a national scandal.' Lorenzo's voice rose. 'It'll destroy her.'

'I'm not sure she doesn't know already,' Larche said quietly.

'Know?' Lorenzo laughed contemptuously. 'She has persuaded herself not to know anything; she denies the truth completely. She's crazy, but she won't be able to hide away from the press. Not once it's out.'

'But it won't be out,' said Larche. 'There's no chance of that.'

'Why not?' Again the flicker of panic in his eyes.

'Because I can stop you.'

'How?' Lorenzo's voice shook and Larche knew that he was winning.

'If you destroy Eduardo's reputation, you'll also destroy Anita. She may be blinkered, but she doesn't deserve that. And you'll destroy her for revenge.' Larche held up a hand as Lorenzo tried to interrupt. 'Listen to me. I can understand how much you hate the establishment of the Church – of the Tomas family – of power and authority in general. You're just a pawn. But you lost the game, Lorenzo. You played on their weaknesses, helped to turn Sebastia from a peasant Bacchanalia into something much more professional.'

'They owed me,' he muttered. 'But I didn't kill them.'

'No – you didn't,' said Larche. 'I know who murdered them.'

Larche's voice was flat; the knowledge gave him no satisfaction – not even for Alison's sake. The one name rang like a clarion in Larche's mind and he owed the sudden immediacy of his deduction to the thoughts he had been having while Lorenzo had been part-manipulating, part-confiding. He felt neither triumph nor elation; instead, he was stale, mentally exhausted, certain that this complex investigation was now almost at an end. He had heard the conflicting confessions and tried to disentangle one from the other, and now that he understood Lorenzo the solution was appallingly obvious.

Larche spoke slowly and carefully, determined to stay in control of the situation. 'Listen to me – you're going to go down anyway, and not just for blackmail. I'm sure there's going to be a lot more you can be done for under Spanish law.'

'There's a lot more can come out.' He smiled a shadowy satyr smile, but his voice lacked conviction.

'No. You'll do a short sentence if you keep quiet, but if a word about Eduardo or the activities here leaks out – then you'll be in for the rest of your life.'

'You can't do that,' he said confidently. 'You just haven't got the authority.'

'Maybe not. But the Spanish security services have. They won't want any of this to get out and they'll lean on you accordingly, won't they? I can see that I'm convincing you.'

Lorenzo lit another cigarette. 'If I don't talk, her artist friend will.'

'Yes – I imagined you two got together; you must have been drawn to each other like magnets. But I can assure you that Morrison will be effectively leant on too. His career as a portrait painter to the rich and famous would be finished. Don't get me wrong, Lorenzo, I'm talking good sense.'

Nevertheless, Larche was very surprised to see him nod –

to see the look of acceptance on his face. Had he really convinced him?

'How long would I get?' he asked indistinctly.

'I don't know.'

'Guess?' Suddenly he was pleading.

'Five years.'

'God.'

'And if you talk – it will be much, much longer. I can assure you of that.'

Again he nodded, his leathery features creased in pain and his hand flattening his thick black hair.

'Do you *really* understand me?'

'Yes.'

'Then you must come with me.'

'Where?'

'To Calvino.'

'I'll go into a cell tonight then?'

'I doubt if you'd get bail. You're too dangerous outside.' Larche put as much authority into his words as possible, knowing that he was really bluffing now.

'I can't do that.' There was agony in his voice.

'But you know the consequences.'

Lorenzo slowly rose to his feet. 'I'm sorry, señor, I can't be locked up. Not for a moment.' His eyes were fixed on Larche's.

'Don't be a fool. Don't you realize the deal I'm offering you?'

Lorenzo wasn't listening. 'I understand what you say. You may even be right. But I can't be locked up. That's what they used to do at the orphanage – shut me in a room, sometimes for days on end. I can't stand it.'

'Be realistic. You could go down for –'

'No chance.'

'You'll be picked up at once. You won't get off the island – not with all this increased security.'

'They know me. They won't stop me going fishing. Night fishing.'

He was horribly right, thought Larche. They'd let Lorenzo buzz around all over the place. It was scandalously inefficient.

198

'*I'll* stop you.'

'I wouldn't get physical, señor.' Lorenzo was standing only a few metres away from him, his bare arms slightly raised, and Larche could see the muscles in them, glistening as darkly as the Mediterranean waves.

Stubbornly Larche stood his ground. 'Do you want to add assault to the list of charges?'

'You won't find me. I know how to disappear on this coastline.'

'I shall have you stopped – alert Calvino.'

'You've come here without a radio and by the time you've reached help I shall have gone. Then I'll make my decision.'

'What decision?'

'Whether to blow the Tomas family wide open – or to encourage the good and foolish Bishop to continue giving me such a generous income. He'd rather pay than press extortion charges. Then there's Mr Morrison to be considered . . .' Lorenzo came nearer to Larche, his thick arms hanging heavily by his sides.

'You're being a fool.'

'I won't be locked up.' Again he moved nearer until he was centimetres away and Larche could smell the garlic and alcohol on his breath.

'Do you see? I can't be locked up.'

'We have to talk –'

'There's nothing to talk about. Nothing.'

Suddenly Larche saw the knife in his hand, the open blade held towards him. Where the hell had he got it from? Had it been on the table? In his pocket? What did it matter – he was holding it, the long steel upwards, pointing at Larche's throat.

'You'll make me think you *can* kill,' he said calmly, knowing that if he showed fear the situation would quickly escalate into violence and he would surely be the loser.

'Get out of my way.'

'I'm having you arrested. Put the knife down.'

'Fuck you.' He was even nearer now. 'Fuck you.' The blade seemed huge, considerably out of proportion to its hilt. Larche could imagine the steel slicing his flesh, feel the hot pain.

'Put it down.' He hoped his voice was still relatively calm.

They were almost touching each other now. Larche remembered how impressed Eduardo had been when he had fought those hooligans in their student days, but then he had been angry and now he was afraid. Why couldn't he be angry now, for God's sake, Larche wondered – the man was threatening his life. But all he could feel was the fear crawling inside him, destroying his attempts at being calm, being reasonable.

'I want to talk.'

The knife was almost touching his throat now but Larche somehow stood his ground. It had been many years since he had experienced any kind of physical violence – and the sensation was far more bemusing and terrifying than he had remembered. In fact, Lorenzo's physicality, his brutishness, his animal concentration convinced Larche that he stood no chance against him. He thought of Monique and then of Alison. Once again he saw the lavender fields in Provence, the radiance of the Mediterranean light. He had played this man along too far; he had failed to estimate his breaking point. Now he was in a situation that he couldn't control.

'Get out of my way.'

'For Christ's sake –'

The knife sliced its way into Larche's shoulder. The searing pain was far worse than he could ever have imagined and he fell back, trying to stop the blood as it gushed down his sleeve in a bright crimson flood.

Lorenzo smiled viciously and punched Larche in the solar plexus. He went down, unable to breathe, his mouth ludicrously open.

Larche had a sensation of drowning, but slowly, very slowly, he caught a miraculous gulp of air and then another. His stomach muscles eased, but it was some minutes before he staggered groaning to his feet, only to feel the dull throb of the knife wound. He looked down and was surprised to see that the blood seemed to have stopped flowing, but it still hurt like hell.

He tried to get to his feet, slid back, tried again and at last managed to raise himself up and half sit, half lean against the table. I've got to stop him, he thought. I must stop him – for Anita's sake.

The door opened and Larche whipped round, wondering if he should prepare himself for another attack, but it was Salvador, dressed in T-shirt and jeans.

'He's hurt you.' He looked glassily at the blood on the floor.

'Where is he?'

'In the church.'

'What?' Larche gazed at the boy as if he was crazy.

'He keeps money there.' There was perspiration on Salvador's forehead and he was shivering, despite the heat of the room.

'I've got to stop him.'

'You can't.'

'Go and fetch Calvino. He'll be in the canvas village.'

'It'll be too late.'

'*Get* him!'

'What about your arm?'

'Go!' Larche screamed at him and Salvador fled out of the door.

As the pain lessened Larche staggered across the room, down the corridor and into the bar which was completely deserted. Looking at his watch he saw that it was just after two in the morning and he lurched across the stone floor and out into the silent street which still felt heavy with the day's heat. His steps ringing out on the cobbles, Larche hurried towards the church and pushed open the heavy wooden door. Inside there was a smell of stale incense and candle-grease. The interior was primitive, with rough-hewn whitewashed walls, and above the altar he could just make out a twisted, suffering Christ, writhing upon a painted wooden cross. The church was in darkness but beyond the nave there was a faint light coming through an iron grille. There was also a muffled, buzzing sound but when he got there, the space seemed to be empty.

As Larche edged slowly forward over the uneven stone flags he could see that it was a small chapel, its bleak stone altar illuminated by wan moonlight coming through the stained glass window above. But when he looked more carefully he could see that it wasn't a stained glass window after all. Instead he could see bars, a frame that was half open, and a figure, cast in iron, standing on the sill.

Larche stared up at it until his eyes became used to the gloom and as he did so, he was conscious of a murmur. It was definitely the sound of muted human voices. But where? Then he saw the narrow staircase leading down on the far side of the darkened chapel.

His eyes returned to the cloaked figure in the window. He supposed it depicted a saint, but to Larche the effigy was more like death itself, and a couple of lines from the English poet, Sir Walter Scott, entered his mind. *And come he slow, or come he fast, It is but death who comes at last.*

Slowly, with his arm now beginning to throb again, Larche walked to the stairway and descended, the darkness becoming more and more impenetrable. The murmur increased and then he was at the bottom, where at last there were a few candles positioned on the stone shelf that ran around what was obviously the crypt. Gradually, very gradually, Larche saw that the space was divided into wooden alcoves that looked as if they had been used for storage. Boxes and crates were piled high in one of them, but in the other five he could see mattresses and on the mattresses the grunting, entwined bodies that were never still. Occasionally there was a groan of desire – a cry of fulfilment as the orgasm came. It was impossible to make out the sexes but Larche knew that this didn't matter – that nothing mattered here. This was Sebastia's bordello; here the clients thrashed in their sanctuary of lust. Larche turned away, sick to his very heart. Three little rich boys, trapped in their island territory. And now there were others – those caged in their positions of power who so desperately needed Sebastia and its unholy crypt. Is this what had attracted Eduardo so much? And his son? Is this what Anita blinded herself to? His arm was now on fire and he turned, his thoughts in turmoil, instinctively trying to find the wooden staircase again. But someone was already standing there. It was Maria Tomas.

'What are you doing here?' she whispered, and Larche registered with surprise that she seemed to be stone-cold sober.

'Looking for Lorenzo.'

'He's gone.'

'Where?'

'Out to sea – in his fishing boat.'

'I'll have him picked up –'

'You're too late. He has a rubber dinghy with an outboard. He'll head for some cove – and lose himself on the mainland.'

'We'll find him. I sent Salvador to get Calvino.'

'He didn't go.'

'Why the hell not?'

'He was too afraid.'

'But *why*?' Larche was furious and there were shooting pains in his arm.

'The men are out – looking for Lorenzo . . .'

'What do they want him for?'

'He's taken the wages from the safe in the office,' she said hopelessly. 'He came here to get the key. This is where he hides it.' She unsuccessfully muffled a sob. 'God – I'm so afraid.'

'He may still be around.'

'I saw him go.'

'You *let* him go.'

'How could I stop him? The men are down at the quayside – they'll take the boats out themselves. Try to catch him and get their money back. But I know he'll be too quick for them.' She sat down on the steps and put her head in her hands. 'He's used to running.'

'Are they after you as well?' asked Larche gently.

Maria Tomas looked up at him in sudden realization. 'No. It's the women – they'll be on the streets soon. They've been patient for too long. They're not so concerned with Lorenzo – except that they want that money returned.'

'What *are* they concerned with then?' he asked her sharply but she didn't reply, merely looking away with a shrug and a strange expression in her eyes – as if she didn't have to tell him, as if he ought to know.

'Where's Jacinto?'

Still Maria said nothing.

'Where *is* he?' insisted Larche. 'You have to take me to him.

He could be in very great danger. These women you talk about – they've seen so much exploitation here.'

She shivered and dragged down her crumpled T-shirt. 'I can feel the atmosphere tonight in Sebastia. It's very raw and I'm afraid,' she admitted reluctantly. Then she noticed the arm that Larche was hugging to himself. 'You're hurt . . .'

'It doesn't matter,' he said brusquely. 'Let's go.'

The night street was completely silent except for the sound of their footsteps, but there were lights on in the majority of the houses now and through the open shutters Larche could see the women sitting silently, waiting. Compared to the wealthy aestheticism of the Tomas estate only a quarter of an hour's walk away, the sight had a primitive quality that was very disturbing. Their dark, shadowed faces were gaunt and watchful and there was a steely patience to them. He was reminded of some peasant farmers he had known in Normandy who had never left their small community and who still believed in the same superstitious life their forebears had lived. Then another image slipped into his mind. He and Monique had become lost while driving near Perpignan and they had stopped to ask for directions in a hot, still, Mediterranean village. But no one had spoken to them and when he had asked an old raven-like crone of a woman sitting by a petrol pump she had given them the evil eye.

'Are *all* the men looking for Lorenzo?' he asked Maria.

'The fit and the healthy – the older ones are tucked up in bed.' Maria looked up at him and he caught the look of terror in her eyes. 'That just leaves the women to deal with the situation as they see fit.'

'*What* situation?' asked Larche impatiently, but it was clear that she was going to hold out on him – at least for the moment.

'Let's move,' she said urgently. 'There's going to be trouble tonight and we don't want to be around when it starts.' Maria's voice wavered, as if she hoped there could still be some doubt about what she was saying.

Larche took another sideways glance at the women sitting

so stoically at their windows. Had they really had enough? Or were they as passive as ever, waiting for their men to come home from the sea? 'Calvino will be here soon,' he said tensely. 'He'll be alerted by the boats going out.' Suddenly he was sure there was a great well of hatred there, an immense dark force which had been thwarted for too long. There was a time when reasoning and deduction and understanding and democratic justice had to stop. That time had come and he felt the primitive anger of the women of Sebastia. Suddenly he wanted them to live up to Maria's fears. Lorenzo and Eduardo had manipulated the community's rough licentiousness to their own advantage; not only had a brothel been established in their church but the villagers had been forced into financial bondage by their corrupt masters.

Then something in his mind stirred. 'What might the women do?' he asked Maria.

'I don't know. Perhaps nothing.' She laughed bleakly. 'They've always been in the background. Their men should have taken the action but they've been bound to Lorenzo for too long. He had so much. Eduardo's patronage. A high salary. The sacrilege at the church. He's used them, abused their religion, become a tyrant. Now he's stolen their wages.'

'They can get that back from the family,' protested Larche.

'Yes, but it's the last straw, isn't it? They want him. I know they do. They want his blood.' She paused at the door of the bar. 'But the men won't get him. He's too clever for them – *and* you. We're the ones who could be in danger – from the women. That's why he must go with you.'

'That's absurd. This is a civilized society.' Larche was flustered, feeling her anxiety reaching out and touching him.

'We're in Sebastia,' Maria replied quietly. 'Things are different here. Eduardo managed to resurrect the past in this place, and all its old values and feelings. Don't you understand?'

'Yes,' replied Larche slowly. 'I think I do.'

As soon as he entered the still smoke-hazed room, Larche knew intuitively that he was right and that he had come to the real source of the hatred. What had so sharply crystallized in his mind earlier he was now sure was true. Jacinto was sitting at the bar, drinking a cognac, dressed in a white linen suit with an open-necked shirt and highly polished black shoes. A gold crucifix hung at his bronzed neck and his whole appearance was immaculate – a total contrast to his dishevelled wife's T-shirt and jeans. His long hair was neatly combed but there was a look of utter desolation in his eyes. As Larche came in, he looked up and gave a half-smile of acceptance. 'Yes?'

'Jacinto Tomas,' said Larche quietly, 'I know that you murdered your brothers Eduardo and Blasco Tomas, as well as Father Miguel Fernandez, and Detective Superintendent Alison Rowe and the man known as Liam Mullen.' He turned formally to Maria. 'Maria Tomas – I believe you are an accessory to those murders.' She stared at him blankly, without speaking, whilst Jacinto drained his cognac. Larche wondered if he could detect a slight atmosphere of relief. It's been such a long time, he thought – all those long Mediterranean days and nights – for his hatred to ferment under the sun.

'I'll make a statement,' said Jacinto flatly. 'But not here. We should go back to the house, and I'll need to ring my lawyer. You can't arrest us, can you, monsieur, or have you been given those powers as well?' There was a faintly ironic note to his voice.

'No,' said Larche, 'but Calvino can.'

'I need a drink.' Jacinto was adamant, going straight to the bar and pouring himself another Martell before they could stop him. 'I'll have this – and then we'll go.'

'We ought to get back now,' said Maria urgently. 'We can't – mustn't hang around here.'

'I'll do what I damn well like,' yelled Jacinto and Larche decided to go along with the last drink for he was sure he would get more out of Jacinto this way.

Maria went to the door, hurriedly glanced outside and then turned the lock.

Jacinto was impatient. 'You've got a thing about the women here. They wouldn't lift a finger to me – or anyone else. They're as passive as ever – as they always will be.'

'I wouldn't count on that,' Maria replied.

'How did you find out?' asked Jacinto. His voice was bright and artificial, but he was very calm and showed no flicker of emotion; even his eyes were grey and dead and without curiosity.

Is it really such a relief to give up, wondered Larche, or is he going to surprise me like Lorenzo did? But somehow he was sure that he wouldn't – that Jacinto Tomas was now just a shell, his personality burnt away by the hatred that had finally consumed him.

'By the usual process of elimination,' replied Larche, his arm beginning to throb even more painfully now. 'You were the little rich boy who hated most, weren't you – really hated the hardest. Once I got beyond Lorenzo, there was only you left.'

'There was no other course open to me.' Jacinto smiled wearily. 'But it's over now, thank God.'

'Think what you're saying . . .' began Maria but her voice tailed away as if she had no enthusiasm for prolonging any further deception, and was only going through the motions.

Jacinto ignored her. 'I might as well tell you now. Yes, monsieur – I killed them. But not just out of hatred. It was me who ran Sebastia's . . . Bacchanalia – although I simply built on the existing reputation. Lorenzo was only a manager who turned a blind eye because he enjoyed the power. Initially Eduardo let me go ahead because I created what he needed – what a lot of people needed. The perfect, private whore-house, protected by its nearness to the family estate and having a very special reputation – that of taking place in the crypt of a church in the proximity of other clients. A truly erotic recipe, don't you agree?' Larche was silent, unresponsive, but Jacinto swept on as if he had assented. 'Of course there were rumours, but they could never be proven. In fact they worked rather like a protective screen. Too many powerful people came here – even tonight I have a cabinet minister and a newspaper editor grappling in the crypt. Maybe I couldn't leave the island that easily, monsieur, but by God I could have been making some much-needed money out of my lucrative little business – except that I wasn't.' He ended on a note of considerable bitterness.

207

'Why didn't you make any money?' asked Larche contemptuously. 'Weren't your fees high enough?'

'They barely covered the costs,' replied Jacinto sullenly. 'My dear brother Eduardo forbade me to make a profit. He always was a hypocrite.'

'You killed your brothers because your time was running out, didn't you?' Larche was insistent.

'Not exactly. And by the way, monsieur, I'm telling you all this, not because you have enough evidence against me, which I know you haven't, but because I can't go on any longer. In spite of everything I'm still trapped on this damnable island. Eduardo took great pleasure in my poverty and Blasco put paid to the archaeological trust as I've already told you, so you must understand, monsieur, that my wife and I just haven't got two beans to rub together so we can't exactly sod off anywhere, can we?'

'Maybe not.' Larche was quietly reticent because he wanted Jacinto to carry on.

'God, how I hated Eduardo – and Blasco, but Eduardo just that little bit more. I tormented him with telephone calls and barraged him with letters. Naturally I was very careful and I was so delighted to see him suffer. Did you know that after a false alarm, he even shat himself in his own swimming pool? The gardener told me there was a turd in the shallows. That gave me so much pleasure.'

'Did you know what he was doing?' asked Larche of Maria.

'Yes.'

'Did you share his hatred?'

'I was sucked into it. You've no idea what hell these years have been.'

'Hooper was a great boon to us,' put in Jacinto. 'Whoever he is – wherever he is – we have come to be exceedingly grateful to him. Eduardo kept me a prisoner here; he could have made it possible for us to leave, given us the support we needed. Blasco hated Eduardo; and wrecked the only valid project that might have given us a new life. I could have capitalized on the discovery, taken up marine archaeology again – *been* someone. Those three little rich boys, monsieur – I do feel you underestimated how ferociously they felt about each other's proximity for so long. You'll never know how much I loved and hated Eduardo, how much I detested Blasco. I *had* to hurt them – and I did, you see – I really did hurt them. But when Eduardo died, I grieved, Monsieur Larche. I really grieved.'

'And you had no thought of Anita.'

'That cold bitch. She sees nothing – nothing except her stupid, obsessive love of Eduardo. Yet she sees everything.'

'What do you mean?'

'She knew what was going on,' said Maria. 'She knew all the machinations here. She just determinedly blinded herself to them.'

'Tell me,' asked Larche quite gently. 'Tell me how you got to kill them.'

Jacinto paused and Maria replied. 'You have to be strong to kill. You have to experience enough hardship, enough frustration to give you that strength.'

'What do you mean?' said Larche sharply.

'She means nothing,' interrupted Jacinto brusquely. '*I* went to the Valley of the Fallen. *I* killed them.'

'But *how*?' There was something horribly wrong about all this, thought Larche, and he began to have doubts for the first time. 'You would have been recognized. Jacinto Tomas can't just walk into a confessional box, blow his brother's and a priest's brains away and walk out again, even if there was an epileptic decoy outside.'

'I set her up,' replied Jacinto stubbornly.

'You would have been *seen*,' insisted Larche. The anger seized him again, throbbing like his arm.

'He's lying to you,' said Maria gently. 'I killed them.'

Larche stared at her incredulously. What kind of crazy games were they playing with him? 'And Blasco – and Alison Rowe?' he asked wonderingly.

'No. Please let me explain, monsieur. You have been very intuitive about my husband, and although he was right when he said you didn't have enough evidence to convict him no doubt you would have proved your case in the end. You are very industrious and you have Calvino's army of policemen to assist you.' She paused. 'The situation we have shared for so many years on Molino has wrecked us both. I married a prisoner – and became a prisoner too. I was always a subsidiary player though. You didn't even bother to question me when you arrived on the island, did you, monsieur? Or at least I was very low on your list of priorities.'

'That's correct,' agreed Larche dispassionately.

'I was just the wife of a playboy, wasn't I? Probably brainless.' Then her tone altered. 'You wouldn't know what it's like being the wife of a prisoner, would you, Larche?'

'You'll soon find out,' Larche snapped, sickened by her self-pity. One of the two butchered Alison and he was determined to find out which.

'I already know,' she replied bitterly. 'Try being married to a victim like Jacinto – and I *mean* a victim. That's why he wants it all to end now – don't you, my darling?'

Jacinto stood up and for a moment Larche thought he was going to hit her, but instead he poured himself another drink.

Maria continued. 'Something was done to him in childhood, something that *made* him stay on Molino, hating his brothers until he could find sufficient personal resources to kill them. In the end we both had to find them. Women are stronger – like the women of Sebastia. When I first married Jacinto I was a superficial convent-educated young Mediterranean socialite making a major social catch – the most glamorous of the Tomas family, the youngest son. For a few years he lived up to his reputation as an efficient playboy and I to mine as a glamorous and rather stupid lotus eater. We started our diving business and it made a little money for us. Then I began to realize, very slowly began to realize, the kind of trap Jacinto was in. And, of course, I shared it with him.' She paused for breath and then added more slowly, 'Soon I began to hate them as hard as he did. I could understand how Jacinto enjoyed torturing Eduardo. I could understand how terrified he was when Father Miguel summoned Eduardo to see him.' She paused again and stared at Larche searchingly. 'I don't suppose we shall ever know now what Father Miguel was going to tell Eduardo. Maybe Jacinto's suspicions were right ...'

'What *were* his suspicions?' demanded Larche brusquely.

'He thought Blasco had found out that he was persecuting Eduardo.'

'How?'

Jacinto poured himself yet another Martell and said, 'He came into the diving school when I was writing Eduardo another little missive. I was very quick to conceal the piece of paper – but perhaps not quick enough. The most frustrating thing is that I shall never know, will I? For some days afterwards I'm sure he was watching me and before he went back to Fuego he said something that convinced me I was right to be very suspicious of him.'

'What was that?' Larche was impatient. He was feeling increasingly tense about what might happen on the streets of Sebastia, yet he didn't want to interrupt this last confessional.

'He said that I might be happier if I accepted my life rather than fighting against it – that it was a life many would be pleased to have. He also told me how Eduardo was suffering – that he thought he was being hounded to his death by an unknown assassin. Blasco said *he* thought the hound was much closer to home. I took this as a warning to stop, but I didn't. It was only when Eduardo said he was going to see Father Miguel that I thought the game was up.'

'And so?' prompted Larche.

'We had no choice,' said Jacinto. 'Blasco and Miguel were very close. Neither of us could face the kind of disgrace that Eduardo would bring upon us. I knew he'd be very vindictive; he'd ruin us.'

'So I decided to kill them,' said Maria. 'By this time my hatred for our jailer Eduardo had increased to such an extent that I thought about nothing else. Everything narrowed down. The ingenuous little girl had gone; Eduardo had destroyed her. Only Jacinto mattered now. I loved him so much that I would do anything to protect him.'

'Like Anita loved Eduardo,' said Larche quietly.

Maria nodded. 'Ironically, you're right.' She paused. 'So I went to the Valley of the Fallen in the disguise of one of the voluntary officials of the Basilica. Together Jacinto and I had already hired our epileptic actress.'

'Bit of luck finding one just like that?' said Larche, anxious to test out the validity of what she was saying.

'Not if you know where to look,' Maria replied evenly. 'Despite the urgency I can assure you that we laid our plans most carefully, and don't forget we are both experts in low-life.'

Larche bowed acquiescence. He was satisfied.

'While our epileptic whore performed so conveniently for us I went into the box and shot Miguel – then Eduardo, through the grille.'

'Simple, wasn't it?' said Larche with quiet sarcasm. He was trying to keep his temper at bay, trying to keep the persistent image of Alison out of his mind.

'Then I put the gun back in my shoulder bag as the little whore's performance heightened. I was still a subsidiary player, monsieur – or so it would have appeared.' She paused. 'It's curious, but I felt nothing after killing them, absolutely nothing at all. Later on, when I got back to the island, when I heard that the killings were being linked with Hooper's name, I was exhilarated. I'd struck a blow for Jacinto's freedom. Monsieur – I love him so.' She went over to Jacinto and took his hand. 'I love him so very deeply. I'd do anything for him.'

'You have,' said Larche quietly. 'You've done as much as anyone could. I don't see you as a subsidiary player.'

'With Eduardo's death, we knew we would also inherit a substantial legacy,' said Jacinto unexpectedly.

'That was a *minor* consideration, I'm sure,' Larche sneered.

'In a way. We would have left the island anyway, but it was convenient to have some money to leave with.'

'But you didn't go, did you? There was unfinished business.'

'Blasco,' said Jacinto. 'That bastard.'

What about Alison, thought Larche as he fought for control. What about her? Wasn't *she* the real subsidiary player? Killed because she happened to be there.

Maria intervened. 'Jacinto – after the killings – he became more and more disturbed.' She squeezed his hand harder

212

and he looked away from her. 'He was certain that Blasco suspected him of killing Eduardo and Miguel. Eventually he convinced me . . .'

'That Blasco had to go as well?' Larche was very still.

'Yes. I have to say I wasn't sure *what* he knew, and now I believe it's quite possible that he didn't suspect Jacinto. Nevertheless, as you say, he had to go. Just in case.'

Larche could see her walking towards him, that first time at Sant Pere de Rodes. He could remember . . . Grimly he tried to blot Alison out of his mind yet again, and yet again he failed to do so.

'We knew that we had to be very careful but, of course, there was Hooper. He was a godsend.'

'I'm sure he was,' said Larche bitterly. 'And were you the executioner again, Maria?'

She shook her head. 'Jacinto shot them – from a distance, using a telescopic sight.'

Something went white hot in Larche's mind. Filled with a blind hatred, he walked over to Jacinto Tomas and hit him as hard as he could in the face with his fist – and then he hit him again. Larche felt pulp and splintered brittle bone. Then Jacinto was on the floor, his smashed face a mass of blood, and Maria was pulling him away.

Larche stood there panting, the adrenalin pumping, seeing Alison on the rocks at Molino. He felt his physical desire for her sweep over him. Hurting Jacinto had been a catharsis, perhaps the same kind of catharsis that Jacinto had felt when he pumped bullets into his brother.

'Don't touch him again,' Maria said furiously, still hanging on to Larche.

'I shan't.'

'You've broken his nose.'

'Let go of me!' he whispered.

Eventually she did and he stood there, motionless, as Jacinto slowly hauled himself to his feet. 'And it was even more convenient that Detective Superintendent Rowe was there – a potential Hooper target.' Larche's voice was expressionless now and he felt drained of both energy and feeling.

'Yes,' replied Jacinto shakily, wiping the blood off his face, gingerly touching his broken nose. 'Yes, it was.'

'And the Irishman?'

'He was just one of those itinerant bums who spend a few months in a place, make a bit of money and then move on. We recruited him in Barcelona quite quickly, just as easily as we recruited the whore – and smuggled him into the cave. As I said before, monsieur, we had become experts in low-life. What we did in Sebastia provided us with such useful contacts. And by condoning it all, it was rather as if Eduardo had given us the weapons himself. So many people came to the church – such diverse backgrounds.' She was watching Larche intently and the force of her bitterness and contempt was as powerful as the blow he had struck Jacinto. He thought of her as she must have been – innocent, frivolous, expecting to be cosseted by the most glamorous of the three little rich boys. Instead she joined a waiting game that grew more obsessive, more claustrophobic, more psychotic by the moment.

'For some time we thought we'd overplayed our hand and taken far too great a risk.' Maria spoke quietly and reflectively now. 'But fortunately Calvino was careless. We'd told our recruit that he'd receive a considerable sum of money to help us out in a robbery and he agreed readily. He had no police record in Spain, and he claimed not to have one in Ireland. In the end, we accepted that risk too. He hid out and therefore had no idea of what had been going on.' She paused and then said almost shyly, 'I kept him company one night – and planted the papers we had prepared on him. The worst bit was throwing the gun down without Lorenzo and Juan seeing.'

'So killing was easier now,' observed Larche.

Jacinto nodded.

'What did you talk about?' Larche asked Maria. 'You and your tame Irishman?'

'Life and its unfairness.'

'It was certainly unfair on him,' said Larche.

'Yes. I shot him and he fell off the cliff – more surprised than anything else. As you can see, he was the result of quick but careful planning – just as the first killings had been.'

'Ingenious.'

'We must go back to the house now,' said Maria suddenly. 'We've been here too long.'

They listened, but there was only silence except for the faint sighing of the waves against the jetty.

'They'll still be after Lorenzo,' said Jacinto confidently. 'There's no hurry.'

'We must go *now*,' replied Maria sharply. 'Besides – you both need medical attention.'

Larche was surprised to find that, once again, the throbbing in his arm had dulled, but when he looked at what he had done to Jacinto's face he felt a wave of self-loathing. There would be questions, of course, and he would have to confess. But surely anyone would argue that there were extenuating circumstances. 'I am not my brother's keeper,' muttered Larche.

Jacinto laughed. He was fairly drunk but the cognac seemed to have made him docile. 'The question is – who kept who? I still feel his presence – his needs. Directing a secluded brothel for such a distinguished older brother made me *his* keeper – just as much as he was mine. I saw to the discretion, he to his real sexual fulfilment. Eduardo was a driving force, Larche; he needed what Sebastia had to offer – what he had made Sebastia become.'

'And all the time Anita shut it out?' Larche could at last see it more objectively.

'She loved him,' said Maria. 'To the exclusion of everything and everybody else. Just like I love Jacinto. Anita and I are two of a kind.'

'And they were three of a kind – Eduardo, Blasco, Jacinto. Spoilt and trapped.'

'You can't say that about Blasco,' said Jacinto grudgingly. 'He'd made his escape – Fuego.'

'But he couldn't help coming back, could he?' said Larche. 'And he came back once too often.'

'Perhaps Blasco was our keeper.' Jacinto smiled. 'Maybe he had my moral welfare at heart all along – and Eduardo's.' He looked at his watch. 'I can see how tense Maria is getting, monsieur. I think we should go with you now – although I'm sure I have nothing to fear from the women of Sebastia.' He turned to Maria. 'All they do is wait for their men to come home; that's all they'll ever do.' Jacinto walked across to Larche. 'I've been a captive on Molino for a long time; I think I'll be able to cope with captivity of a different kind. I suppose we shall be split up?' His voice was emotionless.

'Undoubtedly.'

'Can we have time together at the house?' Maria asked Larche. 'Just a little.' The tears were spilling out of her eyes and again Larche was reminded of Anita suddenly and so unpredictably weeping when he had first arrived on Molino. These women were so strong, Larche thought. Far stronger than their men.

Slowly the three of them walked out into the street.

The little square was full of women – young, middle-aged, elderly, very old. They stood not in groups but alone, silently waiting, their eyes on Jacinto. For a long time absolutely no one moved. Jacinto looked quietly amused but Maria seemed numbed, quite unable to respond to the extraordinary sight. Larche could sense the fear beating inside her, but he felt, perhaps as she did, oddly helpless in the face of something that had to happen – that like Jacinto's hatred had been brooding for a very long time.

Larche tried to be reasonable. These women were ordinary enough – wives, mothers, grandmothers. They would have understanding, compassion, sensitivity – the way women did. There was nothing for anyone to be afraid of. Surely all this was only in the nature of a protest. There would be harsh words, condemnation no doubt, and then they would disperse.

A gnarled stick of a grandmother took a couple of steps forward and immediately a chill swept over Larche. She was holding something in her hand. They were all holding something in their hands. What in God's name, he wondered frantically, are they going to do? The night was cat grey now and he could just hear the ocean licking at the harbour wall. Faint strains of dance music drifted from a radio in one of the houses and a dog, woken by the activity, howled mournfully in a backyard.

'Señora.' The woman's voice was dry and hard.

'Yes?' asked Maria despairingly.

'I would ask you to step aside.'

'Why?'

'We have business with Jacinto Tomas.'

'Get rid of them,' whispered Maria. 'Tell them to go.'

Larche tried to exert his authority but he knew that his efforts would be useless. 'Go home. Go home – all of you.'

'Step aside, señor, and you, señora – please, step aside.'

'Go to hell,' shouted Jacinto, his voice rising, his amusement gone. 'Go home.' Now he, too, was afraid – horribly afraid.

The old woman moved nearer and in her dark, lined face Larche could see the final firm resolve of unrewarded patience. There was a hard glint in her eye, so hard and so determined that Larche could feel the passion in her, the fire that had been smouldering for so long. 'Señor Tomas. You have used Sebastia, committed our church to sacrilege. Our men won't punish you – our men do nothing but talk and watch, but that is natural. In the end it is the women who must stop watching – it is the women who must take action.'

Jacinto took a few steps away from them.

'No,' Maria shouted. 'Don't move, my darling. Don't move. That's what they want.'

'Stay with us,' said Larche authoritatively. 'Stay with us and we'll protect you.'

But Jacinto took a few more steps and they were the signal for the hail of stones to begin.

Maria ran to hurl herself over Jacinto, to shelter him as the missiles rained down, but several women dragged her away, letting her scream helplessly on the sidelines whilst Larche made ineffectual attempts to stop them. But there were too many, far too many – perhaps sixty or more – and all of them held stones and broken cobbles.

'Stop this immediately,' shouted Larche. 'You mustn't interfere with the course of justice. He's going to be punished by the courts . . .'

Jacinto Tomas was squirming on the ground now, fresh blood flowing down his face. He had curled up into a foetal position, with his torn hands covering his head. Despite Maria's imploring screams and Larche's ineffective commands the women continued to stone him, their faces impassive, only their eyes intent and enraged. Frantically Larche struggled with a couple of the women but they pushed him away and he fell backwards on to the cobbles, pain shooting up his wounded arm.

The stoning continued relentlessly while Jacinto rolled and screamed and begged and implored, but they showed no mercy as they hurled their missiles, united in their self-appointed mission. Soon a helicopter came buzzing and clattering overhead and a jeep could be heard, roaring at high speed towards them. Calvino's too late, thought Larche, as he looked across at the bloodied, broken heap that was now still – and had once been Jacinto Tomas.

'Murderers,' screamed Maria. 'You're murderers – all of you.'

'And so are you,' capped one of the retreating women as they all hurried into the anonymity of the shadows and closed the shutters on their homes.

Soon their men would be home from the sea, thought Larche, but the real job has been done here – by the women. He walked over to Maria who was kneeling by Jacinto, but could find nothing to say to her. He remained beside her as dawn slowly began to break over Molino.

Epilogue

Anita Tomas and Marius Larche stood together, looking down at the sea boiling around the old harbour quayside, its massive Hellenic rock darkly brooding over the long, flat beaches. It was early evening and the gulls were feeding on the waves, sweeping, calling, soaring over the gleaming Mediterranean.

The cicadas rhythmically sounded in the grasses around them, while the shadows stole over the monolithic columns and stone fragments of the forum and the villas of the Graeco-Roman ruins. The site of Eduardo's proposed grave was a fenced-off mound of earth, but a pile of marble slabs indicated this was to be no modest edifice. Cypress and conifer trees were dotted amongst the crumbling stonework and the lowering sun spread a mellow warmth through the ancient remains of the old city. Empuries was at its most mysterious, the crimson light of the recent sunset making the stone insubstantial, shifting, almost distorted.

'You really didn't know?' murmured Larche as he turned away from the translucent sea. He had spent the rest of the night in hospital, having his arm attended to, but although he was completely exhausted the pain had been reduced to a soreness that was bearable. Early that morning he had spoken to Calvino and been agreeably surprised by the conversation. After they had discussed the recent traumatic events, Calvino had said, 'I knew I shouldn't have been so accepting, but the pressure was barbaric – and I just wanted time. What was more, I knew you would get much further than I with the interviews, and much more quickly. After all, you were a friend of the family.'

'Yes,' Larche had replied hesitantly. 'But you know, I only

219

started out as an acquaintance. I became a friend – a necessary friend – as it all happened.'

'You became the family confessor,' Calvino had replied.

In the end he probably came to resent me, thought Larche, as he stumbled over the rocky, barren ground. Walking with his arm in a sling hadn't been as easy as he had imagined, but Anita steadied him maternally and he was grateful for her cool, matter-of-fact assistance. Around them, in the gloaming, were a scattering of security guards, watching them with clinical detachment.

'Of course I knew,' she said. 'But I blotted it all out – and I shall continue to do so. Eduardo and I had a very special love – one that was private and exclusive to us – and to no one else. I'm very sure of that. That's why I was able to talk so intimately to Mr Morrison – he was a sounding board to me.' She held up a hand in protest before Larche could intervene. 'I know he's a dangerous man – a very shallow and self-seeking man – but I shall keep him on because he's a very fine painter and he'll bring Eduardo alive again for me.'

'Have you changed the background?'

'Sebastia? No – why should I? Eduardo recreated an industry there. It doesn't matter what else he did; that was not part of what we meant to each other.'

'You can really make this separation?' Larche was still incredulous.

'You know I can. I was delighted when they discovered that unfortunate Irishman but I should have known that it was only a passing charade. Señor Calvino may have been controllable but you were not, Marius.' She smiled sadly at him. 'Why should you be?'

'You were the only one who didn't see me as a father confessor,' said Larche drily.

'No – certainly that was not a role I saw you in. As for the others, I don't think you received very accurate confessions, did you? People told you only what they wanted to express – or like me they just practised to deceive. However, I suppose that's what you're used to in your profession.'

220

'Yes,' he replied carefully. 'I have to interpret what my penitents say in the confessional.'

'As you can imagine,' said Anita Tomas with uncharacteristic hesitation, 'I wanted a quick result to keep Eduardo's name clean. I didn't achieve that but I'm sure I can rely on your continued discretion.' Her tone was not threatening but pleading and Larche winced inside at the fragility of the woman. She had built her life on quicksand – and occasionally, very occasionally, she looked vulnerable.

'I'll do what I can,' Larche muttered in an attempt at reassurance. He was tired of the abuse of power. 'You'd already asked Father Miguel to look into Lorenzo's background, hadn't you? And you'd spoken to Blasco.'

'I could see all the connections, Marius. I'd just rather not understand the answers,' she said with a return to her fortress mentality.

'What happens if Morrison – or Lorenzo – talks? There's nothing I can do to control them,' he reminded her.

She shrugged. 'I can shut them out. Unlike my brothers-in-law, Molino is not a prison to me. Despite what has happened – it's still a haven.'

'What about your career?'

'I shall retire.'

He nodded, knowing how little the world of concert performances meant to her now. Eduardo's memory was all-consuming and Larche knew that eventually it would submerge her completely. 'And you'll really stay on Molino, with Sebastia so near?' Larche felt he needed to play the devil's advocate.

She nodded. 'It pleases me to think of those other women having done their duty, returning to those shuttered homes to serve their menfolk again. But they are the powerful ones in the end. It was they who meted out justice while the men were out hunting.' She smiled at Larche again with the same sad look. 'I could never be like them; someone from my background can only sit and lick their wounds and live in the past with a painting.'

And a conveniently truncated memory, thought Larche.

Anita spoke softly, exactly reading his thoughts. 'As you

know, I have this ability to seal myself off – to make myself an island. And I'm successful at it, Marius.'

'For how long?'

'For as long as I wish. I assure you I can be very single-minded and I don't need the kind of senseless protection Bishop Carlos lavished on me. He has made me very angry.'

'Why do you think he *did* protect you in that way?' asked Larche curiously.

'The Church has always protected the Tomas family – through the centuries.'

'So it's a habit?'

'It's a method of ensuring that the old bastions of Spain remain intact and untrammelled.'

'But will they remain that way?' said Larche. 'With the enemies you must have?'

'Frankly, I don't care. I have the island. I have *my* island.' She sounded very certain. 'Molino may have ensnared the poor little rich boys you talk about but, as I've said, the place is a haven to me – a sanctuary. I shall remain here.'

'Do you . . . will you be giving evidence against Maria?'

'If I have to. But I don't know what I could say that would be . . . helpful.' Her voice was neutral.

'Do you hate her?'

'I can feel nothing for her.'

'And Jacinto?'

'He tortured Eduardo and for that I can never forgive him, but I think the women of Sebastia did all the avenging.'

'What about Salvador?'

She paused, her answer unready for the first time. 'What you told me about him was appalling. I don't want him to grow up like them – trapped here, following a path that can only make him another prisoner. So I'm sending him away – to my sister in Madrid. He'll go to school there and I'll . . . I'll take him away in the holidays.'

'Leaving your island?'

'Not for long.'

'You realize he may . . . pursue the same path in Madrid?'

'There is that risk,' she replied slowly. 'But he can't stay

222

here.' Anita turned back to the darkening sea, its mantle broken here and there by the lights of a fishing boat. 'You can just see Molino,' she whispered. 'Do you know Benjamin Britten's opera, *Peter Grimes?*' she asked him.

'A little.'

'Balstrode sings,

> *'This storm is useful: you can speak your mind*
> *and never mind the Borough comment'ry.*
> *There is more grandeur in a gale of wind*
> *to free confession, set a conscience free.'*

Larche peered into the fading light and saw the indistinct cluster of rock. 'Yes. I can see Molino.'

'Think of me then, Marius. Think of me in my island fortress, sealed off with my free conscience and the Eduardo I understand. Occasionally I'll play my cello and maybe hear his voice in a gale of wind.' Anita began to speak more briskly. 'Of course I shan't entirely be a recluse. There's Sebastia – and its fishing industry. I may even have a hand in running that myself. I feel I would be well supported by the women there – don't you?'

'Yes,' replied Larche with confidence. 'I think you would.'

'Will you be staying for the funeral, Marius?'

'Yes – but if you don't mind, not at the guest house. I've booked into a hotel on the mainland.'

'Of course.' She proffered her hand. 'I don't suppose we'll be alone together again. Thank you for your wisdom – and your intuition.'

Larche nodded. A little night breeze sprang up, rustling the trees. He thought of Alison Rowe, and closed his eyes fiercely against her memory. Marius Larche was not a man who could take refuge.